Always a Place

A Novel

by Maureen Gaynor

This book is dedicated to all of my family, my friends and all the people who believed in this novel. A special thanks to my late, great friend, Peter Falk, for his tireless efforts with polishing up this novel.

Salute!

Chapter 1

The sound of a basketball bouncing on the driveway echoed down Crawford Street. A canopy of trees shielded the Cape Cod and Colonial style houses from the harshest of summer suns and the wickedest of winter winds. On this humid July evening, a line of cars formed a barricade in front of the Reed home.

In the backyard, charcoal smoke and bug repellent permeated the air, as Kate and Meg watched the men shoot baskets. The orange paint on the rim had peeled off many cruel New England seasons ago. The humidity brought the men to a standstill. Eric wiped the sweat from his face with his shirt. He walked over to Kate and plucked a bottle of beer from her lap.

"Doing okay?"

"Yeah." Kate nodded.

"You're gagging all the mosquitoes with that smoke," Eric said to Meg.

Unfazed, Meg continued to puff on her cigarette. "I have to die of something? Might as well be emphysema," Meg quipped.

"Yeah, well, just keep it away from my wife, please."

"Certainly!" exclaimed Meg, with a touch of sarcasm.

Eric smiled and went back to shoot more baskets. "Double or nothing?" he asked Kate's brother, Brian.

"Sure," Brian said, starting another game of Horse.

Meg raised the bottle of beer to Kate's mouth; Kate sucked on the straw. She and Eric were moving the next day, and a few beers would take the edge off her nerves for a while, or that was what she hoped. She wanted to be numb to it all. After two beers, Kate's muscles were relaxed. Words flowed easily from her lips. She sensed every syllable, every sound. She loved the calming effect beer had on her rebellious body.

"I'm gonna miss you," Kate said to Meg.

Meg put her hand on Kate's shoulder. "Me, too. Finish this," Meg said, as she guided the straw to Kate's lips.

Through the clamminess of the midsummer night came the thunderous noise of Joe's beat-up Chevy truck. Eric looked at Kate with annoyance and walked down the driveway toward his brother.

"Sorry I'm late!" Joe exclaimed.

Eric approached his brother. "Joe, what the hell are you doing here?" Eric looked at Joe who was dressed in grungy jeans and a torn T-shirt. His hair hung down over his gaunt face. Eric smelled the booze on Joe's breath.

"This is a goodbye party, ain't it?" asked Joe. "I came to say goodbye to you and Kate."

Eric blocked him from walking any closer to the house. "Yeah, but I didn't invite you," said Eric. "Now get in the truck. I'll drive you home."

"Just let me say goodbye to Kate," said Joe.

"Don't make us look like fools in front of my family, Joe." Eric's words were quiet but forceful.

"I'm the only real family you got, little brother!" Joe shouted. The words pierced the hot, dense air like a bullet through grease. Eric turned around and saw that Kate and the others were getting nervous. Eric pushed Joe back toward the truck.

"Get in the damn truck," Eric said. "You're scaring Kate."

"What's the matter, Mr. Big-shot Syracuse man, too good to be caught in the company of your own alcoholic brother?"

"Now you're pissing me off!" Eric said and grabbed Joe by the arms. "Either get in the truck, or I call the cops," he explained. "Pick one."

"Okay, okay. Just get the hell off me," Joe said. He had become well acquainted with the police in recent years and didn't want to face another night in jail.

Eric released him. "Get in the truck now!" Joe started to walk around to the driver's side and Eric grabbed him again. "This side, Buddy," Eric said and led him to the passenger's side. Eric jogged around to the driver's side. "Can somebody follow me, please?" he called to the others.

Brian volunteered.

Joe reached for the keys in the ignition.

"Don't get cute," Eric said, grabbing Joe's hand. "How old are you, Joe, two?"

Brian got in his car and followed Eric and Joe. Crude bumper stickers were plastered over the back of Joe's truck. They fit Joe's crass personality. Brian wondered how Joe could have got his license back so soon after his arrest for drunk driving.

The unexpected intrusion of Joe deflated the mood of the

party like a hot air balloon punctured by the beak of a crow. Kate and the others moved inside, in the hopes of restoring some air to the celebration. Kate was on her third beer. She was feeling relaxed and impaired. The kitchen was the gathering place, inviting and comfortable, where several conversations went on at once. Kate's mother loaded the dishwasher, plate after plate, glass after glass. Kate remarked to herself on the precision with which her mother placed each item according to size and shape. Mrs. Reed made loading the dishwasher an art form. She was tall and well-proportioned, with a strong presence that commanded respect. Her long blond hair was pulled back into a tight bun. The wrinkles on her face provided the only clues to her actual age.

Mrs. Reed hated to have things out of order in her life. Change did not come easily to her. She still lived in the same ash-blue house for 30 years.

"Want another beer?" Meg asked Kate.

"Yeah," Kate answered.

"Hang on, I'll be right back." Meg left to retrieve another beer outside.

Mrs. Reed wiped the counter. "I have to go to work early in the morning. I have a presentation to prepare for."

"We'll clean up," said Kate. "Go to bed." The stove clock read 9:47 PM.

"Okay. Tell Brian to lock up the house."

"I will."

Mrs. Reed kissed Kate on the forehead. "Good luck in Syracuse. I guess I'll see you at Christmas."

"Yeah. We'll be home for Christmas."

"Good night," said Mrs. Reed.

"G'night," said Kate, as her mother retreated upstairs. Kate felt an overwhelming hole in the pit of her stomach.

Meg returned from outside. "Where's your mom?"

"She went to bed," Kate said. "She has to get up early tomorrow."

"She's not going to see you guys off?"

"I guess not," said Kate, sighing.

"Are you okay with that?" asked Meg.

"Oh, yeah." Kate cracked a grin.

"You big liar," Meg said.

"I lie good when I'm drunk, don't I?" Kate conjectured.

Eric parked in front of Joe's apartment in South Boston. It was the worst area in the city and looked like a part of a third-world country. Brian pulled up behind Eric and shut off his headlights to avoid drawing attention from the invisible eyes that he felt peering out at him from porches and second-floor landings. Eric followed Joe up the exterior staircase. Joe navigated the rot-infested steps quite well, while Eric cautiously stepped on each frail tread and hung onto the wavering handrail. Joe opened the door of the apartment. Eric lunged inside, as if the landing was giving way.

The smell of alcohol pervaded the hot, stagnant air. Eric fumbled for the light switch. A dim bulb overhead was all the light there was in this small space. Joe had already found his bed. Eric speculated that Joe had done this many times in a drunken stupor.

A brown shag rug covered the floor. Dirty clothes were strewn all around. Eric struggled to open the only window that wasn't painted shut. It wouldn't budge and he screamed in frustration. He hated this place and the circumstances that faced his brother. He managed to crack open the window slightly. He went to the kitchen and turned on the fluorescent light over the sink. The kitchen was tiny and the countertops were crowded, with empty Jack Daniels bottles. In the sink, glasses sat waiting to be washed; some were broken. Eric picked up the shards of glass and carefully tossed them into the trash. He opened the ancient refrigerator and was greeted by darkness and a horrid smell from a two-month-old carton of milk. Eric's stomach turned. He poured the chunky contents down the sink, as he held his breath. He opened the faucet and brown water spurted out.

Joe was sound asleep on his bed. Eric removed Joe's ragged sneakers. In the gloom of the bedroom, Eric stared at Joe and wished for better days for him. He agonized over moving so far away from Joe. This last look at his brother would haunt him for weeks.

Eric picked up all the liquor bottles and threw them down to Brian. As he gingerly descended the stairs of the crumbling structure, his heart raced again. Each step felt like his last. He didn't breathe or blink, so afraid he would fall to his death. Eric jumped off the fourth step to the ground. He released all the air from his lungs. The empties were loaded into the backseat of Brian's car.

"What a dump," Eric said.

"Looks like it," Brian replied. "Why the hell is he driving? I thought he lost his license."

"He did," said Eric, "but that hasn't stopped him from driving. I'm taking the keys to his truck." Eric took one last look at the staircase. "Let's get the hell out of here." Brian wasted little time complying.

A string of red, yellow, and green traffic lights punctuated the darkness. The night had cooled a little and the rush of air made Eric feel alive again.

"Is your new apartment ready?" Brian asked.

"Yep," Eric said, spiritedly. "The landlord called today and said everything is finished."

"I know Kate is excited about her new job."

"Yeah," Eric said. "She can't wait to get there."

"She's something else," said Brian. Brian and Eric looked out at the road, as their thoughts created a pause in the conversation.

"Do me a favor, Eric," Brian said.

"Sure."

"Keep her safe and happy," Brian said. "I know you will, but she'll be far away and I just want her to have everything she deserves."

"I'll take good care of Katie. I promise," Eric said.

"Thanks," said Brian.

They arrived home to find a small gathering of friends in the kitchen. Eric knelt down in front of Kate and hugged her. From the intensity of his embrace, Kate sensed her husband was upset by his encounter with Joe. She whispered her love for him. As Brian watched on, he grew confident that Eric would keep his promise.

It was almost midnight when Eric and Kate said their goodbyes to remaining guests, promising to keep in touch.

Suddenly, the house felt empty. Kate felt sad and found herself counting the hours until morning. Eric retired to bed to regenerate himself for the long drive the next day. Kate, Meg, and Brian stayed up for another hour to clean, but even more to prolong their time together. After two more beers, Kate sensed a headache coming on. Brian stood tall and slender at the sink, with his young face and brown hair in loose curls. He was kind and gentle to everyone around him. Meg had a strong body that complemented her strong personality. Her straight, dirty-blond hair was tied back in a ponytail. Her face was pretty.

Tears started to run down Kate's cheeks. Brian had always been her protector, and Meg, her best friend for years. Meg and Brian's eyes welled, too. Meg cracked a joke, breaking the tension, if only for a moment. Kate's headache grew worse, as she tried to keep from completely falling apart. Brian and Meg hugged Kate and allowed her to cry. It was past one when Meg declared it was time for everyone to go to bed. Meg helped Kate into bed. Minutes later, Kate was asleep.

At 6:32 AM, the sun pierced through Kate's bedroom window. She felt the aftermath of the previous night. Her head felt like a sound stage for a heavy-metal rock band and her stomach felt like the floor the overly enthusiastic audience was jumping on. Seized by a desperate need to hover over a toilet, Kate managed to crawl into the bathroom. Eric awoke and rushed to her side. He rubbed her back as the past night's evils came raging out of her stomach. Kate broke down in Eric's arms.

"We're gonna be okay, Babe," Eric said softly.

Kate draped herself over his shoulders like a wet rag and cried easily.

Eric held her tight. "Christmas is just around the corner, and we'll see everyone then."

With every word Eric spoke, she regained more of her composure. "I know," Kate struggled to say.

"You're okay?" Eric asked as he stroked her short hair.

"Yeah, I'm okay."

Eric smiled brightly. "You know, Syracuse is going to be great for us."

"I know it is," Kate said and returned his smile.

He kissed her forehead. "Let me go find some Advil. I'll be right back."

Kate wiped her tears. She dreaded this day for the past six

months. It was the day she had to say goodbye.

"I defizzed some Coke," Eric said, as he knelt down.

"I love you," Kate said softly.

"Yeah, yeah—you only love me for my Advils," he teased. Kate grinned. Eric put the Advils in her mouth, gave her a sip of Coke to wash them down, and wiped her chin with the palm of his hand. "You're okay?"

"Yeah, I'm good," she said. "Thank you."

"It's still early. Why don't you go try and sleep for a little while?"

Kate nodded. Eric carried her to the bed.

"I'll be back in a little while," Eric said. He laid her down.

"Okay."

Standing in the kitchen, Eric heard a car door slam. He looked out the window and saw Mrs. Reed leaving in her blue Volvo. Disappointment came over him, as he thought about her lack of consideration for Kate. Soon, his disappointment turned to anger and he felt his blood boil, as his heart pound. Brian entered. They greeted each other just like any other day. Brian offered to help load up Eric's pickup with essentials for the couple's first night in Syracuse.

Two hours later, the truck was fully loaded with a box spring and mattress, cardboard boxes, a few chairs, and Kate's power wheelchair. Brian secured the cargo under a tarp. Meg packed her car and waited to say goodbye before heading back home to New Hampshire. Kate's eyes welled, as Meg and Brian hugged her goodbye. Brian put Kate into the passenger seat. Her headache returned, as she fought her emotions. As they drove off, Kate struggled not to break down. Eric touched her face, and with his touch the tears came freely.

Thick fog blanketed the Massachusetts Turnpike. Inbound traffic was unusually heavy for ten in the morning—Mercedes, BMWs, and other high-priced European cars were backed up for miles going into Boston—the westbound lane was moving freely. Eric drove with a Dunkin' Donuts Big One coffee cup between his thighs. Kate watched in the side mirror as the Boston skyline receded out of view. Her short, dark hair fluttered in the warm air.

A five-hour drive wasn't the best remedy for a hangover. Kate wanted to sleep. Her mouth was as dry as a desert and her eyes were like the desert sand. She regretted drinking too much. Alcohol only let her true emotions show through. She wanted to go back and do the night over, better.

Kate was on the verge of deep slumber when Eric said, "Hey, we're about 20 minutes from the New York border. I'm gonna make a pit stop. You want anything?"

"A bed would be nice," Kate said, with her eyes closed.

Eric chuckled. "Oh, Sweetie," he replied, "I'll put something soft over there when we stop." He touched her arm. "Want a soda or something?"

"Yeah, okay."

"Okay." Eric took the next exit and pulled into a gas station. Returning the convenience store, he opened Kate's soda can and inserted one of the straws that were scattered around the truck. He held the soda for Kate, while she took a few gulps.

"Enough?" he asked.

"Yeah, I'm good."

He pulled a large towel out of the back and tucked it beside her head. He started up the engine and threw the truck into reverse. There was a screech of metal on metal, as Eric wrestled with the stick shift.

"This piece-of-shit clutch!" he cursed. "I swear, we are getting a van very soon."

Kate sat, amused. "You've been saying that for two years now," she said. "When are you gonna give it up?"

"What, the truck?"

"Yeah," she said.

"I can give it up any time I want," Eric said with conviction.

Kate broke into a chuckle. "I'll believe *that* when I see it."

"I will, you know." He let a smile slip.

The white lines on the black tar oscillating on highway lulled Kate into a deep sleep. Eric shuffled his eyes between the road and his wife, making sure she was comfortable. She looked so peaceful, as the wind swept through her hair. At times, Eric touched her arm, all along remarking how soft her skin was. He loved the feel of her.

An hour later, Kate stirred. She squinted in the bright sun.

"Hi, Sweetie," Eric said. He held her left hand.

"Where are we?" she said.

"We are just about into Albany," he said. "Hungry?"

"I think I could eat," she said and pulled herself up in the vinyl bucket seat. "My butt hurts."

"Okay, Sweetie," Eric said, laughing. He took the next exit and followed the signs to the fast food restaurants. "How's the head?" He massaged her temple.

"Better."

"Need to pee?"

Kate smiled. "Do I dare?"

"It's now or never."

"Okay, okay."

"Where do you want to eat?"

"Anywhere but Burger King," she said. "If I even smell a Burger King, I'll throw up again."

"Let's look for a Wendy's," Eric said. "Is Wendy's okay?"

"Yeah," Kate answered, spiritedly.

They drove along the busy strip past every kind of store imaginable. It was the main drag of Albany. You could buy a car, shop for groceries, take in a movie, go to dinner, and drop off and pick up your dry cleaning all within a two-mile radius. It was truly a 20th century indulgence. At night, the strip was all bright lights and neon. Flashes of white, green, and pink lights invited people in to eat and drink.

Like all cities, Albany had hatred and crime, and the well-lighted areas weren't necessarily safe. People feared for their lives, unlike fifty years ago when the world seemed more benign. In this age, there was no guarantee that a neighbor would intervene on a stranger's behalf. It was kill or be killed.

"There's Wendy's," Kate said.

"Great," Eric said. He pulled in and parked near the entrance. "I'll carry you in. There's no way I can get your wheelchair out from under all that junk."

"I figured," said Kate in an appreciative voice.

Eric stepped out and opened the passenger's side door. "Ready?"

"Yeah." She moved her legs out of the cab, one at a time, and leaned on him as she stood. "Anyone looking?"

"No, don't worry," Eric said and massaged her backside. "Feel better?"

"Yeah."

"Okay, here we go." Eric picked Kate up and carried her

inside. A blast of cool air welcomed them in. Eric approached a young attendant wiping a table.

"Excuse me," he said.

The girl looked up, surprised at the sight of Kate in his arms. "Yes?"

"Would you mind looking in the ladies' room for me to see if there is anyone in there? I need to take my wife in there."

"Oh sure," said the girl. She went into the bathroom and found it empty.

"If you can, just guard the door. We'll be right out," Eric said and carried Kate to one of the stalls. He lowered Kate down to the seat. "Comfortable?"

Kate looked up at him. "Yeah," she said.

Eric left her and went to relieve himself in the next stall. He heard Kate giggle. "What?" he said.

"Remember that time—"

"Oh, yeah," Eric interrupted. "How could I forget that night?"

"That woman thought you were a nut." Memories filled her mind. "I thought she was gonna have a heart attack."

"She almost did. She went out of that bathroom, screaming like she saw somebody being axed to death or something." Eric returned to Kate's stall. "You didn't help much, laughing like a fool. She thought you were a nut, too."

"It was funny!" she exclaimed. He pulled Kate to her feet and pulled up her shorts.

He made sure her clothes were all properly tucked in, snapped, and buttoned. "Ready?"

"Yeah."

Eric hoisted Kate on his waist and clasped his hands tightly around her. He nudged the door open. He found the attendant standing outside. "Thanks a lot," he said.

"Sure, no problem," the girl said. She followed Eric to the entrance and held it open for him.

"Thanks again," he said.

"Thank you," Kate said. Her eyes met the girl's.

Eric situated Kate in the truck and returned to the restaurant. He went over to the girl. "Here are a few bucks for all your help."

"Oh, sir, you don't need to give me anything," the girl said, but Eric insisted she take the three dollars. She looked at him again and took the money. "Thank you, sir. That's very generous."

"You're very welcome," Eric said and waved goodbye. He walked up to the counter to order.

"In my day, those kinds of people stayed home, or were put in institutions," said a man behind Eric in line.

Hearing these words, Eric turned and saw a short, wiry old man. "Excuse me?" Eric asked.

The old man adjusted his glasses. "That cripple out there," said the man. He pointed his thumb toward the truck. "You should leave that kind of person at home. People don't need to see that in public places." His voice was gravelly.

"Excuse me," Eric said angrily, "that's my wife." He managed to keep his voice at a reasonable level.

"I'm telling you for your own good, sir."

Eric had had enough of this old geezer's warped ideas. "Listen," Eric said, "I don't care to hear anymore of your opinions."

"Certainly, sir," said the old man in a condescending voice.

It was Eric's turn at the counter and he ordered. He was anticipating another bold statement from the old man, but it never came. When his food came, Eric turned, glared at the old man and left.

"Some people should be shot," Eric said to Kate.

"What the hell happened in there?" Kate asked.

"This guy, he was an old guy, was behind me in line and he starts getting on my case for taking you out in public." Eric pulled the food from the bag.

"No way!" she exclaimed. "What did you say?"

"I asked him politely to shut up."

"What did he say to that?"

"He said he was telling me for my own good. I just told him I didn't want to hear anymore of his dumb opinions and I left."

Kate smiled, as Eric fed her a French fry. Sympathy overflowed her chest, but she hid her emotions well. It was her fault that Eric was put in that position. Kate reminded herself that she couldn't fix everything that he might face. She wanted things to be easy for him. "Thank you," she said.

"Now, don't go and get all mushy on me. I would have done

it for anyone." Eric fed her a bite of cheeseburger.

"I know," she said, trying to speak with her mouth full.

"Let's get back on the road," Eric said. He put everything in place in order to keep feeding her and himself, and to keep driving all at the same time. Eric thought of this as a special talent.

Kate nodded.

Cerebral palsy had claimed Kate's body, but it would never claim her mind. To her, CP wasn't a curse, it was a challenge that was placed on her when she was born, and it would be a challenge until the day she died. She couldn't control the movements of her arms and legs, hands and feet, and fingers and toes, but she fought hard to minimize the jerky motions. It was as if a puppeteer was hovering above Kate and manipulating her at every turn. The disorder also affected Kate's speech, making her words slurred and mispronounced, as if she were constantly intoxicated. She yearned to better articulate her words, so that the average person could understand her without her voice synthesizer or another person interpreting. Sometimes, Kate wished people had ESP, so she could express her thoughts in real time. She wondered what it would be like not having to rely on others to care for her basic needs. She was acutely aware of other people's perception of her, and she always wanted to give a good first impression. While strangers often failed to see her as a real person rather than a wiggling figure in a wheelchair, most people recognized her intelligence as soon as they made eye contact.

She had an engaging smile and beautiful blue eyes that sparkled like the stars in moonlight. At times, her facial expressions were skewed by CP, but that didn't take away from her attraction. When Kate spoke, the words were exaggerated due to her lack of control around her jaws. But she had the will of a thousand men and the courage of a billion. And even though she would never know what it would be like to walk or to talk normally, she was content with her life. She was deeply in love with Eric, who saw through her blunt facade and recognized the spirit inside. Eric was her island, and she could survive on just him. He was her best friend and her husband. They were beginning a new life in Syracuse, New York.

The late-day sun blinded them, as they turned off the highway. They were only ten minutes away from their new apartment. The air was cooler now, but the humidity still lingered. Eric turned onto Lancaster Avenue and moments later, he and Kate gazed at their new home. Their apartment was in a three-story building with a small porch. There were trees in the backyard. The smell of fresh paint pervaded the air.

Eric got out and went up the porch steps. He rang the bell and waited. Kate gazed at her husband, studying every part of him. A V-shaped stain of sweat darkened his khaki shorts. He was a strong 5′7″. He looked back at Kate. He had sharp facial features that stood, out as if a famous artisan had sculpted them. The late-afternoon sun highlighted his short, curly blond hair. Kate wondered who or what had made such a beautiful figure and dropped him down to her.

Their new landlord, Rich Davison, opened the door. Mr. Davison was an average-looking man, with thinning hair that encircled a bald spot. His youthful disposition and his wire-framed circular glasses made him seem younger than his 49 years. He had a round face and a friendly manner. He wore a gray T-shirt and denim cutoff shorts. His little potbelly barely could be noticed.

"How was the drive?" Mr. Davison asked Eric.

"It was long, but not a lot of traffic. We made good time." Eric noticed the ramp Mr. Davison had installed for Kate. "The ramp looks good."

Mr. Davison turned. "Yeah, they finished it yesterday. They did a good job."

"We appreciate all the things you did in the apartment."

"Oh, it was no problem at all," said Mr. Davison. "It's not every day you can find good tenants like you and Kate. It's important to keep good tenants, however you can."

"Well, we thank you."

With a smile, Mr. Davison nodded. "Can I help you take in some things from the truck?"

"I could use some help with Kate's wheelchair and the mattresses," Eric said.

"Okay, sure. Just let me run upstairs and put on some sneakers."

"No rush, Mr. Davison." Eric walked back to the truck.

"How's your butt feeling?" he asked Kate.

"It's okay," Kate said.

"Mr. Davison will be right back."

"Good," Kate said, smiling. "I was watching you. You are a sexy, sexy man."

"Oh, did you just realize this?" he asked, playfully.

"No, I just wanted to tell you."

Eric grinned. "I already knew I was a sexy, sexy man." He leaned over and kissed her.

Mr. Davison appeared and approached the truck. "How are you doing, Kate?" he asked.

"I'm fine. How are you?" Kate extended her arm and encouraged Mr. Davison to take her closed hand in his.

He grabbed her hand. "That's good, Kate," he said, pretending to understand what she said.

"She asked you 'How are you?'" Eric said, trying not to make Mr. Davison feel uncomfortable.

"Oh, I'm fine, honey," Mr. Davison added.

Eric and Mr. Davison unloaded the truck. Kate used her power wheelchair to push box after box up the ramp and onto the porch. Within an hour, everything was in their apartment. As the sun set, their appetites were overrun by exhaustion. Eric set up the mattress and box spring and they were asleep within minutes.

When Kate awoke the next morning, Eric was the only familiar thing. He lied in a perfect sleep. Kate pulled her naked body closer to him and kissed his shoulder. She smiled when he opened his eyes. "Hi," she said.

"Good morning," he said, and ran his fingers through her untamed hair. "I bet you feel much better today, don't you?"

"Oh, yes," Kate said with a chuckle. "How about you?"

"I slept like a baby." He pulled her onto his chest. "You feel nice and cool." His hands traveled up and down her back.

"Oh yeah?" Kate kissed his lips as she drowned in his gaze. "Can we stay in bed all day?"

"What about the movers?"

"Damn," Kate joked, "I forgot about the movers! What time are they coming—around ten?"

"Yeah, that's when they said."

He checked his watch. "It's only 8:30. Feel like attempting a shower sitting on a towel?"

"Yeah, that'll be okay."

Eric kissed her forehead. "Okay. Let me get things ready and I'll be right back."

Kate rolled onto her back. Eric fumbled through some boxes, grabbed a few towels and disappeared into the bathroom. He turned the shower on. "Ready?" he said, reappearing.

"Yeah," she said.

He picked her up and carried her to the bathroom. The first stop was the toilet. Then, he carried her to the shower and let her down gently onto a soaked towel. "Feel okay, Sweetie?" he asked.

Kate heard him, but the muscles in her left foot were forcing her big toe into the tile, causing excruciating pain. She struggled until her foot found a comfortable position she exhaled hard. "Yeah, I'm okay."

"How's the water temperature?" he asked.

"It's good," she said.

Eric soaped up the washcloth and began to wash Kate's body. "Are you hungry?"

"Yes," she answered.

"I'll go out and grab something fast to eat." Eric started to shampoo her hair. "Is tea and a muffin okay?"

"Sure," Kate said with enthusiasm.

"What are you looking at?" he asked.

"My gorgeous hunk of a husband," she answered, grinning widely.

Eric chuckled. "We can't be late for the movers."

"We have five minutes, don't we?"

"Oh!" he exclaimed. "That was a low blow." He squatted down and playfully sprayed her in the face with his fingers. He kissed her on the lips. "Are you ready to get out?"

"Yeah."

He turned off the shower, dried Kate off and carried her into the bedroom. He unpacked the day's clothing and began dressing Kate. "Keep those toes still," he said jovially, as he slipped a sock on her foot.

Kate wiggled her toes even more.

"D' you think the movers will have any problems getting the

stuff through the hallway?"

"Do I think what?" Eric asked.

Kate prepared to speak clearer. The invisible puppeteer tugged on her arm and leg strings and they became rigid. "Can the movers get the furniture through the hallway?"

"Mr. Davison said they've never had any trouble before." Eric grabbed her wrists and sat her up on the edge of the mattress.

Kate felt the puppeteer pulling her every which way, trying to topple her. She was too strong, but if she tried to talk the puppeteer would gain the upper hand. She remained quiet, as Eric finished dressing her.

"Are you okay there, while I get your chair?"

Never looking up, Kate nodded. It took all of her concentration to not let the puppeteer pull her over. When he was about four feet away, Kate relaxed.

"Ready?"

"Yes," Kate said.

Eric picked her up in the usual way and situated her in the wheelchair. He buckled the seatbelt. "All set?"

"All set." Safe and secure in her wheelchair, Kate could now talk. "You think everything is going to fit in here?" she asked, as she judged the size of the bedroom.

"Sure, everything's going to fit," he answered. "Will you stop worrying so much?"

Kate smirked. "Okay, okay."

"Everything's gonna be fine," he said and put on his sneakers. "Will you be alright while I go get something to eat?"

"Yeah, I'm good," she said and followed him to the front door.

"I'll be back in a few minutes." He planted a delicate kiss on her forehead and was gone.

Kate explored the empty apartment. The walls were a light cream color. The doorways were trimmed in a natural wood stain. She went into the living room and looked out the bay window. A few cars passed by. She heard a lawn mower in the distance. She spotted a young couple across the street. They appeared to be arguing. Their body movements were abrupt. Their expressions seemed tense. Kate sensed their anguish towards each other. Their frustration was palpable. She wanted to know what they were saying, so she continued to watch them feuding. Kate wanted them have peace. The young man abruptly got into a car and drove off, while the woman went back into the apartment. Vapors from the hot summer sun began to rise up from the street. A wave of loneliness struck Kate.

Eric returned with breakfast. They sat at the counter and ate. Eric fed Kate. She sipped her tea through a straw. On occasion, the puppeteer yanked on her left arm and her hand collided with the edge of the countertop. After 27 years of hitting inanimate objects, she was used to the pain. She imagined the puppeteer getting a chuckle at her expense.

The movers arrived. Eric went out to greet the two men. Kate followed. The movers carried boxes and looked at Kate with utter astonishment, as if she was not of this world. Kate's anger rose. She was convinced the two men were time-capsuled here from the Paleolithic Age.

As the men went in and out of the apartment, they always caught a glimpse of Kate, as if in the hope of seeing her do something strange. She rolled up and down the driveway, trying to appear deep in thought. But she wondered if her constant pacing made the cave-dwellers think she was more diminished. The blatant stares stopped and soon the movers were gone.

By day's end, the apartment was starting to feel like home. Eric stretched out on the couch. Kate attempted to set the VCR clock.

"Need any help?" he asked.

"I got it," answered Kate. She scraped her knuckles on one of the hard plastic edges of the VCR, determined to set the time.

"Need your headstick?"

"No," Kate kindly declined. "I almost got it. Just take it easy over there." She smiled at him.

He smiled back and continued to watch her do battle with the VCR. There was a knock at the door. His rest was over. "Come in."

Liz Young was very neatly dressed in dress blue shorts and a white blouse. Her dark hair hung down to just above her shoulders. "I see the movers came," she said.

Eric stood and greeted Kate's new personal care assistant. "How are you?"

"I'm good," Liz said.

Success was finally achieved—the clock was set. "I'm sorry. I didn't mean to ignore you," Kate said directly to Liz.

Liz looked uneasy. "I'm sorry, could you say it again?"

Kate grinned at Liz to show that she appreciated her patience. Kate repeated herself.

Liz looked intensely at Kate. Kate glanced at Eric.

"Kate wanted you to know that she wasn't ignoring you when you came in."

Liz turned to Kate. "Oh, oh, I didn't think you were. I'm just happy to be here to begin working with you." Her expression was still one of concern.

"Don't worry," said Eric, "you'll learn to understand her with no problem in a couple of weeks. At the beginning, have Kate spell everything."

"How long did it take Eric to begin to understand you?"

"Three days," Eric said.

"Three days? Wow!" exclaimed Liz. "You guys must have hit it off right away."

Kate glanced at Eric. "Yeah, kind of," she said.

He and Kate had met Liz about a month earlier on another visit to Syracuse. After Eric placed an ad in the local newspaper, he and Kate had spent an entire weekend interviewing potential candidates for the job. It was an exhausting and frustrating process. The majority of candidates were older women who couldn't let go of the old myths that all people with cerebral palsy were mentally deficient in some respect. Eric explained Kate's condition, but the facts didn't seem to replace the old myths. One woman praised Eric for his devotion to Kate, as if he had taken some priestly vow of celibacy and sacrificed his life to care for her. Kate wanted to demonstrate for this woman right then and there how well she could fulfill her wifely duties for her husband.

They were relieved when they interviewed Liz. She had experience. She had youth. And above all, she related to Kate as a real human being. They knew they had the right person.

The aroma of Chinese food filled the apartment. The conversation was friendly. Liz tried her hand at feeding Kate. Kate thought it was cruel to start Liz off with Chinese food, but Liz did well. Pieces of food were soon scattered on the floor. Slowly, Liz began to understand Kate's words. When the words got too difficult for Liz to decipher, Eric stepped in. He explained the "beer phenomenon" to Liz: "Give Kate a beer or two and she pronounce her words better." Kate didn't want to illustrate that fact, still recovering from two nights prior. There would be other opportunities to prove that theory.

The night drew to a close. Kate remembered the feeling of loneliness that had plagued her earlier. Now, that feeling was gone.

Chapter 2

Blaring electric guitars came bursting out of the radio at 6:49 a.m. It startled both of them. Eric hit the snooze button. Four minutes later, a disc jockey strung out on caffeine screamed as he talked. Eric silenced the shrieking lunatic and rose, giving a quick glance toward Kate as she stirred. Kate turned onto her back and allowed her arms go where they wanted. As she listened to running water, she felt anxious for Eric on his first day of work. It was as if he was her child going off to Kindergarten. Kate tried to occupy her mind with something different, but her thoughts always returned to Eric.

"Hi," Kate said softly.

"You're awake?" asked Eric, returning. "It's early."

"You think I would let you leave without a kiss?" she asked. "No way, baby!" She grabbed for the towel around his waist. After a struggle, she got hold of it and pulled it to her.

Eric smiled. "You think you'll be okay with Liz today?"

Kate used the towel to wipe off the nightly gunk from her lips. "Yeah, I'll be okay. She did a good job this weekend."

"I agree," Eric said, as he slid the closet door open. "Don't hesitate to call me if you need anything. Ray is very flexible about you."

"What if I need a little afternoon delight?" Kate struggled to ask with a straight face.

"I don't think he's that flexible, Sweetie."

"I'm kidding. Is that a new suit?"

"Yeah, why? Do you like it?"

Kate nodded.

"Good," he said with conviction. "I don't want to look like a total schmuck my first day." He put on his gray socks and black leather shoes.

"I'll call before I come home to see if I need to pick up anything," he said.

"I think we are okay for a while. We almost bought out the store on Friday."

"Please call me if you need anything."

"I will," Kate said more seriously. As she looked at him, she felt how much she loved him. "I love you," she said.

Eric leaned to kiss her. "I love you," he said and kissed her again. She put her strong arm around his neck and brought him down to her. He reciprocated her embrace. Eric waited patiently, as Kate's arm fought to let go of him. He stood over his wife. "Alright, I'm out of here. Do you need to pee before I leave?"

"No, I'm good," she said. "Have a good day."

"I will," Eric said. He grabbed his keys from the kitchen counter. "Hopefully I'll be home around 5:30."

"Okay," said Kate loudly. She listened intently to Eric's light footsteps, as made his way through the living room; the pocket door slid open and then closed. The outside door closed soon after. She then heard the familiar engine start in the distance. The sound of the engine faded. Once again—silence.

A breeze blew the window blinds a bit. The air was refreshing. Kate studied the room and wondered about the pale yellow paint. The rest of the apartment was almond. *Why was the bedroom yellow?* She pondered this for several minutes. *Maybe the hardware store ran out of almond-colored paint. Maybe it was some artistic expression I'm not familiar with. Maybe someone thought it was good luck for the bedroom to be painted a different color? Maybe Mom would know? Mom would hate this place,* Kate imagined. But her mother would never make the trip to Syracuse, so Kate didn't have to worry.

Kate had always been an anomaly to her mother; something different than a daughter. She was rather an obstacle in her mother's life; something she had to step over. Business was put above everything else. Even Brian, the unaffected child, took a backseat to her professional life as an architect. That fact brought Kate some comfort. For years, Kate had settled on the idea that she was brought into this life to provide Brian with a sibling. Her parents hadn't planned on having a child with a moderate disability. She loved her brother and he loved her. She missed him very much.

It took Eric two minutes to drive to Syracuse University. Old and new, the campus architecture was fantastic and bold. Greek, medieval, and contemporary architecture were all represented. His mother-in-law would be impressed, he realized as he took it all in. It was still remarkable to behold. Situated on top of a hill, the campus had a perfect view of downtown, almost reminiscent of the Parthenon looking over the city of Athens. A mosaic of red brick walkways and the greenest grasses connected the campus, enmeshing century-old buildings and contemporary structures.

Eric pulled into the athletic building's parking lot and walked up a flight of stairs to his pool of offices. Seated behind an expansive mahogany desk was Mrs. Colenza, talking on the phone. She smiled and signaled to Eric that she would soon be with him. Eric noticed that all of her fingers had rings. The joyful middle-aged woman was dressed in dark-green pants and a silk blouse, with electric-blue, green, and black streaks, like something out of one of Van Gogh's paintings. Mrs. Colenza's obviously dyed-red hair clashed with her shirt.

"Eric," Mrs. Colenza said. "Nice to see you again."

"Same here," Eric returned, with almost the same zest.

"Mr. Colberg will be out in a moment," said the colorful secretary. "How's Kate doing?"

"Oh, she's great," he said, smiling.

Before another word was uttered, Mr. Colberg sprang out of his office. "Good to see you," Colberg said, as he extended his right hand. "How have you been?"

"Great!" Eric said, and they shook hands. "I'm happy to be here—finally."

Colberg leaned his back against the desk, as he continued his conversation. He was a tall man, though his height made his gait a bit awkward. He wore a white dress shirt and gray trousers. A pile of salt-and-pepper hair waved atop of his egg-shaped head. He had a bushy mustache. Eric guessed he was in his early 40's.

"Hope the move went smoothly," Colberg said.

"It went well I'm happy to say."

"Great, great," said Colberg. "And how's Katie doing?"

"She's happy to be here, too," answered Eric. "She's doing well—thanks for asking."

"Happy to hear it." Colberg glanced at his watch. "Come on into my office, while we wait for the others."

Eric waved goodbye to Mrs. Colenza and followed Colberg.

Colberg sat down at his desk. "Have a seat," he said to Eric.

Eric sat down on the couch. "I want to thank you for introducing me to Davison."

"Oh, yeah," Colberg said. "How is the apartment working out?"

"It's beautiful. Mr. Davison did a great job." The buzzer sounded from the front desk and a balding gentleman entered. "Hey, John," Colberg said, "I'd like you to meet Eric Hollis, our new trainer."

Eric rose to his feet and stretched out his hand.

"Eric, this is John Griffy, our equipment manager," said Colberg.

"I've heard a lot about you," John said.

"Same here," Eric replied. Eric figured John was between 35 and 40. John stood a few inches above him, with proportions a little bit wider.

"I heard you just moved here from Boston?"

"Yeah, yeah, I used to work at Boston College High School as an assistant coach," Eric said. The buzzer rang again. "It was a fun job, but not a lot of chances to move up."

"I grew up in Newton and came here when I was 18."

Mr. Colberg showed in three people. "Everyone, this is Eric Hollis, our new trainer," he said. "Eric, this is Coach Dave Hill; sports manager Doug Conners, and Dianne Jensen, our team nurse."

Eric shook their hands.

"Hey, Ray," Hill announced in a jesting manner, "are you sure this kid isn't a freshman rookie?"

Colberg and the others broke into laughter. "No, Eric isn't a rookie player."

"How old are you, kid?" asked Hill.

"I'm 29," answered Eric with a well-accustomed smile. He surmised that Hill was the oldest in the room. Eric remained quiet, while the others talked amongst themselves. Dianne Jensen had frizzy red hair and stood about 5'9". She was listening carefully to the conversation. She was very attractive and self-confident. Eric guessed she was in her early 30's.

"Am I right, our first game is on November 14th?" Dianne asked.

"That is correct," Colberg answered.

"Great," Dianne said. She scribbled on her notepad, as if she was catching the front-page story for tomorrow's headlines.

"There's a meeting with the sports administrator at nine.

Everyone must be there," Colberg said. His statement was met with groans by the veteran staff.

"Is it that bad?" Eric asked John beneath his breath.

"You haven't experienced anything until you've been to one of these meetings," said John.

Eric chuckled. He hated meetings and felt they were a waste of everybody's time and energy. But Eric knew he wouldn't need to say anything, nor did he want to. He wouldn't even have to say his name. Colberg would do those honors.

Kate's mind wandered, as her eyes gazed around the bedroom. *The walls were too naked,* she determined. She scanned her memory for pictures that still needed to be hung. This occupied her head for several minutes. Suddenly, she realized she was thinking like her mother. She didn't want to think like her mother. Considering she spent most of her time away from her mother, Kate questioned how her mother had so much influence over her. She tried to imagine her mother's life. Sadness overcame her, as she pondered how *alone* her mother lived her life. Surrounded by material items, her mother seemed to love them more than anything else. Kate could hardly remember her father in the house. She was four when they divorced. He would show up on occasion and shower her and Brian with birthday or Christmas gifts. Kate always wondered what their life would have been like if she hadn't been born into the Reed family.

Engrossed in thought, Kate didn't notice Liz walking into the bedroom. She startled when she saw Liz out of the corner of her eye. Liz apologized. Kate smiled to show Liz no harm was done.

Their daily routine began. Liz fetched the shower chair from the bathroom and successfully transferred Kate onto it. Liz wheeled Kate into the bathroom.

"What time did Eric leave for work this morning?" Liz asked, while adjusting the water temperature.

"Around 7:30," Kate said.

"7:30?"

Success was hers; Kate nodded in jubilation. She rolled into the shower and water splashed all over her rigid body.

"You see, I'm getting this," Liz said, proudly. She soaped up a washcloth and proceeded to bathe Kate. "What time will Eric be home?"

"Around 6:00," answered Kate. She figured Liz would have a better chance hearing "six" than "five-thirty."

"That's a long first day," said Liz.

"Yeah, I know."

The awkwardness of having somebody new shower her was one of those things Kate had learned to accept. For years while, she attended a residential school, she had little choice about who bathed her. Kate was always assigned to the new counselors at the school because she was so easy to get along with. Now, Kate had chosen Liz to take care of her and had confidence in Liz's abilities.

"So, what are we going to do today?"

"I thought we could—" Kate paused to give Liz time to understand the first four words.

"I don't—"

Kate shook her head graciously and repeated herself.

"I thought—" Liz guessed.

Kate nodded. "We could..."

"Where—"

"We," Kate tried to speak again. When she failed to verbalize, she resolved to spell: "W."

"W?" Liz guessed.

Kate continued, "E."

"We..." Liz said and waited for more letters.

Kate was silent for a moment, as Liz rinsed the soap off of her body. "We!"

Kate nodded in elation. *Only 20 more words to go,* she thought. Kate could have gone right to the significant words—clean cabinets, hang pictures, shop—but she believed in the importance of a complete sentence and not sounding like a caveman.

#

After a three-hour excruciatingly dull meeting, the attendants were free. Eric, Ray, and Dianne went outside into the warm sun. Eric thawed out from the conference room's air conditioning; his lungs enjoyed breathing the fresh air. They walked across campus to the cafeteria, an immense room with a 20 foot-high coffered ceiling that looked like an upside-down dinosaur egg crate. They went through the food line and sat down.

"I apologize for the length of that meeting," said Colberg. "Mr. Brabeck was just getting back at some particular idiots that ticked him off last week."

"Thank you," Eric replied. "I'll make sure to stay on Mr. Brabeck's good side." Eric peeled the plastic wrap off his chicken salad sandwich. He caught a glimpse of Dianne cutting her very small salad.

Colberg sipped his coffee. "Brabeck is not a bad guy after you've known him a while."

"How long have you been here, Mr. Colberg?" asked Dianne.

"Seventeen years," said Colberg. "I started here when I was Eric's age." Colberg took another sip.

"So, you just moved here?" Dianne asked Eric.

"Yeah, from Boston," Eric said. "We moved into an apartment about a half mile from the campus."

"Oh, you're married?" Dianne asked, curiously.

Eric wiggled his gold wedding band. "It'll be two years in October," he said. "How 'bout you?"

She hesitated. "Oh, yes, I am—we've been married eight years. We live just off of Route 81."

"Have you lived in Syracuse long?" Eric asked her.

"Just about nine years. I was a nurse at the local hospital for all that time," Dianne explained. "After a while, it just got monotonous so when I knew this job was open, I jumped on it."

Colberg said, "You should have Katie come in one of these days, so Dianne can meet her."

"She starts work on the 15th of August," said Eric. "She'll be on campus every day."

"What will she be doing?"

"Kate is the new assistant manager of the Resource Center," Eric said, proudly.

"Is that part of the library?" Dianne asked.

"Not exactly," Eric answered. "The Resource Center is a place where students can get help, those kinds of things. Katie will be in charge of supervising the disabled students, making sure they get what they need."

"Does she have a lot of experience in that area?" Dianne asked.

Eric chuckled, as he bowed his head. "Yeah, a little more than she deserves, actually. Kate's in a wheelchair—she has cerebral palsy."

Embarrassment claimed Dianne's facial expression. "I'm so sorry."

Eric was puzzled by her overly sympathetic response. "You don't have to be sorry—that's just the way it is. It doesn't bother Kate that she's in a wheelchair."

"Oh, I just thought—" Dianne didn't know how to end her statement. "Please excuse me for a minute." Dianne stood and walked away from the table.

"Oh, I see Kate is going to become best buddies with her," Eric said in a sarcastic tone.

"I don't know her too well." Colberg took another sip of his coffee. "How 'bout this damn baseball strike?"

"It's an ugly display of greediness," said Eric, not missing a beat. "They've taken the game of baseball and flushed it down the toilet."

"I agree," said Colberg.

A few minutes later, Dianne returned. "Did I miss anything?"

Colberg quickly glanced at Eric before he answered Dianne. "No, no, nothing at all. Let me explain what things are like during our basketball season. Traveling from town to town may seem exciting at first, but it's gonna get old very quickly. Being home is going to be like paradise."

"You wouldn't think that if you saw my place," Dianne said, trying to be witty.

Eric grinned and drew his attention back to Colberg.

"Crowds are going to get loud and unbearable at times. Hotels are going to be another place to sleep and meals will be always eaten on the go," Colberg concluded. "You two think you'll be up to the test?"

Eric nodded.

"I'm up to it," Dianne said.

"Do you have any other questions I can answer for you?" Colberg asked.

"Is there usually a physician that travels with us?" Eric asked.

The question brought a grimace to Colberg's nonchalant expression. "That's a very touchy subject," he began. "For the last 20 years, our M.D. has traveled with us. But last year, the administration decided they needed the money for something else."

"I take it you don't agree that we shouldn't have a physician?" Eric said.

"I don't," Colberg said. "I just think there are too many reasons to keep a doctor with us, but the higher-ups see it differently."

"So Dianne and I are the only true medical staff on the team?"

"Yes," Colberg answered. "But we have a good track record for healthy kids."

"I know I'm qualified," said Eric.

Dianne looked at Eric and took the same outlook. "There's nothing I can't handle."

"Well great!" Colberg exclaimed. "Shall we head back to the office?"

The other two rose and followed Colberg out of the cafeteria.

The next informal meeting only lasted two hours. Eric was encouraged to speak. When he did, he held the attention of his audience, including Dianne, who listened to his every word and studied his every gesture. The thought of him being married to a woman with cerebral palsy intrigued her. At 5:30, the meeting ended. Eric went to his office, which he shared with Dianne. He called home. Liz answered. Nothing was needed at the store.

Observing Dianne's inquiring expression, Eric explained in greater detail Kate's disability. More absorbed, Dianne became sullen.

A streak of late-day sunlight spread across the pocket door. Liz had nearly finished cooking dinner when Eric arrived. Kate hurried to greet him. His hands were upon her face, as he kissed her lips. The scent of Eric delighted her. Ten hours in his suit was all Eric could handle, so he changed into shorts and a worn *1981 Boston Marathon* T-shirt.

The aroma of potatoes engulfed the kitchen. Eric took over the stirring for Liz. Kate rubbed the lower part of Eric's back with her closed fist.

Liz left. Eric took a seat on his wife's chair and lap. She relished being close to him. Managing her sometimes incorrigible left arm, Kate directed it around his waist. Her left arm and hand were full of spasticity, and she worried about hurting him. He noticed her anxiousness and quickly put his hand on hers. She rested her head on his back. She wanted to remain there for all eternity.

Soon the day-old sun disappeared. An evening storm was developing. Empty dinner plates were scattered on the countertop. Kate sipped the last of her Pepsi. Eric cleaned up the kitchen.

"Did anyone call today?" he asked.

Kate shook her head. "No one but you." She rested her left elbow on the counter. The puppeteer pulled on her wrist and hand strings constantly; her wrist twisted back and forth.

"Tired?" Eric asked.

"A little," she said. "It's hard doing nothing, and I have nothing to do for the next month."

"Want me to rent some movies?"

Kate sighed. "Nah, I'll become a couch potato."

"You could always come to work with me a couple times a week. We're not doing too much some days."

"I don't think so," she said. "I don't want to get in the way."

"You won't get in the way, Sweetie."

Watching Eric washing dishes relaxed her. "So, tell me about this woman, Dianne. She sounds interesting."

"Time will tell."

"Is she from around here?"

"She said she moved to Syracuse about nine years ago. She didn't say where she was living before."

"So she freaked out when you told her about me, uh?" Kate asked.

"A little, I think." He grabbed the dishtowel. "I think she felt sorry for me. Maybe she once saw someone really involved with CP and figured all people with CP are like that?"

"And she's a nurse," Kate said, with disbelief.

"How was your walk to the shopping plaza?"

"Not bad—it took about ten minutes," Kate said. "But you are gonna have to go in the winter because I'm not walking down there in five feet of snow."

"Oh, yeah?" Eric leaned on her armrests and looked into her eyes. "Gonna make me?"

"Yes, 'cause you have the truck."

Eric kissed her lips. "Okay, I will."

She loved the feel of his lips on hers. Aware of her left arm moving dangerously close to him, she extended it down by her side with force. The puppeteer fought hard to pull her arm upward toward Eric, but she won this round. Her muscles contracted feverishly in her left arm, causing soreness after her struggle with the puppeteer.

Eric put her onto the couch. The clouds were dark. Lightning lit up the sky, thunder clapped and rain poured. The rumbling noises and the flashes of light played havoc on her body. Kate lay on her stomach to keep her arms still.

During the day, no part of her body remained motionless for long; some finger, hand, or toe was always in motion. At night, everything settled down.

Clap! Kate jumped. *Clap!* Kate startled again. Anticipating the claps of thunder, Kate tensed every muscle. *Clap! Clap! Clap!* Eric stroked his fingers above her ear in an attempt to calm her. Eric talked and she answered with an occasional yes or no. Finally surrendering to exhaustion, they retired to bed.

The alarm clock sounded. Kate was used to the obnoxious voice on the radio. Eric was already in the shower. A cool breeze whirled about the bedroom, which now had familiar pictures on the walls.

Eric appeared and leaned over. She pulled him down for the first kiss of the day. They joked, in utter appreciation for one another. It was a good way to begin her first day of work. Kate had been a bit anxious—she doubted her skills and experience—but Eric's encouraging words soothed her mind and she grew increasingly excited. Eric held her close.

Liz arrived. Eric dressed for work. The couple made plans to meet for lunch. They exchanged "I love you's" and kisses, while Liz got Kate's clothes out for the day. Eric left.

At 8:30, Liz and Kate set out on the 15-minute walk to campus. The daughter of two architects, Kate naturally appreciated the remarkable quality and grandeur of these buildings. The large hills of Syracuse brought back memories of the familiar hills of New Hampshire's Monadnock region that Kate had grown to know so well in her childhood.

The hills did not impede Kate's electric wheelchair. Her right hand remained steady on the joystick. Liz struggled to keep up with Kate. At Kate's building, Liz opened the door and wished her good luck.

Inside, Kate rolled down a maze of corridors drowned by antiseptic-white fluorescent light. As she approached her offices, she was briefly possessed by a fear that whoever was there would have forgotten who she was and what she was doing there. Then she remembered Eric's reassuring words from that morning. She had renewed confidence.

Her supervisor, Mr. Leonard, greeted her warmly. He was stocky and short but had a spry, youthful character. His rusty-red hair and beard matched his corduroys. His wire-rimmed glasses were perched on the tip of his nose. Kate was reminded of Kris Kringle.

"Welcome," Mr. Leonard said. "I hope there is enough room for you to get around." He pushed a couple of chairs out of her path.

Kate nodded, with enthusiasm. She opened her laptop computer and gestured to Mr. Leonard to retrieve her headstick from the back of the wheelchair. She had to repeat the gesture a couple of times before he recognized the signal. He knew about Kate's headstick from their interview back in the spring when she'd described how the device works. He reached behind her, retrieved the headstick, and placed it on her head. She used her headstick to tap out several words on the laptop. She hit enter and the synthesized voice boomed: "I'm sure I will have enough room."

"Great!" Mr. Leonard exclaimed. "The rest of our crew should be along in a second. They are eager to meet you."

Kate typed several more words: "I look forward to meeting them." She looked up at Mr. Leonard.

Leonard took a seat. "So, do you like Syracuse?"

Kate nodded and typed: "It's very nice."

A middle-aged woman entered. "Good morning."

"Good morning, Ellen," Mr. Leonard said. "This is Kate

Hollis."

Ellen extended her hand. "I've heard a lot of good things about you."

Kate lifted her right arm and Ellen grasped it. Ellen had an engaging smile and wavy brown hair. Kate typed: "It's very nice to meet you."

"And here's Pauline Lawson, our math advisor," Mr. Leonard said, as Pauline entered.

"Hello everyone," said Pauline. "You must be Kate."

"Hi," Kate said, using her natural voice this time. Pauline had a round face and a plump body. Her hair was silver. Kate guessed she was in her 50's. Kate extended her right arm and Pauline grasped her hand.

"Nice to meet you," Pauline said.

Kate typed at a hurried pace and struggled to avoid making a mistake: "It's good to meet you finally," the computer articulated.

A telephone rang and Leonard excused himself.

"If I remember, you are from around this area?" asked Pauline.

Kate quickly pecked away on her laptop. She knew that most people weren't used to waiting so long for an answer. Besides, the muscles in Kate's neck got tight when she typed a lot, especially if rushed; she'd learned to keep her sentences short and to the point.

"I'm originally from Boston," she said. "My husband and I just moved here about a month ago."

"Really," Pauline said. "Does he work here?"

Pauline's slight but noticeable reaction didn't surprise Kate. Kate noticed that people often assumed she was as slow to comprehend—until she showed them otherwise. "He's the new athletic trainer for the basketball team."

"Impressive," Ellen said. Her surprise at the fact that Kate had a husband was understandable.

"We have ourselves quite a girl here," concluded Pauline. "Will you two excuse me, I got a few calls to make while I'm thinking about it. You know how the memory goes when people get to my age."

Kate negotiated her way into Mr. Leonard's office and closed the door. The room was claustrophobic, as it had no windows.

The fluorescent light gave the walls a pinkish tinge.

He sat behind his desk and stared down at some papers. Kate felt certain that his glasses were going to fall off his nose, but they didn't budge.

He spoke extensively about the students their department serves. Kate asked a few questions, never wanting to be overbearing in the conversation. To Kate's relief, Mr. Leonard moved the discussion into the conference room across the hall with Pauline and Ellen. The two women provided Kate with profiles of several students she would be encountering during the semester. Kate was grateful for this information. They discussed the issue of the accessibility of the campus. Kate listened intently, etching the facts into her mind. Mr. Leonard assured Kate that if any problems with accessibility arose, accommodations would be made. The meeting ran until noon.

The air was refreshing, as Kate headed for the cafeteria. She felt ragged from typing all morning. She flexed her neck in all directions to loosen the muscles.

"Boo!" a familiar voice called out behind her.

Kate turned around.

"Sorry I'm late," he said and kissed her. "Honey, I'd like you to meet Dianne. Dianne, this is my wife, Kate."

"It's nice to finally meet you," Kate said.

Dianne looked on with befuddlement and anxiety. Dianne looked to Eric.

"She says it's nice to finally meet you," Eric said.

"Oh, nice to meet you, too," Dianne said, mechanically. "Eric has told me so much about you."

"I hope it was all good," Kate said, trying to smile. She sensed that Dianne wanted to be anywhere but there.

Dianne stared despairingly at Eric. By the time Eric had repeated Kate's words, the humor had dissipated.

"Why don't we get some food and sit down?" Eric said. He saw Kate's guarded expression.

Kate followed Dianne through the line.

"Don't worry, Katie won't run you over," said Eric, sensing that Dianne didn't trust Kate's driving skills.

Dianne didn't look back again.

Eric placed his tray upon the nearest table and made room for

Kate.

"How did the morning go?" Eric asked Kate, as he closed her laptop and peeled the wrap off her sandwich.

"Good—it went by fast," she answered.

"Where's her office?" Dianne asked.

Eric shot a glance at Kate and saw the disdain rising in her eyes. "Next to the English building."

"What does she do again?" Dianne asked.

Kate felt frustration over Dianne's unwillingness to address her directly. "I'm the assistant manager of the Resource Center," Kate answered.

Eric gazed at his wife in amazement at how clearly Kate spoke and her raw emotion. He repeated Kate's words for Dianne.

Dianne directed her attention to her tiny salad with its thimbleful of low-calorie dressing.

"Hey, guys," said Colberg, appearing from the food line. "Sorry I'm late." He greeted Kate with a smile and a wink. "How is your first day going, Katie?"

"It's going very well, thank you."

Colberg was determined to understand what she said, but failed. "I didn't catch it. Please give me another try."

Almost as if she was preparing for a rocket launch, Kate hunkered down in her wheelchair and repeated her words.

"'Very well' was part of it, right?" asked Colberg.

Kate nodded, enthusiastically.

"Help me out, Eric," said Colberg.

Eric grinned. "'Thank you.'"

"Oh, sure, sure," Colberg said. "Are you going to come over to our office for a visit soon?"

Kate smiled at the kind offer. "I would like that."

Colberg got the gist of her reply. "Great," he said.

Dianne remained befuddled with Kate and everything about her. "I'm heading back to the office," Dianne said. "I have to get some things done."

"Okay," said Eric. "We'll be back in a little while."

Kate felt relieved when Dianne left. She disliked meeting new people over a meal. She had a tendency to bite her tongue, cheek, or lip when she ate, causing her to gasp and startle, and strangers often assumed she was choking. She grew tense and often she would stop eating just so that she could relax. She hated to make a scene. She picked the easiest foods to eat when she ate with mere acquaintances or in restaurants. In movie theaters, Kate always turned down popcorn, candy, and soda, to make sure she didn't cough during the show. She hated to draw attention. She enjoyed loud concerts, since nobody noticed if she happened to bite her tongue, cheek or lip.

After lunch, Eric escorted Kate to the bathroom.

"Well, that was interesting," Kate said. "Dianne hardly knew I was at the table."

Eric sighed. "Yeah, I noticed," he said. "Maybe she hasn't been around people in wheelchairs?" He unbuckled her seatbelt and lifted her onto the toilet.

"Yeah, maybe," said Kate. "I'm just a little unnerved by her."

"Don't worry, we won't be inviting her to dinner anytime soon," he said.

Kate laughed. "That's good to know."

"She may be the kind of person that will never understand."

"Could be," said Kate. "You get off at 5:30?"

"Yeah. Want to meet at my office?" he asked.

"Yeah, sure." Back in her wheelchair, they walked outside under the late-summer sun and they parted with a quick kiss.

That afternoon, Kate was already feeling more relaxed at work. Mr. Leonard invited her on a tour of the campus, and she prepared her computer for the jaunt. Kate listened attentively to Leonard describe buildings, departments and classrooms. The glare of the sun made it hard to see her computer screen, turning away from it. Mr. Leonard introduced Kate to several faculty members whom they encountered. All were impressed with Kate's accomplishments, as Leonard boasted about his newest employee. Two faculty members mentioned specific problems and asked for Kate's help. She welcomed their offers to do whatever she could.

Eric's fingers struck the keyboard harder and harder, but the computer wouldn't accept his inputs. The keys were like little punching bags. New software programs baffled Eric.

"Dammit," he said.

Dianne looked over at him. "What's the matter?"

"The stupid computer won't accept anything!"

She approached. "I think you're in the wrong mode," Dianne said. "Press Control-F."

Eric obeyed. "Now what?"

"Just put in the information you want to enter."

Eric tapped the keys. "You really know what you are doing, don't you?"

"They didn't hire me because of my face, you know," she said.

"Thanks a lot," he said. "Hey, you seemed a bit uncomfortable around Kate."

Dianne looked away. "I've never met anyone like her," she said. "I wasn't sure what to say."

"Just talk to her like any other person. The fact that Kate has cerebral palsy doesn't mean she can't understand," Eric said. He straightened papers on his desk. "Kate can think just as well as you and I."

"Okay," Dianne said. "I'm sorry if I caused you any problems."

"No problems at all." Eric picked up a crumpled paper off the floor. "In nursing school, didn't you come across patients with cerebral palsy?"

"No one," she answered. Dianne retreated to her desk. "You want a soda from downstairs?"

"No, thank you."

"I'll be right back," Dianne said and was gone.

The clock said five minutes to five. Kate took a moment to stretch, raising her arms and arching her back. Mr. Leonard returned and told her that he was heading home. Kate expressed her gratitude for her position at the Resource Center. He appreciated her kind words.

The sun was high in the western sky, as Kate went to Eric's office. She contemplated her first day of work, while admiring the scenery.

The elevator call button in Eric's building was difficult to reach, but Kate stretched and got it. On the second floor, Mrs. Colenza sat at the front desk. Her bright red hair set off her flowery yellow blouse. Mrs. Colenza informed Eric by intercom that Kate had arrived.

"Hi Sweetie, come down to the office," Eric said, as he emerged in the hallway. "I have a couple things to do before I can take off."

"Okay." Kate followed him into his office.

He placed a copy of *Sports Illustrated* on his desk. "Here, look through this for a few minutes." Eric placed her headstick on her head.

"Don't you guys have *Cosmo* or *People*?" Kate asked, sarcastically.

"Sorry, Sweetie, it's just us jocks around here. I'll be right back."

Sports Illustrated wasn't her favorite magazine, but she flipped through the pages. The exhaustion of the day slowly reached her. Dianne appeared.

"Oh, God!" Dianne exclaimed. "I didn't see you there."

Kate just smiled. If she tried to say anything, Dianne wouldn't understand her.

"I'm sorry." Dianne left the office.

Kate shook her head in disbelief and continued flipping through the magazine.

"Ready to go?" Eric asked, as he returned.

"Yeah."

"Let's go," Eric said. He closed her laptop and removed her headstick. "Tired?" he asked, taking the wheelchair controls.

"Yeah," she said. "Let's go home."

After seven years, Eric was an expert at feeding Kate. But their first time going out to a restaurant was different.

Knowing each other only two weeks, Eric asked her out on a date. Kate was hesitant to except his invitation, but after a lot of reassurance from her friend Meg, she agreed.

Something in his eyes made her trust him. He drove up to New Hampshire from Boston. She was a student at The Miller School. Nervous, she didn't eat a thing that entire day. But he quickly put her at ease. He was so elated to see her. He lifted her into his truck. The apprehension and the excitement of the date made it difficult for her to stay still, but after a few minutes she regained some composure. His new truck traveled well on the winding roads. A green wall of leaves soared upward toward the blue vaulted sky. It was a summer's day, everything bright and alive. When Eric engaged her in conversation, she flourished like a rose. Her restaurant of choice, Alberto's, was an Italian joint housed in an old New England bungalow with a farmer's porch. Eric parked and got Kate's wheelchair out. He cradled Kate in his arms like a china doll. She reassured him that she wouldn't break. They were met with a few curious stares, but nothing out of the ordinary. Eric didn't seem to mind. He spoke for Kate when the waitress took their order.

Eric stuffed some quarters into the jukebox. *Who is this guy?* she asked herself. *Is he real? What the hell does he see in me?* She could tell by looking at his hands that he was gentle and disciplined. They were not the hands of a barbaric creature. He slid her hand into his, struggling to overcome the spasticity of her right arm. Eric waited, with sensitivity and compassion. At that moment, Kate knew she would never grow tired of looking into his eyes.

During the meal, Eric dropped only a couple of pasta shells, while feeding Kate. She held her left arm underneath the armrest of her wheelchair. Her left bicep strained and her arm soon grew tired. She let her left arm hang down alongside the wheel. Her fingers kept grabbing the wire spokes, so she positioned her arm against her chest. As Eric held up her soda, her arm sprang forward and knocked the glass from his hand onto the checkered tablecloth. A small amount of soda spilled, but she felt overcome with embarrassment and apologized repeatedly. In a brilliant display of chivalry, Eric tumbled over his almost empty glass of Sprite. Kate laughed. She had come through the date unscathed.

On the drive back, they talked about anything and everything. Eric held Kate's hand. Before leaving for Boston, he promised he would return. They spent half an hour saying goodbye. Under a crescent moon, they shared their first kiss.

Kate sipped her soda, as Eric cleaned up the kitchen. Kate heard a car door slam; voices could be heard. She crawled to the bay window and saw the couple she'd witnessed arguing a month earlier. Sensing tension between them Kate watched their every move, their every gesture. So absorbed, she failed to notice Eric was standing over her. He looked across the street and asked her what was so fascinating. She pointed her eyes to the couple. He asked Kate who they were. She didn't know. All she knew was that they were unhappy. Eric returned to the kitchen.

Kate continued to watch until the cast of characters left their stage. The scene prompted her to consider her relationship with Eric. She suspected the couple had been happy once; all couples are happy at some point. *What'd caused them to be so embittered toward each other?* Kate admired the way they kept trying to bring themselves back together and she wondered whether she and Eric could reassemble their pieces, if something ever happened to them.

She settled into her usual spot in front of the couch. Eric soon joined her and lifted her up on the couch. She rested her head on his lap. They watched reruns.

When she awoke, it was past ten—she could tell by the television show. Eric was out like a light. She kissed his bare knees.

"Eric, wake up, hon," she said softly.

Eric lifted his head and rubbed his eyes. "What time is it?"

"It's after ten," she answered.

"Do you still wanna call Meg?"

"Yeah. She should be home by now."

"Alright," he said. "Let's get you settled in bed." Eric carried Kate into the bathroom, then to the bedroom. He dialed Meg's number and activated the speakerphone.

"Hello," Meg squawked.

"Hi," said Kate, always glad to hear Meg's voice.

"So, how was your first day of work?" Meg asked.

"Good. It was busy, though."

"Did ya have lunch with any cute campus guys?" asked Meg, playfully.

"Nah, only Eric," Kate said. Eric rolled his eyes.

"How are you doing, Meg?" asked Eric.

"Same shit, different day," Meg said with a laugh. "How are you and your wife doing these days?"

"We're doing great. She likes to freak out people, though," Eric said, chuckling.

"It's not my fault she gets freaked out every time she sees me."

"Who gets freaked out?" Meg asked.

"This nurse, Dianne, who I work with," Eric said. "For some reason, she gets all flustered when Kate appears."

"Have you turned into the elephant man, Kate?" Meg said.

"No, I don't think so," Kate said. "But I can't figure the girl out."

"Yeah, well. Some people just don't get it," Meg said. "So, tell me about this boss of yours."

"He's cool—Mr. Leonard."

"What's his name again?" asked Meg.

"Mr. Leonard," Eric repeated. His hands began to wander up Kate's T-shirt.

Kate tried to push them away. "Stop, I'm on the phone."

"Is he getting frisky again?" Meg asked.

"Yes, and he better stop." Kate gave him a hand to hold, pacifying him for a few seconds.

She kept talking to Meg, while defending against his roaming hands. "I'll call you back when he's not bugging the hell out of me," Kate said in mock frustration.

"Okay guys, don't stay up too late," Meg said.

"Bye, Meg," they said in unison.

"Why do you have to get me going, while I'm on the phone?" she reprimanded.

"'Cause I just have to," he said. "It's just something I must do."

She coiled her arms around him. Kate pulled Eric closer to her. Kissing ensued. Sleep would wait for a little while.

Chapter 3

The bustle on campus was like a big city. Students rushed from building to building, trying to find their assigned classrooms. On this first day, it rained mercilessly. Kate avoided going outside. She looked up from her typing and saw a disheartened face of a young man sitting in a wheelchair outside her office. His jet-black hair and worn denim jacket were soaked.

"May I help you?" asked Kate, using her synthesized voice.

The young man seemed confused about where the robotic voice was coming from. He looked reluctantly at Kate. "Is there someone who can help me?"

"Sure. What do you need?" Kate kept her sentences short, so that she wouldn't lose his attention.

"I mean, is there someone who can help me?" the distressed young man asked.

"I work here. I can help you," Kate said. At times like this, she wished the synthesized voice was more expressive.

The young man pulled a crumpled piece of paper from his jacket pocket and stared at it. "Is there a Kate Hollis around here somewhere?"

Kate smiled and typed: "I'm Kate Hollis. What's your name?"

Bewilderment spread over the young man's face. He looked Kate over and ended up staring at the black tip of her headstick. "My name is Carl Delane," he said. "You're my counselor?"

"Happy to meet you," the computer said. "You look like you could use a towel."

"Yeah, I guess so."

"Give me a few minutes," Kate typed. She approached Sue Clark, the student secretary, on the other side of the office. "Do we have any towels around here?" she asked Sue. Sue had known Kate for a short time, but already respected her. "I don't think so," Sue said.

"Would you mind calling Eric to see if he has any?"

"Sure," said Sue.

"Thanks." Kate returned to her office. "Someone is bringing towels right away," she typed to Carl.

Carl looked at her with amazement. "Thanks."

As she typed, Kate smiled in Carl's direction. "No problem," she said. "Did you say you needed help with something?"

"Yeah, one of my classes is on a floor I can't get to."

"What class?"

Carl looked at the paper again. "Chemistry lab."

"Now, there's a fun course," she typed. She pulled up his class schedule on her computer. "Where is CL380?"

"Chemistry Building. Room 380 is on the third floor," Carl said.

"No elevator?" Kate typed.

"No, not in that building, but there's another chem lab in the Science Center, I'm pretty sure."

"Okay, let's see if we can move your chem lab," Kate typed.

Carl listened attentively to the computerized voice. "No problem if you can't move it. I took chem in high school."

Kate gave him a smirk. "College chemistry is required, Carl."

"Oh, well—at least I gave it my best shot."

"I think we'll get along just fine," the computer said. She asked him about his other courses. Before long, Eric walked in with a garbage bag full of towels.

"Here he is," Kate said in her natural voice.

"Hi," said Eric. He handed a couple towels to Carl. "My God, you're sopping. You should get a rain poncho."

Kate nodded. "Eric, I would like you to meet Carl Delane."

"Del—?" Eric prompted.

"D-E-L-A-N-E," Kate spelled.

"Nice to meet you, Carl," Eric said and extended his hand.

Intrigued by Kate's strange way of talking, Carl stared at her. He shook Eric's hand.

"Carl, this is my husband, Eric," the computer voice said.

Carl looked dumbfounded. "You're her husband?" he blurted.

"Yes, I am," said Eric, smiling.

"You know, Carl, he can get you tickets to all the Syracuse home games if you want to go."

"Can you?" Carl asked Eric, excitedly.

"Sure," Eric said. "But I don't want to hear you have been giving my wife a hard time." Eric smiled.

Carl laughed and promised to be nice to Kate.

"Okay." Eric looked at his watch. "I gotta get back," he said and put his hand on Kate's shoulder.

"See you home around six?"

"Yeah, around there." Eric zippered his jacket and looked at Kate again. "See you later." He turned to Carl. "See you sometime, Carl."

"Yep. Thanks," Carl said, as Eric left. "He seems like a cool guy," Carl said to Kate.

Kate pecked at the keys. "He is."

Sue helped Kate contact Carl's chemistry professor. They had a frustrating time convincing Professor Wilcox that this issue needed to be solved. Kate persuaded him to meet with her. She drove across campus to the Chemistry Building. As she waited, she kept reassuring herself of her abilities. Soon, he appeared. His suit was unmistakably out of the 60's; the putrid white-and-green plaid polyester clashed, with the orange walls. He sported a pale yellow dress shirt without a tie. The combination was a disgrace to fashion. He introduced himself and pulled up a chair. Kate began to type, struggling to be fast so not to waste his precious time. She needed to correct typing mistakes. She pressed the Enter key.

Wilcox disagreed. He refused to move Carl's lab class, and even refused to keep Carl in lab. Kate was appalled. Her nervousness turned to frustration. She assured Professor Wilcox that Carl would be physically able to do all the chemistry experiments himself. Wilcox rejected letting Carl participate, for fear that Carl might endanger himself and others. Carl could only participate in the classroom section.

Kate had heard enough and parted graciously. She went back to her office. A young woman was waiting.

"She's waiting for you," Sue said. "Her name is Emily Harrod. She's a second-year communications major. She's blind and wants help finding textbooks in Braille."

Kate returned to her desk. "Hi Emily, my name is Kate Hollis. I'm going to try to help you find your books in Braille. I'm not promising anything, but I will try."

Emily had long brown hair and a face like a porcelain china doll. "You must be new here," Emily said.

"Yes, I am," said the computer.

"It's not so easy to find textbooks in Braille, especially specialized books."

"Have you checked to see if they are available on tape?"

Emily said they weren't. "If you request a book to be recorded, it might take two or three years."

"What if we find some volunteers who could read to you? How would that be?"

"I guess that would work," Emily said.

"How many textbooks do you need readers for?" Kate typed.

"Just two books, I think."

Kate typed quickly. "Okay, just give Sue a call, tell her the titles and we'll take it from there."

"Thank you very much, Ms. Hollis," Emily said. "I'll call her tomorrow."

"Okay, Emily. Have a good night," the computer said. Emily rose to leave. Kate worried whether Emily could get to her next destination. She looked out the window a few minutes later and saw Emily waiting, cane in hand. Kate went to see if Emily needed assistance.

Kate approached Emily slowly. She turned up the volume on her synthesizer. "Emily, do you need help getting somewhere?" she asked.

"Oh, Ms. Hollis," Emily said, without hesitation. "My friend is supposed to come at three o'clock and walk me back to the dorm."

Kate looked at her watch. "It's almost four. How about I walk you back?"

Emily didn't want to impose, but she suspected that her friend was not coming. "Okay."

Kate typed: "Can you give me a moment, while I run inside and ask Sue to take off my computer and headstick? We won't be able to talk too much, but I'll be more comfortable."

"What's a headstick?" asked Emily.

Instead of trying to explain, Kate placed the tip of her headstick in Emily's hand. Emily felt her way up the aluminum stick to the plastic brace on Kate's head.

"You're a unicorn!" Emily exclaimed. "Go take your horn off."

Kate was amused. "I'll be right back," she said in her natural voice. Emily seemed to understand her words. When Kate returned, Emily was waiting patiently.

"Can I hold on to your wheelchair?" Emily asked.

"Yeah," Kate said and guided Emily's hand to the chair.

"You know, Kate," Emily said, "the people who worked in your office last year couldn't see past their noses. If I had asked them to help me find these books, they would have told me to go talk to my instructor."

"Really?" Kate kept it short and clear, speaking above the brisk wind.

"Yeah, I heard Mr. Leonard hired someone new, so I decided to try again. I'm glad I did."

"Good," Kate said.

As they neared Emily's dorm, several people said hello. Emily knew considerably more people than Kate. "Thanks, Kate. I can make my way easily from here."

Kate was taken aback by Emily's perfect sense of where she was. Kate mumbled how impressed she was.

Emily laughed into the gray sky. "I know every crack in the pavement, even with my shoes on."

Kate felt inadequate for a moment. "Oh, oh, okay." She looked down at the bumps and divots in the sidewalk. Her sense of inadequacy soon mellowed into admiration for Emily's spirit.

Saying goodbye, Emily was met by a passing friend before she reached the entrance.

"Okay," Kate said. "G'night!" Kate was glad it was almost time to go home. She returned to a quiet office. Sue helped her put her headstick back on. Kate's thoughts drifted to Wilcox and his unwavering feelings about Carl. She gathered her thoughts to present the issue to Mr. Leonard. She composed a report, stating the facts and the actions to resolve the problem. Like a woodpecker, the rubber tip of her headstick struck the keys at a furious pace. Words soon filled the screen of her laptop. Kate pressed Save. Feeling the stress on her neck, Kate stretched her neck. After a day's work, she was tired. She sat uncharacteristically still. Even the puppeteer left her alone. Before Kate turned off her computer, she delivered the report to Mr. Leonard. He was horrified that Professor Wilcox refused to admit Carl into a course. He promised to help her find a solution. Kate reaffirmed her confidence in her abilities.

Already dressed in her sweats, Kate was in front of the TV

when Eric got home. It felt like days since she had seen him last, but it had only been seven hours. Liz had prepared dinner for them before going home.

Eric kissed Kate and sat down on the couch. "You look exhausted," he said.

"I am," Kate said. "I found myself a battle to fight today."

Eric grinned. "Who with?"

"Professor Wilcox—he teaches chemistry," Kate said. "He won't let Carl into lab."

"Why the hell not?" he asked.

"'Cause he's afraid that Carl will get hurt, or hurt someone else."

"That's such bullshit!" Eric exclaimed.

"I know," she said, "but Professor Wilcox doesn't see it that way."

"What did Mr. Leonard say?" Eric asked.

"Oh, he couldn't believe it," Kate said. "He says he'll help me through it."

"Good," he said. "Not to say you can't handle it by yourself."

"I know, I know," Kate said. She rubbed her weary eyes. "How was your day?"

"Okay, I guess. I met with some of the players. Gotta meet a few more tomorrow."

"Are they nice?"

"Yeah, most of them."

"That's good."

"Do you want a beer?" he asked.

"Sure," said Kate. After her strenuous day, one beer would relax her.

Kate and Mr. Leonard focused their efforts on getting Carl into chemistry lab and relocating the class to an accessible room. Professor Wilcox continued to resist letting Carl participate. Kate got to know Carl. She was struck by the agony he had in his heart. The future seemed unreachable to him.

Carl talked about wanting to do well for his father's sake. His father, a high-priced corporate lawyer in Manhattan, had always dreamed of having a son attend Syracuse, play a little basketball or football, and graduate magna cum laude. Carl looked at the floor and wondered aloud how he would ever live up to his father's expectations. His lack of confidence moved Kate. She vowed to do her best for him.

Eric arrived at the office. He was the first one there and he started brewing the coffee for Mrs. Colenza. He began his paperwork early so he could meet with a few students at eight o'clock. The quietness allowed him to get most of his paperwork. A few minutes before 8:00, Dianne arrived and greeted Eric with warm sincerity like she did every morning. They asked each other how their evening went, discussing the popular television shows.

Eric arranged the papers on his desk. He looked handsome in his charcoal pinstripe suit and silver tie. Dianne inspected his clothes. She left the office before the two students arrived. Eric greeted the two African-American youngsters. "Please come in and sit," said Eric. "Can I get anything for you guys?"

"No thanks, Eric, we're all set," said the larger man.

The smaller man nodded.

Dianne returned.

Eric stood. "Guys, this is Dianne Jensen, our nurse. Dianne, meet Derrick Johns and Stuart King."

Derrick and Stuart stood and shook her hand.

"Nice to meet you." Dianne sat down.

"I need to find out a little about you both. I won't ask you any personal questions until after your physical exam next week," Eric explained. "Both of you are freshmen, right?"

"I am," Derrick answered. "This little thing is a sophomore."

"Shut up," said Stuart.

"Yes, I apologize for reading that wrong," Eric said. "You had a pretty good year last year."

"Yeah," said Stuart. Though physically smaller than his friend, Stuart had a commanding presence.

"So, tell me, what did you guys do this summer?" Eric asked.

"We grew up together," Derrick said. "Most summers we work for the Cleveland Indians organization, but this summer we worked for a friend."

"Very cool," Eric said with excitement. "What did you guys do for the Indians?"

Stuart looked at Derrick to see who was going to answer.

"We started out as bat boys when we were 13, and then every year after that we had more responsibilities," Stuart said. "My Dad is one of the higher-ups in the organization."

"No kidding?" Eric said. "I'm jealous."

"Next summer you should come see a game. We'll have a great time," said Derrick.

"Sounds like a plan."

"Is Ray around?" asked Stuart.

"Yeah, he should be here in a few minutes," Eric said.

"I haven't seen him yet this year. It'll be good to see the man," said Stuart, with reverence.

"Don't worry. He's coming on the road with us."

"He was so funny last year," said Stuart. "One time, we were in the Kentucky, I think it was; Ray comes out of the locker room after the game with a jock strap taped to his back. I think he walked around like that for a couple of hours."

"Who taped it to his back?" Eric asked.

"Oh, God," said Stuart. "I think it was George."

"If you hadn't cracked up," Derrick said to Stuart, "he would have worn it through the airport."

All three laughed.

"Now I know what I'm in for with you guys," said Eric. "So, were you guys healthy this summer?"

Both young men answered yes.

"Any health problems with either of you?"

Both men answered no.

"Are you being safe with yourselves and others?"

"Do you mean sex?" Derrick asked.

Eric nodded.

Derrick chuckled. "Stuart here hasn't had sex in months. Isn't that right, Stu?"

"Shut up."

"Come on guys, this is serious," said Eric.

"Sometimes," Johns mumbled.

"You guys have to use condoms every time," he said, looking at the two men.

Stuart squirmed in his seat.

Eric turned to Dianne. "Can you get these gentlemen some condoms please, Dianne?"

"Certainly," said Dianne. She stood and walked out of the

room.

"Thanks, Dianne," Eric said. "Derrick, I have scheduled your physical for next Wednesday at eight in the morning. That doesn't conflict with any of your classes, does it?"

"No, not at all," said Johns.

"And Stuart, yours is next Thursday, also at eight," Eric said. "Any problems with that?"

Stuart shook his head. "That's fine," he replied. "Is it the same idiot doctor we had last year?"

Eric picked up a letter from his desk. "Dr. Paul F. Freham?"

"Yeah, that's him," Stuart said. "I take it you haven't met him yet?"

"No, I haven't," Eric answered. "Is he a real bonehead?"

"Wicked!" exclaimed King. "Last year, Roy had a slight cold—I mean, slight. Freham puts him in the hospital for four days. Nothing was wrong with him."

"Really?" Eric said.

Stuart nodded.

Dianne returned. "Here you go, guys," she said and handed them each a strip of condoms. "And don't use them as Hindenburg balloons."

Laughter filled the office.

"Okay, guys," Eric said and stood. "I'll see you next week. Anytime that you have any questions, health issues, or just want to chat, my door is always open."

"Okay," Stuart said.

"And if anyone needs more condoms, every RA should have a supply. If they don't, let us know," Dianne said. Her deep voice commanded their attention.

"Okay," Derrick said. "We always wanted to be condom narcs."

Eric grinned. "See you guys next week."

"What's the matter?" asked Dianne after the young men were gone.

"I got the impression that Freham is an idiot," Eric said at low volume.

"You got to be kidding?"

"Well, that's what Stuart said. We shall find out."

After a draining week of going over the same concerns, it was decided that the safety concerns voiced by Professor Wilcox were unfounded, and Carl was allowed to participate in the lab. Kate felt proud to have won her first battle. No wheelchair accessible laboratories were available, except for the newly renovated labs across campus. Professor Wilcox demanded that the lab in the assigned classroom not move.

The autumn sun glowed through the tinted windows of Kate's office. Pauline Lawson noticed Kate's tired eyes and suggested she leave for the weekend. Kate took her advice and promised Pauline she would stay late for her one day.

A stiff, cool breeze whipped Kate's hair back, as she headed for Eric's office. She found Eric looking vacant into his computer screen. Sensing her presence, he turned and caressed her cold cheek. He was just finishing up. As he typed, Kate kissed the side of his neck every now and then.

On the way, home they decided to go out to a nice restaurant and celebrate their wedding anniversary a few days early. It would be the last full weekend they would spend together before the college basketball season began. It was their first real date in a long time. Eric wore a button-down shirt and a pair of nice blue jeans. Kate put on a white blouse tucked into black dress pants; her black leather boots completed the ensemble. She wore the gold necklace Eric had given her a year before.

Kate found the restaurant's ambiance warm and inviting; she felt unusually elegant. They sat next to a window. As she looked out at the evening, she noticed her muscles were more relaxed than ever. They talked and laughed about their recent months. Neither of them paid attention to the occasional looks Kate's wheelchair drew from other patrons.

Two years earlier, on a bright and beautiful Saturday in the early fall, New Hampshire's trees were decorated with the colors of red, orange, and gold. Only a few close family members and friends gathered for Eric and Kate's wedding under the vivid canopies. Eric had proposed only two weeks earlier, but they couldn't wait to wed. The justice of the peace presided over the small ceremony with great joy. Kate was adorned in a simple white dress, pretty and dainty; no accessories were needed. On that special day, Eric wore an elegant gray suit.

During the ceremony, Eric kneeled by Kate's side, so as to be eye to eye with her as they proclaimed their vows. The wind blew gently, as the justice pronounced them husband and wife. Their smiles revealed their great love and happiness. A small reception at Meg's gathered everyone in celebration. It was the perfect day. Now, here they were, two years later, embarking on a new life together.

The wind had grown brutal outside. Winter was quickly approaching. The front caster wheels wobbled furiously, as Eric pushed Kate's wheelchair. Eric hurried Kate inside the truck and blasted the heat. All of her muscles were trying to warm up. As Eric pulled into their driveway, the truck was finally getting warm.

"Damn, it's even cold in here," he declared on entering their apartment. "Need to pee?"

Kate nodded, as she changed her bladder into home mode—whereas she stopped worrying about finding a bathroom.

They settled in the living room and their usual spot. Eric fetched a bottle of Champagne and two plastic cups. "Maybe this will warm you up," he said.

"When did you get this?" Kate asked, as he poured the bubbly.

"Yesterday. Don't drink too fast!" he exclaimed.

Kate took a few sips. "God, that's good." She took a few more.

"Warming up yet?"

She nodded.

"What would you like to do tomorrow?"

"I don't know," Kate said. "Let's see tomorrow."

"Okay. Whatever my favorite girl wants," he said, lost in her gaze.

"I better be your favorite," Kate said.

"You are," he returned.

"I love you."

"I love you, babe," Eric said and kissed her. He unbuttoned her blouse. Kate was consumed by his touch, as he slid off her blouse. He slowly removed her bra. He cuddled her soft breasts and kissed her lips. Clumsily, Kate reached up her right hand and slid it down the front of his shirt to signal what she desired. He removed his shirt, while she attempted to help. Kate knelt and put her chest to his. He lowered her to the floor. The carpet tickled Kate's back. She ached for more. Her eyes conveyed her wishes. Eric finished undressing her, then himself. With him so close, Kate was mindful to control her muscles as best she could to avoid hurting him. Eric held her left hand, as they made love.

Clouds diffused the morning sunlight that poured through their bedroom windows. The room was unusually cold. Kate opened her eyes. The clock read ten past eleven. She gazed at her sleeping husband. For several minutes, she stared at the beautiful creature next to her. She studied his smooth eyelids, his perfect nose, and his soft lips. She wished cerebral palsy did not possess her body. She would have given anything to be able to caress his perfect features with her fingertips. She used the tip of her nose as a substitute, gently drawing it across Eric's stubbly cheek; her lips found his. Eric awoke and pulled her onto his chest.

"Good morning," he said.

"Guess what time it is?" Kate said. "It's past eleven!"

"It is not?"

"Yes it is," said Kate, with exaggerated authority.

Eric chuckled. "I guess last night went pretty well, uh?"

"Yeah, it did," she said tenderly.

"How did you sleep?"

"Good," she said. "How 'bout you?"

"Like a baby," Eric said. "What do you feel like doing today?"

"Oh, I don't know," she answered. Her chin rested upon his chest. "What do you want to do?"

"Let's go for a drive somewhere; maybe around the Finger Lakes, or somewhere like that?"

"Okay. I'm up for anything."

He kissed her forehead. "Oh," he said, "I just remembered I haven't checked you lately."

"Do it now." Kate rolled onto her back and he examined her breasts for changes. "They're fine."

"I gotta find a doctor around here."

"Have you asked Liz? She might know somebody."

"She's got some old guy," Kate said. "I want someone I can relate to."

"I know, I know; keep looking," Eric said and rose to his feet. "Ready for a shower?"

"Yeah," Kate answered.

A little after noon, Eric and Kate started on their trip. Maps cluttered the dashboard. Eric had brought them just in case. He stopped for doughnuts and coffee—tea for Kate. He fed Kate as he drove, a talent that he'd perfected over the years. Occasionally, Kate would bite one of his fingers, if he didn't remove it fast enough. She would often laugh, knowing she hadn't caused him great pain. The invisible puppeteer got a thrill out of catching Eric's finger in her teeth.

Two hours passed and they found themselves near the Finger Lakes. The sun filtered through the autumn-colored leaves over the winding roads. The shimmering light reminded Kate of her years in southern New Hampshire.

As the day wore on, the temperature dropped considerably and Kate's light-gray Syracuse sweatshirt wasn't enough to keep her warm. Eric turned on the heat in the truck and frequently slapped the dashboard to kick-start the thermostat. Fearing a lecture from Kate, he kept quiet about the decrepit condition of the truck. He hoped the truck would survive the winter, and then they would buy a new van in the spring, if they could afford it.

They stopped for a bite on the way home. Once home, they exchanged anniversary gifts. Kate crawled into the bedroom to retrieved Eric's gift. She reached under the bed and retrieved a small box wrapped in maroon-and-silver-striped paper; a matching bow decorated the box. She gently punted the box out toward the living room, as she crawled behind it.

"I hope whatever's in there isn't breakable?" Eric asked, teasing.

"Just open it."

"You first," Eric said and retrieved a framed picture from the closet. "Ready?"

Kate nodded with excitement.

Eric unveiled the picture.

"Oh wow, Eric." It was an engraving of an old New England

barn in winter. Kate was flooded with memories of all the times they'd spent in Meg's barn in New Hampshire. "It looks just like the barn," she said.

"I know. I knew you would like it."

"I love it," she said, without taking her eyes off of the picture.

"Where shall we put it?" he asked.

"How about over the TV?" Eric mounted the picture. He stepped back and admired the engraving.

"I love it!" exclaimed Kate.

"Me, too." Eric lay down next to Kate. "What would this be?" he asked playfully, shaking the maroon box.

"Just open it."

"Okay, okay," he said and unwrapped the box. "Oh, a gold watch!" He put it up to his ear. "It's not ticking," he joked.

"Funny guy," she said, wearing a huge smile. "Turn it over."

"Ooh, there's a message?" Reversing the watch, he saw that there was an engraving. He read it aloud: "Two or two thousand years, I will always love you. Love, Kate." He pulled her down to his chest and kissed her. "I wish we had two thousand years together."

"Me, too," she said and kissed him.

As the summer ends and fall begins, people swap their beach chairs for couches, and tranquil seascapes are replaced with 27" television screens—a truly American rite of passage. At the start of the pro football season, men speculate on which team will make it through January. Commentators and sports analysts give their own spins. But no one can consistently predict the Super Bowl champion.

Most young boys dream about being a professional athlete. Dreams of hitting the winning homerun in the bottom of the ninth, a three-pointer in the last seconds of a basketball game, or sinking a birdie on the 18th hole at Augusta to win the prestigious Green Jacket are popular. These are dreams that seldom come true. Long after such dreams recede, men and women settle to watch their favorite sports on TV.

Kate and Eric invited the Griffys over for lunch. Kate sat on the floor and awaited their arrival. When Eric greeted them at the front door, she rose to her knees and waved hello. John and

Roberta Griffy followed Eric into the living room and hugged Kate. Roberta had a beautiful face that distracted people from her slightly convex figure. Blush shaded her defined cheekbones; the blue tine of mascara intensified the color of her eyes. Dirty-blonde hair hung down to her shoulders. Kate was careful not to accidentally pull it, as they embraced. Roberta tried her best to understand Kate, watching Kate's ever-changing facial expressions. Kate relied on Eric to intervene when needed. In time, Roberta would be able to master Kate's unfamiliar speech.

Eric brought sandwiches, potato chips, and soda out to the coffee table. He sat on the floor and leaned against the arm of the couch. Kate rested her head on his chest. Her left arm dangled at his side and she grabbed onto his shirtsleeve for stability. She fought to keep her legs relaxed. Her head flopped from side to side on Eric's chest. She could feel his beating heart.

Eric turned on the football game. Kate loved the humorous chitchat, chiming in frequently.

With winter approaching, the sun set in the late afternoon. When the game ended, John and Roberta offered a gracious goodbye. Eric gathered all the empty glasses and plates and dropped them into the sink. She crawled to the kitchen.

"You look very tall from this angle," Kate said.

"I always wanted to be tall. You're the only one who appreciates my tallness."

"Me and an ant," she said.

"You and a what?" he asked and turned to her.

"She repeated herself: "An ant; A-N-T."

He chortled, as he dried off a glass.

"So, tell me what your practice schedule looks like."

"It's a killer. I have to be in at 12:30 to do paperwork for three hours, wait for the kids, tape them up for the six o'clock practice, and then untape them afterwards. I probably won't get home until ten or so."

"I will hardly see you," Kate said.

"Yeah. It sucks."

"You have practice every day?"

"No, just Mondays, Wednesday, and Fridays. Tuesdays and Thursdays, we have team meetings that run at least until nine."

Eric saw her distraught expression and his heart sank. He squatted in front of her and held her face. "It's going to be a change for us, but we can handle it. We've handled everything else."

Kate nodded. "At least we'll see each other in the mornings."

Eric's expression turned serious.

Kate grew anxious. "What?"

"Colberg wants me to open the weight room at seven."

"I thought John was doing that?" Her voice was tense.

"Colberg wants me to be there, too. There's a new law that two trainers have to be in the weight room when the number of occupants exceeds ten."

"Do a lot of kids get up that early to work out?"

"Surprisingly, they do. God, remember me in college? I couldn't get out of bed at five of nine for a nine o'clock class."

"I remember that time the guys fooled you into thinking it was Friday morning when it was really Saturday. You never got out of bed so fast."

"Yeah, I thought I had a final," he said. "I was gullible back then." He stroked his wife's cheek.

"We'll manage."

"You know how to reach me, if you ever need me. I'm only two minutes away."

"Yeah, I know." She kissed his hand.

"It's going to work out, I promise." Kate clinked her gold wedding band against his. It was their sign of unity.

Stuart and Eric sat outside Dr. Freham's office. It was 15 minutes past their scheduled time and Eric was frustrated with the doctor's tardiness. His legs bounced, as though he had his own private earthquake under his feet. The previous day, Freham had cancelled his morning sessions. From Eric's brief time with Freham, he knew that he didn't like his approach to medicine. Eric's rank, however, didn't allow him to make formal complaints about Freham.

The door opened and Dr. Freham walked past Eric and Stuart, and into his office without uttering a word. After another five minutes, Freham stepped out and stood like a statue. He was 50-ish, short and pudgy, with a stern look engraved on his face. "You two can come in now," he declared.

"Good morning, Dr. Freham," Eric said cordially.

Freham didn't respond. They entered the exam room and Dr. Freham closed the door. "You should have had this young man ready for his exam, Mr. Hollis."

"I apologize, Dr. Freham," Eric said, holding his composure. "I didn't know the room was unlocked."

"Try the door next time."

Eric was growing tense, but remained steady. "I do apologize, Dr. Freham."

As Stuart undressed, Freham's body language conveyed his annoyance with the delay. "How's your eyesight?" Freham asked Stuart.

"Fine," Stuart answered.

Freham listened to Stuart's heart and lungs with his stethoscope. "Everything sounds fine." After feeling his neck and chest, he looked in his mouth. "Eric, can you prepare the treadmill for him?"

"Sure," Eric answered. "Let me stick these pads on you, Stu," Eric said. Stuart walked to the treadmill.

"Did you have this test last year?" Eric asked Stuart, as he stuck circular nodes to his chest.

"Yeah," Stuart answered. "I passed with flying colors."

Eric looked up and grinned. "Glad to hear that." Eric started the treadmill.

Stuart was jogging and then running. He breathed hard.

Eric examined the electrocardiograph, as the strip of paper flowed out of the machine. "Everything appears good." The test lasted ten minutes and Eric scrutinized the printout. Near the end of the strip, Eric noticed a slight abnormality in the lines.

Stuart observed Eric examining the strip intently. "Is everything okay?"

"Oh yeah, yeah," Eric said. "I'm just looking it over." Eric was not a cardiologist, but he knew something was amiss on the electrocardiogram. He let the strip fall to the ground. "Okay, we're done." Eric removed the circular nodes from Stuart's chest.

Dr. Freham came back into the exam room. "Are we done?"

"Yes," Eric said.

"Okay, King, you're free to go," Dr. Freham said and

retreated into his office.

Like a nervous recruit, Stuart listened to the orders of his commander and hastily dressed. "See you later, Eric," he said and headed for the door.

"I'll talk to you later," Eric said and gathered up the electrocardiograph from the floor. He checked the readout again. He knocked on Dr. Freham's door, awaiting the command to enter. He saw Dr. Freham in his big, butterscotch leather executive chair.

"What is it, Mr. Hollis?" Freham asked from behind his big desk.

"There's something you should look at on Stuart King's ECG."

"Show me," Freham ordered.

Eric laid the strip of paper on Freham's desk and pointed out the abnormality.

Freham glanced at the ECG. "I see no abnormalities. Those are normal rhythmic outputs," he explained dismissively.

"That's not abnormal?"

Dr. Freham shot Eric a menacing look. "No, that's normal rhythm!" exclaimed Freham. "Now, please leave my office. I have work to do."

Eric glared briefly and left, closing the door behind him with such force that the wall shook. He went to the file room and pulled Stuart's medical records from the prior year. He could not locate an electrocardiograph. Stuart's records revealed no medical concerns. He began to question his judgment, sitting until his calm returned.

Kate had completed her work for the day. The university van was running late, so she decided to try to catch Eric before he left for practice. She was still adjusting to his new schedule.

Leaves had fallen to the ground and drifted in the wind. As she headed for the gymnasium, the cold air chafed her cheeks. She had familiarized herself with all the sidewalks around the campus, and knew where all the cracks and bumps were located. She had learned her lesson many years ago when she got stuck in a ditch in the pouring rain and vowed never to let it happen again. The gentle hum of her power chair relaxed her. Nearing the gymnasium doors, several members of the basketball team emerged and confirmed that Eric was inside.

The long and wide corridors invited Kate to speed up. The doors into the gym were blocked open and Kate breezed through. The bright fluorescent lights and the high gloss of the vast waxed floor distracted her for a moment. Eric called out. He stood among a circle of athletes lying on the floor, stretching their legs up to the gods. He signaled that he would come over in a minute. She watched him interact with the young men and sensed a trust between them.

Dianne rushed in, threw down her bag and went over to Eric. Whatever Dianne said to Eric made him laugh. Dianne took over for Eric and he made his way toward Kate.

"Is the van late again?" he asked.

"Yeah."

"I'll call them tomorrow and find out," he said.

Kate nodded. She sensed he was in a hurry. "You're busy."

"Yeah—working my butt off, actually. Dianne was late, so I had to do all the taping and stuff myself."

"You look tired."

"I'll be fine. "You're the one who looks tired." He rubbed her temples.

"Yeah," said Kate. "You mind if I stick around here for a little while?"

"Not at all." He looked over and saw Dianne waving for his attention. "I gotta go. See you later, okay?" He kissed her on the forehead.

"Okay."

Kate found a good spot to watch the practice. The squeaks of Air Jordans barely startled her, too tired to contend with the puppeteer. Periodically, she looked at the clock. The minutes passed slowly. Eric stood next to Dianne. She never stopped talking. She always had a smile on her face. It bothered Kate. It had been a long day, and Kate just wanted to go home.

She checked the clock again. The van was due outside of her office in ten minutes. Like a pianist striking middle C without a glance at the keyboard, her right hand found the joystick on the first try. She headed for the exit. She kept looking at Eric, and trying to signal that she was leaving. He saw her and bid her goodbye, with a wave and a wink. Her unsteady arm jerked to wave goodbye. Things were only going to get more demanding for Eric. Kate prayed the season would go smoothly for him.

The van was waiting outside Kate's office when she returned. On the ride, she began to miss Eric. Her body felt stiff and she was relieved to be home. She was greeted by the aroma of garlic and onions. Liz helped her change into sweats. Kate stretched all of her muscles, as she crawled into the living room.

Liz and Kate spent a lot of time together and quickly became loyal friends. Instead of having dinner with Eric, most nights Kate shared the company of Liz. Communication was easy now. Kate would talk about her day with Liz. Liz's feedback differed from Eric's. Of course, Kate didn't tell Liz everything. Eric understood her, as if there was some external force responsible for their connection, for their love for each other. From their first encounter, Kate had always been intrigued about why she and Eric had met and why they had fallen in love. She perceived herself as different from everyone else. She was very tough on herself. She knew she didn't have to be, she just was.

Liz left for the night and Kate had at least two hours alone. Like every night, Liz placed Kate's phone and headstick on the floor near her. Footsteps from Mr. Davison's apartment upstairs gave Kate a sense of security. Feeling a chill, she crawled into the den and retrieved a pillow and a blanket. By the time she returned to the couch, the blanket was unfolded from its travels. She positioned the pillow in front of the couch, grasped a corner of the blanket and fell back onto the pillow. She let go of the blanket too soon. She got up and tried again, succeeding in pulling the blanket over her.

Within minutes, she was fast asleep in front of the television.

The meeting ended late. Eric's office was silent, as he packed his duffel bag. He heard footsteps. Dianne appeared at the door.

"Going home?" she asked.

"Yep. I'm late as it is," said Eric, struggling with the zipper on his bag.

"I thought maybe we could go out for a drink or something," Dianne said, casually.

"I gotta get home to Kate. She's probably asleep on the floor."

"That's right," Dianne said, haphazardly remembering that Kate existed.

"Maybe some other time?"

"Sure, sure."

"I bet your husband, Mark, is it?" Eric paused and she nodded. "I bet Mark is waiting for you?"

"He works the graveyard shift. He won't be home until morning."

"That's tough," Eric said. He sensed Dianne's distress from her sullen features. "If I may ask, is everything okay?"

"Our marriage has been shaky for quite a while," Dianne said freely. "Actually, I don't know why we're still together." She crossed her arms and bowed her head.

"I'm sorry."

Tears rolled down her face. "We were young and foolish. We thought love was something else."

"I'm sure things will work out for the best," Eric said.

"Yeah, I'm sure they will," she answered, looking down.

Eric searched Dianne's face for permission to leave. "Can I walk you down to your car?"

Dianne smiled and took him up on his offer. Few words were exchanged. He feared saying too much.

Eric slid open the pocket door and saw Kate asleep, curled up on the floor. Guilt consumed him. The blanket was barely covering her back. Quietly, he knelt down and kissed her on the forehead. She awoke and glanced up at him. She asked what time it was. "A little before eleven." The only light came from the television. She rose to her knees and leaned on him awhile. Few words were exchanged. They just sat and held each other before retiring to bed.

Chapter 4

The days grew shorter, but for Kate they seemed twice as long. The clock looked down at her, reminding her how much time was left in the day. She made an effort to ignore it.

Carl rolled in without making a sound. When she noticed him, she startled.

"Well, aren't we a little jumpy today?" he said.

She typed: "I'm sorry. I didn't hear you."

"You should go easy on that Halloween candy," Carl said jokingly. "Too much of that—fry your nerves."

"Thank you very much for your concern." She shot him a sarcastic grin. "But I stopped eating Halloween candy long before you went out on your first trick-or-treat."

Carl smiled.

"What can I do for you, Sir Carl?" she typed.

"Well, Sir Carl is having a problem with that egghead Wilcox again. He doesn't want to give me the same test he's giving everyone else."

"Why not?" Kate asked, without the assistance of the computer.

"I have no idea."

"Are you doing all the work you are supposed to?" she asked, reverting to her synthesized monotone.

"Yeah, I am. Ever since I started chemistry, it's just been one problem after another. I'm sick of it. I'm not going anymore."

Kate typed at a furious pace: "You have to keep going. Otherwise, it will stay on your transcript that you failed the class."

Carl groaned. "I can't take that guy anymore."

"I'll go over and talk to him," said Kate. She continued to type: "Promise me you'll stay in the class. So far you're doing well. Please don't blow it. I busted my butt to keep you in chemistry. I expect the same effort from you."

Carl debated what to say. His eyes arbitrarily focused on various things: a red folder on the desk, a paper clip lying on the carpet, the triangles twirling on the computer screen. Kate waited patiently for a reply.

"Okay, I'll stay in, but I'm not promising anything."

"Good man. I'll try to see Wilcox this afternoon," she said.

"Yeah, okay," Carl said, acquiescing.

"And remember to have respect for your instructors. Please don't call them names."

"Yeah, right," Carl said with contempt. "When they show me a little more respect, I'll do the same. I'll come by tomorrow."

Kate nodded. "Okay." She understood his frustration, and directed Sue to call Professor Wilcox and arrange a meeting.

Outside, the wind was gusting—typical for the first day of November. The sun was bright. Kate steered her wheelchair over the concrete sidewalks, avoiding any bumps that might make her hand fly off her joystick. As if she was piloting an airplane through a clear blue sky, the ride was smooth.

The secretary informed Kate that Professor Wilcox would be right with her. Kate wished secretaries would come up with something more original to say. What would have amused Kate was if Wilcox's secretary had announced: "Professor Wilcox will be right with you. He's just changing into another awful outfit."

As Kate waited, she studied the corkboard over the secretary's desk. It was cluttered with memos, calendars, the usual odds and ends. There was the requisite picture of a birthday party, with children covered in birthday cake, complete with the pointed hats on their heads. *Must be her grandchildren,* Kate surmised.

The door opened to reveal Professor Wilcox in a hideous red, white and blue plaid suit. He might as well have been wrapped in an American flag. Kate struggled not to chuckle.

"May I do something for you, Ms. Hollis?" asked Wilcox in a condescending tone.

Her muscles tightened, trying not to be bothered. "Carl said the test you are giving him is a different test from the rest of the students," she typed. "I want to know why." The robotic voice lacked the emphasis and emotion she wanted to convey.

"I caught him cheating on a quiz last week," Wilcox bluntly stated. "I know he's hanging around with another kid. All their homework appears the same, down to the dots over the 'I's."

Kate felt like a tire bursting. "He didn't tell me this."

"Why would he?" Wilcox said. "Your boy Carl isn't an angel

by any stretch of the imagination."

Kate breathed and resumed typing: "What is this test going to prove?"

"Well, I hope it will indicate to me how much stuff is getting into his head. After I see the results, I can take it from there."

"Okay," said Kate. "Do you want me to talk to him?"

"Just tell him he's participating in one of my experiments," said Wilcox. "Or I can tell him."

Wilcox's demeanor made Kate very uneasy. "I think it will be better coming from you," she said. "When is the test?"

"Friday morning."

"Friday afternoon I want the results," Kate said.

"Stop by around four," Wilcox said.

"Okay. Thanks."

Professor Wilcox nodded goodbye. Kate closed her laptop and headed back to her office.

Exiting a building was much easier for Kate than entering. In the distance, she saw Eric and Dianne walking toward the athletic building. She was too far behind to catch up to them or be heard, if she dared to shout. She decelerated. They disappeared around the corner. *If Wilcox hadn't made me wait so long, I might have caught Eric,* Kate imagined. She knew the thought was silly, but she missed Eric. She wanted to see him, talk to him—if for only a few minutes. Her yearning scared her. She knew she would see him that night.

When she got back to the office, Emily Harrod was waiting. She quickly turned on her laptop to talk, so Emily wouldn't think she was being ignored. Kate's frustration over Wilcox hindered her muscles, as she tried to release the lever on her laptop. She took a deep breath and sat for a moment. Regaining control of her emotions, she tried again. The latch popped open and booted up the computer:

"I'm sorry it took so long to open my computer. May I help you, Emily?"

"Oh, it's quite alright," Emily said. "It seems Kathy, my reader, forgot she was reading today."

"I'm sorry," the computer said. "I talked to her yesterday and she knew she had to read for you today."

"I tried to call her, but her brother said she was at school,"

Emily said. "Maybe she got caught up somewhere?"

"Yeah," Kate said in her natural voice. "How much do you need to read?" asked the computer.

"Not much. It's just a page or two. The rest of the chapter is on cassettes that Kathy taped for me."

"If you're free for the rest of the afternoon, I can have the computer read to you."

"How are you going to do that?"

Kate began to type. "I'll type the words myself."

"All two pages?"

"Yeah," Kate said, reverting to her natural voice. Then she typed: "It won't take long. Would you like to join me in the conference room?"

"Sure," Emily said. She stood and gathered up her knapsack and her cane. She was in her own darkness, never knowing what surrounded her. She stood statuesque, looking at nothing. Kate guided her wheelchair to Emily and touched her arm to alert her that she was nearby. Emily found the rear wheelchair handle, and Kate escorted her to the conference room.

"I think I left off around page 237," Emily said, as she settled at the table. She opened the book and found the bookmarked page.

Kate pulled up close and glanced at the textbook. She typed: "Did you leave of at 'The Rules of Speech Writing'?"

"Yes, that sounds right."

"Okay," Kate said. "If you need a sentence repeated, just tell me please. I'll go sentence by sentence. It's easy to repeat sentences."

"Okay," Emily said.

Kate typed the first sentence and the laptop spoke the sentence for Emily. Kate typed as quickly as she could, so that Emily wouldn't lose the flow. Kate typed for nearly three hours. Her back and neck muscles ached for relief, but she was motivated by the joy of assisting Emily. Kate forgot all about Wilcox, keeping her focus on the task.

Kate left work early to try to catch Eric before she went home. Just as she was about to enter Eric's building, he emerged from within. Her heart leapt with joy.

"Hey, I know you," Eric said. He kissed her. "Sorry but I'm

gonna have to stay later than usual tonight." He gauged Kate's reaction. She was irritated. "The coach is having an extra practice and I gotta be there."

"Don't they know that you have a life outside of basketball?" Kate asked, frustrated. "I've only seen you for an hour the whole week!"

"What am I supposed to do, Kate? This is my job."

"I know it's your job, Eric," said Kate. There was a long pause. They stared at the ground.

"What do you want me to do, quit?"

Kate couldn't believe he had asked such a question. "I gotta go," she said.

"See you tonight," he mumbled.

"Yeah," she said and headed home.

Kate rode slowly and thought about what had just transpired. She felt bad for taking her frustrations out on him—frustrations that had been building up the past week. She regretted putting unfair demands on him. *There was no excuse for my insensitivity*, she thought.

Professor Wilcox stumbled out of his office, wearing a brown polyester suit that represented a dramatic improvement over the checkered-flag suit.

"Hello, Professor Wilcox," she typed.

Wilcox got to business. "Carl got a 43 on his test. He didn't even answer half of the questions."

Kate typed: "I'd like to hear your suggestions."

"I want him out of the class," Wilcox said bluntly.

"Isn't that a little drastic, without confronting him first?" Kate asked.

"I don't stand for dishonest students, Ms. Hollis."

Wilcox's defiant demeanor irritated Kate. "I want to talk to Carl first," stated the computer.

"If you want, but my mind is made up. Carl is out, plain and simple."

Kate didn't care to argue with this hardened man. "I will contact you sometime early next week," she typed.

"There's no need to waste any more time talking about this, Ms. Hollis," Wilcox said and retreated to his office.

"Nice suit," Kate muttered under her breath, as she left.

The beer went down easy. It was Friday night and the beer was well earned. Kate searched for something good on television, but as usual for a Friday evening nothing kept her attention. Around eleven, she heard Eric's footsteps on the stairs. He walked in. She studied his demeanor for some sort of sign.

"What's in the fridge that I can eat?" asked Eric, heading for the kitchen.

"I think there's some chicken left over." Kate crawled into the kitchen. "I'm sorry for blowing up today."

"I must apologize, too," Eric said, tenderly. "The last comment was not called for."

Kate grew upset. "I'm sorry."

Eric knelt down beside her. "It's okay, Katie." He rubbed her back.

"It's not okay," Kate managed to say through her tears.

"Why isn't it okay, Sweetie?" Eric asked, looking at her weary face.

Kate tried to compose herself. "It's not okay." She breathed deeply. "I've had such a bad week."

"What the hell happened?"

"Carl is cheating in chemistry—or that's what Wilcox says."

"Cheating?"

Kate nodded. "Yeah. I met with Wilcox a little before I saw you."

"How did Carl do on the test?"

"He got a 43. Wilcox wants him out."

"Have you talked to Carl yet?" Eric asked.

"No," Kate said quietly. "He doesn't know that Wilcox thinks he's cheating."

"What do you think?"

"I don't know what I think," she said, gazing upward. "The only thing I know is that Wilcox is driving Carl crazy."

"You'll sort it out. I'm sure of that."

Feeling his arms around her was what she longed for all week. She reveled in his love. "God, I miss you."

He kissed her on the lips. "I miss you, too."

"The other day I saw you walking on campus."

"Why didn't you call to me?"

"I couldn't—you were too far away," she said. "All I wanted

was to say hi."

Eric held her tight. "I'm sorry." He kissed her head.

"It's okay."

Eric spent Saturday paying bills and cleaning the apartment. In the late afternoon, he got called in to work—not unusual for a Saturday. Alone, Kate peered out the window. It had been a long time since she had observed the couple across the street. Leaves had fallen off the birch tree in front of the apartment, affording her a better view. Her mind wandered, as she looked out. One car sat in the driveway, but the guy's beat-up Honda Civic wasn't there.

When Eric returned, Kate was asleep on the floor. She awoke. He expressed concern that she wasn't getting enough sleep. She reassured him that she was fine. She listened as he told her that a player had sprained his ankle. From years of listening to Eric's descriptions of human anatomy, she knew how long it would take for the ankle to heal. She could have listened to him all evening.

Sunday, Eric and Kate went to the Griffys. Still drained from her week, Kate didn't want to spoil their plans. Even though her eyelids appeared heavy as bricks, he failed to notice her weariness. She wanted to close them for a little while. She fought the good fight for Eric's sake. He was having a good time with John. Strangely enough, Kate was managing to speak very clearly to Roberta. Kate hadn't been drinking, but her tiredness relaxed her.

The phone rang and it was Colberg. John picked up the phone. Eric was being called out again. Eric urged John to stay and watch the game. John insisted on going along. Eric reluctantly agreed and promised they'd be back soon. Before Kate could even propose the idea of going home, Eric and John were gone. Kate resolved that she was there for the duration. All she wanted to do was to shut her eyes.

Daylight dissipated into the evening. After three hours, Kate became anxious. It was the longest that Eric had been out on a call. Roberta passed the delay off as an emergency-room visit.

When the two men returned, they seemed unusually spirited.

"Why are you guys so cheery?" Roberta asked.

"Eric and I stopped for a beer on the way home," said John,

as he walked into the living room.

"So, the call was nothing serious?" asked Roberta.

"Nah," said Eric, "a minor sprain." He saw the irritation on his wife's cast.

"Three hours?" asked Kate. Eric stared scornfully at Kate. Before speaking the words he wanted to say, Eric thought twice. "I had to make sure he was okay."

Kate made no reply.

"We are going to head home, but we thank you for the day," Eric said for the both of them.

"Oh, I was hoping you'd stay for dinner," said Roberta.

If the tension wasn't noticed by John and Roberta, it was certainly felt by Kate and Eric.

"I have to do some work tonight," Kate said, "but thank you."

Eric carried Kate to the truck and buckled her in. "I'd appreciate it if you wouldn't humiliate me in front of our friends."

"I'm sorry, but you could have called to tell us that you were gonna stop for a drink."

"What is the big deal? We only stopped for a damn beer!" Anger entered his voice.

Flustered, Kate had to put together the words that she wanted to say. "I was tired and I just wanted to go home."

"I'll remember to clear it with you whenever I have to take a piss, Your Highness!" he exclaimed.

Kate didn't say another word. The drive home was painfully silent. The silence continued inside the apartment. It was one of those times when Kate wished she had the ability to care for herself. Eric changed her for bed. The tense emotion radiated to all of her muscles. She hated feeling this way. One involuntary movement could end their night even worse than it was already. Kate tightened all of her muscles to prevent such a catastrophe.

When Kate sensed that Eric's anger had abated, she relaxed.

The noise of the pocket door closing awakened her. It was Eric leaving. Kate stared at the ceiling, mentally preparing for another workweek. This was the day she would interrogate Carl. The past weekend had not brought her the regeneration.

She thought of 20 things she would rather do than to accuse Carl. Eating dirt was at the top of her list. The closet door was open and she tried to recall where each piece of Eric's clothing had been bought. A gray striped suit reminded Kate of the time Eric got trapped in a dressing room, her wheelchair jammed against the door. She wished for more silly times with Eric.

Liz arrived and her presence cheered Kate up. Liz remarked upon the tired look in Kate's eyes. Liz had never seen Kate looking so worn on a Monday morning. "You sleep okay last night?" Liz asked, gathering Kate's clothes.

"Yeah."

"How was your weekend?"

Kate pondered the question, while Liz fetched the shower chair. The weekend passed by Kate's eyes like a slide show, scene by scene.

"Okay," Kate answered. "How was yours?" She was hoping to change the subject.

"Fine. I went out with a couple of friends and saw a crappy movie. Then, we went out for drinks to forget the crappy movie. That kind of stuff," Liz said. She transferred Kate into the shower chair and wheeled her into the bathroom.

"We didn't do much," said Kate. "We went over to John and Roberta's yesterday. We can't go too far, in case Eric has to go into work."

"Did he have to go in?"

Kate nodded. "Two times."

"Twice?!" Liz repeated in alternative words. "That sucks."

"Sure did suck," Kate said.

Liz chuckled. "Every now and then, your words come out crystal clear," she said and turned on the shower. Kate closed her eyes and reveled in the warm, cleansing rush of water. The puppeteer was unusually subdued for a Monday morning. *Maybe he's on vacation?* Kate wished he and Professor Wilcox would go on permanent sabbatical.

At breakfast, Kate silently composed the words she planned to say to Carl. The bagel and tea perked her up. The bleak weather reflected her grayish mood.

Locking up the weight room, voices echoed down the narrow cinderblock hallway. Eric returned to his office and found

Dianne crying. He asked what was wrong. Sobbing hysterically, she was unable to answer. Eric locked the door and tried to calm her. Tentatively, he put his arm around her shoulders.

Through heavy sighs and streaming tears, Dianne began to tell him the events of the previous night. She recalled every moment in striking detail. Her hand movements embellished the action of the story. Eric was engrossed and horrified, as she explained how she and her husband, Mark, got into an argument. She told of plates flying across the kitchen and shattering on the floor. Her arm motioned a throw, as she relived the terrible night. She recollected every fierce word Mark said, and what she had said back to him. Eric sat motionless, feeling the anger build up in his gut. Dianne said she spent the night at a friend's apartment.

Telling her story seemed to calm her. Tears ceased and her hands stopped shaking.

Eric brought her a cup of coffee. She sat quietly for a while, her eyes fixed on Eric as he did paperwork. She felt safe and content in his presence.

For Kate, the day could not end fast enough. Eleven o'clock and her energy was already fading. She expected Carl at any minute. She prepared the words she would say to him on her computer, but figured it was foolish to predict the path of their conversation.

Carl rolled in and Kate took a deep breath. "Let's go into the other room," she typed and gestured toward the conference room.

"This must be serious," Carl said, not thinking much of it. He followed Kate into the empty room. She closed the door with her foot.

"This is serious, isn't it?" Carl asked.

Kate positioned herself in front of Carl. Her headstick started pressing keys: "Yes, this is serious," said the synthesized voice. She was running on adrenaline. "You know that test you took on Friday?"

"Yeah. It was a joke," said Carl.

"You got a 43 on it."

"I'm not surprised. I couldn't answer half the questions,"

Carl said, dismissively. "So, did I pass the experiment?"

"It wasn't an experiment. It was a special test to find out if you were cheating or not."

"Cheating?! I don't believe this! What the hell makes him think I've been cheating?" Anger entered Carl's voice.

Kate typed: "On the last test, Wilcox saw you lean over another student's desk."

"I was leaning over to pick up a stupid pencil. I was two feet away from Matt's desk. I did not cheat!" Carl said, without hesitation.

Kate looked into his eyes and saw no flicker of doubt. "Wilcox says your homework is very similar to Matt's."

"Yeah," Carl said, with unwavering confidence. "I help Matt with his homework. I don't do it *for* him—I *help* him! Is that a crime?"

Kate shook her head. "Why would Wilcox accuse you of cheating?" It was a question for both of them to answer.

It was evident to Carl that Kate should know the answer. "Have you forgotten you couldn't get Wilcox to move lab?" Carl asked. "Wilcox would do anything and say anything to get me out of chemistry."

Kate considered this possibility. "How come you couldn't answer the questions on the test?"

"I guess Wilcox didn't show you the test."

"No, he didn't," Kate said.

"It was a simple multiple-choice test, but I had to do the formula out to get the answer," he explained. "I spent ten minutes on the first problem, refiguring and refiguring, but each time I did it I got the same exact answer. It wasn't among the four choices. I moved on to the second question and then the third—the same thing happened." Carl paused to breathe. "And I know the formula was right because Wilcox allows us to use our notes."

"Are you saying that Wilcox fixed the test?" asked Kate.

"Yes, I really think he did."

Kate sat back and stared at the wall, overwhelmed and discouraged. Everything Carl said made sense. She felt defeated by Wilcox, an imbecile. Kate promised not surrender to Wilcox.

"Just get the test and have somebody look it over," Carl said.

"Like a chem tutor?" asked Kate.

"Yeah!" Carl also wanted to be part of this battle. "I promise I didn't cheat, Kate."

Kate smiled.

"I just—I just wanted to—" Carl took a deep breath. "Thank you for believing in me. I would never lie to you."

At that second, Kate's energy returned. "I have to believe in someone. It's what I'm here for," she said. "I'll see if I can see Wilcox today."

"He cancelled class today. Maybe he went to buy a new suit," said Carl.

Kate chuckled. "Wilcox may not let you back in class. He made it clear that he wanted you out."

"He got what he wanted, didn't he?"

"Yes, I guess he did," Kate answered in her natural voice. Then she typed: "You're going to need to take chemistry again with another professor."

"Whatever," Carl said.

"I'll let you know," she said. "You can open the door." In parting, Kate touched his shoulder with a closed fist, reaffirming her promise to him.

The cafeteria was bustling at quarter to twelve. People talked and dishes clanked. Kate waited for Liz by the door. Kate spotted Mr. Leonard. He always invited her to sit with him during lunch. She accepted his offer. Soon, Liz arrived to feed her.

Kate sat alone while Liz and Mr. Leonard braved the long food line. This was her time to relax. Among the waves of colors drifting around the large dining room, Kate spotted Wilcox's plaid jacket bobbing toward the door. His confident stride reminded Kate of a big plaid peacock displaying his plumage. Kate was annoyed with his cocky strut. She would confront him. She wouldn't relax until she resolved this issue with Carl.

Sue answered the office phone. It was Wilcox mournfully confirming Kate's appointment. Sue helped Kate on with her jacket and headstick. Sue wished Kate luck.

Kate arrived at the Science Building. The wind blew fierce, as she waited for someone to open the door. Thankfully, a student appeared within seconds. Kate wheeled down the long hallway. Today, she was calm. She wouldn't be intimidated by Wilcox's condescending antics.

The secretary greeted Kate with a pointed finger. Wilcox was awaiting her arrival in the lounge area outside his office. "I haven't much time," he growled.

Kate typed: "I want to see the test you gave Carl on Friday."

"Absolutely not."

"Why not?" she asked.

"You have no right to see it," he said.

"Do you know what discrimination is, Professor Wilcox?"

"And do you know what slander is, Ms. Hollis?"

Her foot stomped down on the footrest. The puppeteer was exercising total control over her body. Wilcox made his impatience known through foot-tapping of his own. "If I don't have that test by tomorrow morning, I will go to the academic board," announced the computer.

"Oh, did I mention I'm a member of the board?" Wilcox hissed.

Kate imagined her hands around his dumpy neck. "This is not over, Professor Wilcox."

"I look forward to our next meeting, Ms. Hollis," he said.

"And so do I," she said. "And by the way, it's Mrs. Hollis." The mechanical speech of her computer failed to convey her hostility. As she turned and drove away, Kate heard Wilcox mumble something. She refrained from looking back.

Eric expected to find Kate asleep on the living room floor, but she wasn't there. He flipped on the light over the kitchen sink. He heard voices coming from the den and saw the familiar flickering of the TV. Kate was asleep on the futon. He shut off the TV, knelt down on the edge of the futon and kissed her on her temple. It dawned on him that he hadn't thought about his wife all day, and resolved to lie with her awhile. He stroked her hair. His gaze never left her face. He loved seeing Kate so still and peaceful, like a newborn baby. He curled up beside her and drifted off.

Kate awoke and discovered Eric beside her. The sight of him

was heaven. Remembering the last time she had seen him, she cursed herself for being so angry. The clock read ten to six. She rolled onto her side, gently put her fist against his chest, and shoved him onto his back, down five inches to the carpeted floor. He jolted awake to the sound of her laughter.

He got right back onto the futon, intending to tickle the perpetrator. They laughed together.

"Do you always sleep in your clothes?" Kate jokingly asked.

"It's the new fashion in pajamas," he said. "It's the new wave: put them on in the morning and when you come home, you can just fall into bed."

"Sorry I wasn't awake when you got home."

"You didn't move a muscle," he said. "Must have been a rough day."

He was right on target. She labored to get up to her knees and ended up on the floor.

"Get back on the bed." With these words, Eric had forgotten about Sunday evening at the Griffy's.

Kate climbed onto the futon beside him. She recounted the events of her draining day. She began to giggle. "Do you realize it's six o'clock and we are sitting here talking about that idiot?"

Eric pulled Kate close. "I'm proud of you."

"And how was your day?" she asked.

"Different. I walked into the office and Dianne was just bawling her eyes out."

"What happened?" Kate asked.

"Well, apparently she and her husband had this knock-down, drag-out fight and he was throwing dishes at her."

"He didn't hit her, did he?" Kate asked, concerned.

"No, no, but she was very upset."

"What was the fight about?"

"She didn't really say. I know they are having some problems, but she never said he was violent."

"Did the police come?" she asked.

"She didn't say."

"Do you guys talk a lot?"

"Some."

"Does she ever ask about me?"

"Sometimes," he answered.

"Don't lie—Dianne never asks about me."

Eric pulled Kate to him and kissed her. "I do, though."

"Oh, you do?" She climbed over and straddled his legs.

"Every minute." He kissed her again.

Kate placed her fist on his zipper and gazed up at his reaction.

Eric grabbed her hand. "Not now," he said. "I have to go to work."

"Please stay."

"I can't." He helped Kate off of his legs. Her dispirited look said it all. "I'm sorry," he said.

The alarm clock went off in the bedroom. Kate crawled into the hall. "I miss you."

From the bedroom, standing in front of the closet, Eric looked back at his wife. "I miss you, too," he said. "I tell you what: tomorrow night I'll come home early and we can spend some time together."

She cracked a tiny smile. "Okay." She sat against the doorjamb and watched him get dressed. "You know, it's sad when we have to set a date to make love," she said.

Eric chuckled. "Yeah, I know." He gave her a drink of orange juice, took her to the bathroom, and quickly showered and dressed for work.

"I love you," she said, as he left the bedroom.

"Love you, too," he bellowed from the living room.

Kate heard a series of doors close in the distance.

Once her workday started, Kate forgot about her morning at home. She updated Mr. Leonard on the Wilcox situation. Ousting Wilcox from the academic board made her mouth water. Never in her life had she wanted anyone to suffer as much as Wilcox. He belonged in a swine's pen. Mr. Leonard advised Kate not to get too worked up. She appreciated Leonard's wisdom.

Lunch came and went. Kate patiently waited for news from Mr. Leonard. At last, he appeared in her office, holding a couple sheets of paper. Like a child wishing for a particular toy at Christmas, Kate prayed that it was Carl's test. It seemed like an eternity before Mr. Leonard placed the sheets in front of her. It was indeed the test. Kate asked how he got it. Like a magician, Leonard refused to explain his tricks.

That afternoon, a respected chemistry tutor confirmed the test was fixed. Leonard advised Kate to submit the case to the academic board. Kate pictured what the board members would look like, all of them educated, finely dressed in gray suits—all but one, of course. She began to question her abilities and reminded herself that she had Carl's future in her hands. *Am I up to the task?* Anxious thoughts weaved through her mind like a rollercoaster.

Carl showed up and Kate informed him what had transpired. He was out of chemistry for the semester but that there would be no mark on his transcript. He would have to take chemistry again. Carl thanked Kate. He looked up to her as a role model and considered her a friend. The indifferent attitude he had at the beginning of the semester was fading.

Since his mother died eight years before, in the car accident that left him paralyzed, Carl had the feeling that someone believed in him. For years, he'd fought for his father's respect by getting good grades, but he knew he would never live up to his father's expectations. The accident had ruined his father's dream of having a college athlete. Carl's hope was to prove himself to his father some other way. Kate assured him that he would find a way.

Chapter 5

It was a day of nonstop pecking at the keyboard, at work and at home. In the den, Kate worked all evening on her report, fine-tuning every word and making sure not to leave anything out.

By ten, her eyes grew heavy. The phone rang. Kate jumped. Her hand circled over the speakerphone button. Finally, a knuckle landed on it. "Hello," she said.

"Hi kid, how the hell are ya?!" squawked the phone. It was her brother, Brian.

"Oh, it's you," she said.

"The hell do you mean, 'Oh, it's you'?"

"I'm only kidding," Kate said. "How are ya?"

"Not too busy. This hockey strike is killing us. Hopefully, it won't last too long."

"It sucks, doesn't it?"

"Sure does. Is Eric working?"

"Yeah." Kate remembered Eric's pledge from yesterday morning. "He should be home any minute." Silence prevailed for a few seconds. "What's Mom doing?"

"Driving herself crazy, as usual. She has a new house she's designing."

"Where is it?" asked Kate.

"It's in Newton, I think."

"Well, good for her."

"Are you coming home for Thanksgiving?"

"No, sorry, Bud. There's a game that Saturday, so we can't make it home." Kate knew Brian would be disappointed. "But I think we're coming home for Christmas," she said.

"Great. I can't wait to see you guys."

"Me, too," she said. "Ah, he's home."

Eric walked into the den. "Who are you talking to?"

Brian heard Eric's question from a distance. "I told you that he'd be home soon."

"Brian, how the hell are ya man?" Eric asked.

"I'm fine. How's it going with basketball practice?"

"Brutal," he answered. "I eat, drink, and sleep basketball. But it's fun." Eric began to scratch Kate's back.

"Mom is signaling me to get off the phone. Good thing you guys don't live in Russia. She'd never let me call you."

"You have to move out of there one of these days," Kate said.

"Yeah, I know, I know. Maybe soon," Brian said softly. "Alright, Mom is giving me the slash-across-the-neck sign. I gotta go. Bye."

"Say hi to Dot for us," Eric said.

"Sure thing. Bye."

"Bye," they said together.

"Sorry I'm a bit late," Eric said. "Dianne wanted me to follow her home tonight because she thought her husband might be waiting for her at her friend's house."

"Are you crazy?!" she exclaimed. "Don't do that again!"

Confusion and anger prompted Eric to raise his voice. "What the hell is wrong with that?"

Kate's body swayed, as if she was a tree caught in a windstorm. "Was he there?"

"No, he wasn't there!" Eric snapped. "What if he was?!"

"You don't know..."

"I don't know what?" he asked with distinct annoyance.

It would have been easier for Kate to sit through a root canal than to pull out the words trapped in her vocal cords. "How..."

Eric's frustration was growing. "Head-spell it, please."

Kate's eyes and head started to draw letters in the air: D-A-N-G.

"What?" Eric said. "You think Dianne's husband is dangerous?"

Kate nodded.

"You think I can't take care of myself?"

"Not if he has a gun!" Kate said clearly, surprising them both.

"Oh, come on," he said. "You're blowing this just a little out of proportion?"

"He threw dishes at Dianne!" Kate said with a stern look.

Eric stared forcibly back. "I can't believe we're having this conversation."

She refused to back down. "I'm trying to make a point."

"And what is your point, Kate?"

"You could get hurt!"

"Thank you for believing in me," he said in a sarcastic tone. "I'm tired. I'm going to bed."

Kate was just as exhausted and decided to drop the issue. They hardly exchanged another word. The promise of a peaceful night was gone.

For days, Kate hardly saw Eric, and when she did it was silence and indifference. He would come home. She would hear the door. She would wait in the den for Eric to appear. She would debate whether to bring up the matter. She never did. He looked so tired. All she would ask of him was a trip to the bathroom. He would fall asleep within minutes. In the dark, she would see his face, wishing that her unruly fingers would obey her so that she could touch him like he touched her. She wanted to hold his hand as he slept, but she resisted, fearing that her jerky movements would wake him. The best thing was to let him sleep. She listened to him breathe. He slept soundly.

Kate's goal was to let this Saturday be peaceful. Eric spoke few words, as he dressed her. She contemplated what to say to him. She considered apologizing for being so stern the other night. She said nothing. The case against Wilcox kept her busy for most of the day. She occasionally crawled out to the living room and found Eric asleep on the couch. Meals were spent in front of the television. At times, the apartment seemed like a monastery. It was like they had the world's problems upon their shoulders. In their seven years together, Kate had never sensed such a disconnection with Eric.

Sunday was typical: the Griffy's arrived in the afternoon and football took over the men's conversation. The women spent time in the kitchen comparing whose workweek was worse. Roberta described her first-grade class. Hearing the horrors of teaching six-year-old's impelled Kate to appreciate her job, even though she had to deal with Wilcox. Kate would often observe Eric, as he lay on the couch. A few times, he looked over at her. She tried hard to appear happy, but Roberta's quizzical gazes proved that she was failing. Everyone seemed to peer into her soul's window.

Another Monday arrived. Kate forced the bagel down with a cup of tea. Two inches of snow had fallen during the night—the first snow. Winter had arrived. Kate thrust her left knee into the counter when the phone unexpectedly rang. She cursed the counter. Liz took a message for Eric: Joe was arrested in Boston the previous night. If Kate needed a reason to talk to Eric, this topic wasn't one to choose. She hated to be the bearer of such news when their communication was at a standstill.

The sidewalks were clear, lined with snow on either side. Kate went straight to Eric's building. One of the team members held the door open. Anxiousness slowed her down. Mrs. Colenza signaled for her to go into Eric's office. He was seated at his desk. "Eric," said Kate quietly from the hall.

Dianne stood up abruptly from her desk. "I'll be back in a while," Dianne said. Detecting Kate's eyes upon her, she walked out of the room.

"What's up?" he asked Kate.

"Joe was arrested last night."

He let out a sigh and ran his hand through his curly blond hair. "What for?"

"I don't know—the cop didn't say. Liz took the message." The somber look on his face upset Kate. "Joe wants you to call him." She indicated a piece of paper on which Liz had written the number.

Eric dialed the number and nervously fiddled with his tie. A policeman answered and they discussed Joe's situation. Kate wanted to create a perfect world for Eric—converting Joe into an upstanding citizen, taking away all the disappointments Eric endured from his brother. With every attempt Eric made to help Joe, he lost a part of himself in the agonizing process. Kate knew Eric would never give up helping his brother, and she would support him unconditionally. Joe was a loner, consumed with the pleasure of addiction. He entered treatment time and again, only to revert to his prior habits. Eric internalized all of his brother's failures.

Eric hung up the phone. "Possession," he said. "They got him for drug possession. Dammit." He put his hand on his forehead. "I gotta fly to Boston. Will you be okay today?"

Kate experienced his agony. "Yeah, of course. Go, go."

"I'll be back as quickly as I can." He moved to her, held her face and kissed her. "Thanks."

"No problem," she happily said. She lived for such tenderness.

He slid his finger down the bridge of her delicate nose. "Wait here, I have to clear this with Ray."

One rung of the long, broken ladder of their relationship had been fixed. Several more rungs needed to be replaced.

"I'm out of here," he said, as he hurried in to get his jacket and keys. "I'll walk you out."

Kate accompanied him down to the parking lot.

He unlocked the truck. "I have no idea when I'll be back."

"Yeah, I know," she said. "Be careful."

"I will," he said confidently. "Get going—it's cold out here." The truck engine finally turned over.

Listening to the wrenching, grinding sounds of the engine troubled Kate. She was thankful that the airport wasn't miles way. The truck left the parking lot. Kate waved goodbye. Snow began to fall, as she headed to her office.

Eric was on her mind the entire day. She wanted to accompany him to Boston, but knew that was unrealistic. He needed to go, do what he had to do and get back to Syracuse. She wondered how much more of this he could handle. Thinking about Eric every minute wasn't doing her any good. She tried to occupy herself with work.

Kate worked with one eye on the clock and one ear on the phone. Every time the phone rang, she was jolted as if receiving shock treatment for cardiac arrest. Being tense intensified her cerebral palsy. Her arms struck the chrome bars that framed her wheelchair. The puppeteer's strings had to be severed.

None of the phone calls were from Eric. Soon, all of her energy was consumed. She was running on adrenaline. The letters on her computer screen seemed to meld together. None of the words made sense.

The snow was still falling at day's end. The heavier the snow became, the more Kate worried about Eric. Exhaustion of the day caught up with her during the short trip home in the van. Liz met her at the front door.

"Eric called," said Liz.

Kate's eyes opened widely, as she stopped her progression inside. "What did he say?"

"Get in before you catch pneumonia," Liz calmly demanded. This irritated Kate, but she obeyed.

"He said he hoped to catch the 7:40 flight out, so he'll probably be home around ten."

"Did he say anything else?"

"That was about it," answered Liz.

"How did he sound?" Kate realized this was a stupid question.

"I don't know—he sounded like Eric," Liz said.

Kate drove her wheelchair in circles on the large mat until the wheels were dry and clean.

"Rough day?" Liz asked. They entered the apartment.

"Yeah, I guess," Kate answered. "I'm sorry I asked such a stupid question."

"What question?"

"How Eric sounded on the phone."

"Don't worry about it. You were just concerned," Liz said. They went into the kitchen.

"I'm just a little worried, that's all."

"How is he anyway?" Liz asked. "I never get to see him anymore."

"Neither do I," Kate said. She leaned on the counter and watched Liz cook. The warmth of the kitchen soothed her nerves.

Liz left after dinner. Kate settled in the den in front of the TV. Time passed and before she knew it, the eleven o'clock news began. Her mind wandered. Fifty-seven channels and still nothing was on. She had her ear tuned to the outside door. Every car she heard pass created hopes that it was Eric, but they were only driving by. The weather man waved his wand across a map of New York State when Kate heard jiggling keys coming from the hallway. She listened, as the keys fell onto the coffee table. Eric was in the den before she was able to throw the covers off.

"You're still awake?" Eric asked, untucking his shirt from his pants.

"Yeah—I was waiting for you," she said. "What happened?"

"Like always—I bailed him out and then he went home."

"Did he say anything?" Kate worked to get up to her knees.

"Like what?" Eric said. "Do you really think Joe would admit his guilt? He might when hell freezes over."

Kate smiled. The fact that Eric was still standing in the doorway puzzled her. She wished he'd come closer. "Are you alright?" she asked.

"Yeah, sure. Why wouldn't I be?" His voice was short.

Kate's muscles tightened up. "I was just asking."

He bowed his head. "I'm sorry," he said quietly. "I'm fine." He rubbed his eyes. "Do you need to go?"

"Yeah," she said and crawled toward the bathroom. She told Eric there was some food in the refrigerator. He wasn't hungry. The bright bathroom light displayed hiss weariness. His shoulders were slumped. It was evident by his solemn demeanor that he was bothered by the day. Kate decided it was not worth it to pick for details—maybe some other time. He put her in bed, shut off the light, climbed into bed and kissed his wife goodnight.

As the college basketball season approached, Kate wondered how the constant travel would affect Eric. It would either bring him relief, or put more stress to his routine. She hoped it would bring him relief, but deep down she knew his strain was going to increase. Time would tell.

Snow had fallen for two days. Snow glistened under the sun, as if the ground had millions of tiny dancing lights. As she sat and gazed out the office window, Kate marveled at the beauty of it all. The campus was under a blanket of snow. Mr. Leonard informed Kate that their meeting with the academic board was postponed until January, during the winter break. The news frustrated her. She wanted to be done with the issue as soon as possible, but she was thankful for the extra time to prepare.

Kate looked up from her computer and saw a well-dressed gentleman.

"Ms. Hollis? I'm Mr. Delane, Carl's father," he said and extended his right hand.

Kate said hi, shook his hand and began to peck on the keyboard: "Nice to finally meet you," announced the computerized voice.

"Same here," Mr. Delane said kindly. "Carl has told me a lot about you. He's very impressed with you."

Kate typed with quick and accurate strokes: "Thank you very much. What brings you to Syracuse?"

"Oh, I had to fly up and see a client of mine. I thought I'd drop by and see Carl."

Kate was struck by his presence: a bullet would ricochet off his steel-like chest. She saw the resemblance between father and son and he had the same defined features, the same facial expressions and the same dark-brown eyes. Even their jet-black hair was similar.

"I imagine he was happy to see you," she typed.

"Yes, he was. He was," he said. "I have noticed a sharp change in Carl's attitude and I assume it's because of you."

Kate smiled at Mr. Delane. "Well, I really appreciate the acknowledgment, but I'm sure it is all Carl's doing," she typed.

Mr. Delane nodded. "Last year was a whole different story," he continued. "He struggled with the simplest of courses and not because he wasn't smart. He knew the material, but he didn't apply himself, almost like he was lost or something."

Kate was impressed by his sincere manner. It reminded her of Carl. "I've heard those reports," said the computer.

"He did," Mr. Delane said, embarrassed for Carl. "What he doesn't know is that I nearly pulled him out of Syracuse. I thought he was having too tough a time."

Kate said nothing and continued to listen with great interest.

"I was going to enroll him in a trade school down in the city. I figured he'd have an easier time with that." Mr. Delane talked softly.

Kate typed: "What made you change your mind?"

Mr. Delane thought for a moment. "Over the summer, Carl looked forward to coming back," he answered. "How could I deny him that?"

Kate calmly pecked on her keyboard: "Carl is a very smart young man and he knows what he's doing."

"That he does," said Mr. Delane, confidently. "So, what's going on with Carl's chemistry class? Carl said the professor gave him a bogus test or something?"

"Yes, that's true," she typed. "A meeting is scheduled for the middle of January with the academic board. I will present my case then. After that, the professor will put forth his case."

"Would I be allowed to attend this meeting?" asked Mr. Delane.

The question caught Kate by surprise. "I would need to check." Kate's palms started to sweat, as she typed. The thought of a Manhattan lawyer at the academic board meeting numbed her brain. She imagined Mr. Delane peeling Wilcox down to his very soul, if he had the chance to interrogate him.

"I apologize. I should stay out of it," he said.

Kate shook her head and typed: "No, I really think you should be there. I'm sure Carl would want you there."

"What makes you say that?"

A long pause ensued, as she typed: "Carl once told me that there was nothing he wanted more than to make you proud of him. He knows he'll never be the athlete you once were, so he has decided on another way to show you how capable he really is."

Mr. Delane swallowed hard. "He really said that?"

"Yes, he did." Kate typed: "I think if you can attend the meeting in January, it would please your son."

"Please let me know if I can attend."

"I will," she typed. "I'm almost certain that the university encourages parents to be present at such meetings."

"Mrs. Hollis, it's very nice to meet you," Mr. Delane said.

Kate typed: "It's very nice to meet you, Mr. Delane. I'll be in touch soon."

"Thank you," he said and departed.

Kate reflected on her responsibility. Briefly, she panicked. *Am I acting in Carl's best interest?* She soon regained her resolve to discipline Wilcox. She had chosen to pursue a career in special education after someone had told her that she would never succeed in the field. She would devote her career to clearing away barriers to people with disabilities. Access to education should start with a ramp and end with a diploma; and along the way, every faculty member should help make sure all education benefits are available to every student, including the physically challenged. Nobody should say it can't be done because it can be done. Sure, a blind woman cannot hope to be a bus driver, and a man in a wheelchair cannot hope to be a construction worker on a skyscraper. But, why can't that man in a wheelchair become an architect? Why can't that blind woman be a city planner? There are no reasons. The prejudices and the stereotypes must go.

In college, Kate had a great academic advisor. From day one, she knew what was expected of her, and the faculty knew what was expected of them. Besides being educated in the academic sense, Kate was also educated in the life experiences of being a student in a wheelchair on a college campus. Those lessons remained with her.

She often wondered what would have become of her, if she had been born 50 years earlier. She probably would have been institutionalized at infancy and spent her life as a ward of the state. She cringed at the horrible thought. Crib bars resembling prison bars and grumbling nurses resembling ill-tempered prison guards. She felt grateful for the life she had and for the opportunity to defend Carl.

Every day for the past month, Eric and Dianne had sat on the wooden bleachers and watched basketball practice. The first game of the season was five days away. The coach screamed at his players, walking back and forth in a fury.

"Are you ready to go on the road?" Dianne asked over the din.

"I have no idea, but I sure could use a vacation before we do," Eric said, as his gaze followed the basketball around the court.

"Maybe Colberg will give us a few days off?"

Eric chuckled at her absurd comment. "Doubt that very much. Even if he was willing, Hill would still want us at practices. We're lucky to have Thanksgiving off."

"By the way, what are you doing for Thanksgiving?" she asked.

Coach Hill screamed furiously at the players. Eric was certain that if Hill continued to scream, his juggler vein would burst. "Colberg invited us over to his place for dinner—before the team party. What are you doing?"

"He invited me, too, but I think I'm going to decline," she answered. "I think I'm going to spend Thanksgiving with Mark."

As Dianne spoke, Stuart King approached the bleachers.

"Are you sure you want to do that?" Eric asked Dianne, casually. He had his eye on Stuart.

"Yeah, pretty sure. It'll be okay," she said, as if reassuring herself.

"Good," he said. Stuart was breathing heavily and Eric asked if he was okay.

"Yeah, fine. Why?" asked Stuart.

"No reason," Eric said without hesitation. "I ask everyone that, I guess." Eric continued listening to Stuart's breathing, secretly noting how long it took his breathing to return to normal.

Dianne moved down a row to where Eric and Stuart were sitting. "You looked good out there, Stuart," she said.

"Tell that to the coach," he said in frustration. "He thinks I'm dragging my butt."

"I think Hill is just having a bad day," said Eric. "He just chose you to pick on today, that's all." Eric noticed that Stuart was breathing normally. He glanced at his watch. His worry dissipated.

"Give it all you got the next practice," Dianne said, trying to boost Stuart's confidence.

"Yeah," said Stuart.

The three went back to watching practice. The moves were rehearsed, as if the players were practicing a contemporary ballet. The ball advanced smoothly from one player to the next. In practice, it had to do with the mechanics and the strategy of the game.

Once the team members stepped onto an opposing court, things changed. The goal of the Syracuse basketball team was to drive every player on the opposing team out of tempo and create havoc with their line of attack.

The Syracuse basketball team started off the season with two easy wins. The cheerfulness around campus was bolstered—Thanksgiving break was a week away. Like everyone else, Kate looked forward to a few days off. Getting from the start of the semester to Thanksgiving was like running a 26 mile marathon. At the beginning, the runners were fueled with energy. By mile 15, they were beginning to feel the road unmercifully pounding the soles of their feet. And by the 25th mile, they were digging deep to unearth energy reserves.

The office was quiet. Sue had stepped out, so Kate had the office to herself. Carl appeared at the door and she welcomed him in.

"Are you the only one here?" Carl asked, surveying the rest of the office.

"Yeah," she said in her natural voice. She typed: "Are you

looking for someone?"

"No, just looking around," answered Carl. "I was bored, so I came to visit."

Kate smirked. "No homework?"

"All finished," he said, smiling.

"I see," she typed. "Hey, your father was in."

"He didn't tell me he came over to see you. What did he say?" Carl asked.

"He was telling me how much you've changed and he's pleased to see you doing so well," she typed. A curious look engulfed Carl's face. "You know, you and your dad should really talk more. He could learn a lot from you and you could learn a lot from him." Carl nodded. "He wants to attend the academic board meeting in January," she continued.

"He does?"

"Yeah," Kate said. She looked toward him, but she continued typing. "He really wants to be there. I told him I would find out if he's allowed to attend."

"And is he?" Carl asked.

"I haven't found out yet," she typed. "I'll find out before Christmas." Carl seemed unusually placid. "Are you excited about the upcoming break?"

"Yeah. It's been a long three months."

"Yes, it has," Kate said, reverting to her own voice. Carl understood her.

"You look tired," he said.

Kate assured him she was fine—running her 26th mile.

"Yeah, well, I think you need this break more than I do," he said. "So, what are you and Eric doing for Thanksgiving?"

Hearing Eric's name reminded her that she indeed had a husband somewhere not too far away. "A friend is visiting. She's flying in from New Hampshire. We always have a good time," she typed.

"Dad and I are going to his mother's," Carl said, without measurable enthusiasm. "We've spent the holidays there the last eight years. My grandmother has this evil cat. Every time I'm there, it attacks. We have to put the damn thing in the basement—the stupid cat."

Something about the way Carl told his story made Kate aware of how profound the loss of his mother was to him. Carl noticed a spot on Kate's desk and rubbed it with his thumb.

"Nobody can come close to Mom's stuffing," Carl said, still trying to erase the spot. "If I could, I would sleep from Thanksgiving to New Year's."

Kate's heart dropped. She typed: "I have no doubt that she's watching you all the time, and she's so proud of you. Do you believe she's watching you?"

"I think so," Carl said, already more positive. "Dad doesn't talk about Mom too much. When I try, he just clams up. Sometimes, I think he would rather have had me die along with Mom." Tears started to fall.

"That's not true," Kate typed. "Your dad loves you."

Carl wiped his eyes with his shirtsleeve. "Yeah."

Sue walked in. Carl was disappointed about the interruption. Their conversation had been derailed. "I really enjoyed our talk."

Kate smiled and typed: "Any time, Carl, any time."

"I better get going," he said and left the office, a few tears lighter.

He rolled down the hall at a pace more confident and relaxed than before. Kate's encounter with Carl stayed with her throughout the van ride home. She stared out the window at the passing cars. She liked to imagine where they were coming from and where they were going. Business types, in their suits and ties, driving their expensive foreign cars were perhaps heading back to the office to do some last-minute work after a meeting with a client.

The van turned onto Kate's street. As usual, Kate glanced at the house across the street. She turned to her driveway and noticed the truck.

Eric came to the front door. "Isn't this a surprise to see me home so early?"

"Yeah!" Kate said, with enthusiasm.

"Hill just gave us the night off. He said we looked tired." Eric took off Kate's jacket and carried her inside.

In Eric's arms, she realized how much she missed him. He carried her all the way to the bathroom. His scent enlivened her. He changed her into her sweats and then started cooking dinner. "What's new?" she said.

"What? With me?" he asked.

Kate laughed. "Yeah, you."

"I'm fine," he said. "It feels strange to be home so early."

"It's strange to have you home so early on a Thursday," she said. "What time is the game next Saturday?"

"12:30, or 1:00. I think it's at 12:30."

"So we can take Meg out to dinner after the game?"

"Meg? I didn't know she was coming," he said.

"She's coming for Thanksgiving. I told you two weeks ago," she said, sensing another argument.

"No, you didn't," Eric shot back. "You told me she might come for the weekend. You didn't say she was coming for Thanksgiving. I already told Colberg we would enjoy having dinner at his house."

"I did tell you she was coming, Eric," Kate said, struggling to stay calm. "Let's not fight about it."

"Maybe we should start writing little notes to each other and leaving them on the refrigerator," he said. "I can read them when I get home." He pretended to read an invisible note on the refrigerator. "Oh, I see that Kate had a bad day at work and I shouldn't disturb her."

She listened in exasperation. Incensed by his unwillingness to find balance between them, she knew arguing wouldn't help the situation. She needed a speaker device that she could plug into her brain so her words would bypass her mouth and go directly to the speaker.

"Did I win this fight by default?" Eric tossed the spatula into the sink.

She didn't answer. Sick of his badgering, she crawled into the living room. If she had had the ability to leave the apartment, she would have. Instead, she was faced with sitting through dinner while he fed her. The morning was a long way off and if she chose not to eat, it would be a night of endless hunger.

She turned the television on. She tried to recall if she did tell Eric about Meg's arrival, almost positive she had. Watching the news, she made an effort not to look in his direction.

Whatever happiness she had felt earlier was gone. Over the anger, she became worried about their arguments. Battling with Eric was alien to her. She searched for answers on how to end her battles with him. The lack of time they spent together was causing the bridge between them to collapse. With the basketball season in full swing, she knew there wasn't much she could do. It remained clear that no repairs would be done this night.

The television gave them an excuse not to talk. After she finished eating, she retreated into the den, away from their conflict. Intentionally or accidentally, Eric banged the dishes and pans much louder than usual, as he washed them. And every time plates clashed, Kate startled, often striking her hands on the computer stand. She had enough of the loud clanks. She finally asked him to stop. He obeyed.

She saw his silhouette against the hallway wall. It crossed her mind to go out to the kitchen and begin the repairs, but she decided against it. She didn't know when the right time should be. She didn't know who should apologize first. She had wished Eric had a night off. This wasn't what she expected. The night was a lost opportunity.

She and Eric remained in separate rooms for the entire night. The only words they spoke came when Eric took her to the bathroom before going to bed. Kate said she would stay up to work, adding she would sleep on the futon. He had no objection.

Retiring for the night, she was haunted by his words. Tormented, in her head she replayed their feud over and over again, in booming stereo. She looked at the clock—*1:27, 2:46, 3:49, 4:13*. She was headed for a fatiguing day and, in all likelihood, a headache.

A door closed and she awoke. She had slept for two hours. She got up from the futon and crawled into the hall. Disappointment consumed her. Eric had already left for work. It was too late to apologize. For an hour, she sat in the bedroom doorway, studying everything around her. The bed lay unmade. It looked like Eric, too, had trouble sleeping. Sunlight entered through the window blinds. Kate couldn't help staring at her wedding ring.

It seemed like hours before Liz arrived. *Once Liz notices the two unmade beds, she'll probably figure out the situation,* Kate thought. Kate didn't care to answer Liz's questions.

It took Liz a few seconds before she noticed Kate sitting in the doorway. "You scared the shit out of me!" exclaimed Liz. "Why are you sitting there?"

"It wasn't a good night last night," Kate finally said. "We had another fight. I slept in there." She looked into the den.

"It looks like you didn't sleep too well," Liz said.

"No, I really didn't," said Kate.

"Want to stay home today?" Liz said, kneeling in front of Kate.

"I can't. I have to go in for a meeting," she said. "I'll be fine."

"You're sure?"

Kate nodded. "Yeah, I'll be okay."

The morning routine started. "What was it about, if you don't mind me asking?"

"I don't mind," Kate said. "It was about Thanksgiving. He forgot I told him Meg was coming. I'm almost sure that I told him. His boss asked us over for Thanksgiving. I can't eat all that turkey."

Liz admired how Kate could laugh at a difficult situation. There was nothing to do but laugh. Kate just wished Eric was laughing, too. By the end of the shower, the critical voices inside her head faded away. She had a long, anxious day ahead of her before she would see Eric again. The night couldn't come fast enough.

All morning, she tried to work but her tired thoughts always returned to Eric and what she wanted to say. She loved his patience. She didn't need to worry about how fast her words came out. He always listened. She'd grown frustrated with people who pretended to understand her when they had no intention of understanding her. It was like they assumed she had a language all her own. He always listened.

Like most meetings, this one was painfully dull. The unrealized previous night's sleep tackled her at two o'clock. She struggled to stay awake, as she listened to Mr. Leonard and Pauline Lawson endlessly discussing next semester's materials to use in the calculus courses. She imagined being fast asleep in bed. She would have given a million dollars to be asleep at that particular moment. The meeting ended and she wasted no time exiting the library.

"Katie," a familiar voice called out. Eric leaned against the library's brick exterior. His hands were in his pockets.

"What are you doing out here. It's cold," she said.

"You have time to come have a cup of tea?" he asked.

She drove toward him. "I have time."

"May I drive?" he offered.

"Yes," Kate said. "I'm really—"

"Wait, I'm sorry," he said, interrupting her. "It seems that I had written down on my calendar, 'Meg for T-day.'" He looked at her with sorrow. "I'm such an ass."

Someone had just lifted two hundred pounds off of her shoulders. "You wrote it down?"

"Yep, I did," he said. He saw Kate's reaching for his hand and he grabbed it. Her hand was the temperature of ice, but he could still feel her warmth.

The cafeteria was empty. Eric chose a table, took Kate's jacket off and got them each a cup of tea. He put a straw in her cup. "I told Ray we were bringing a guest to the party," he said.

"Thank you," Kate said, gracefully. She was regaining some energy. "You know, I hate fighting with you. We seem to be fighting a lot these days." She took a sip of tea.

"I know, I know," he said. "You didn't get much sleep last night, did you?" He put his hand on her knee. Her leg stayed unusually calm.

She shook her head. "I could sleep right now."

"I'm sorry, babe." He pulled her toward him and she rested her head upon his shoulder. "I didn't know how difficult it would be."

"You think we could have some time together this weekend?" she asked.

"Let me check my schedule and see if I can fit you in," he said, jokingly. "I recall I have an hour free Saturday morning around eight."

She pretended to contemplate her answer. "I think I'm free also." She leaned over and put her lips to his. "Boy, I miss that," she said.

"It has been a long time, hasn't it?"

"Too damn long." Her tiredness made it easier for her to move her hand without much of a detour. All at once, Eric became familiar again, like viewing a lost photograph that had been hidden away for years.

"Let me take you home," he said, observing the fatigue in her eyes. "Do you think Leonard will mind if you go early?"

"I'm sure he will."

"I'll give him a call," he said. "We'll walk straight home from here." He stepped away to make the call. She closed her eyes, feeling tremendous relief that they had begun to be kind to each other again.

Eric got the nod from Leonard. They finished their tea. He dressed Kate warmly in gloves and a scarf.

"Sure wish we had a van," Kate hinted, as they ventured into the bracing chill outside.

"I promise, soon," he said, amused.

Chapter 6

Kate stared out the window, awaiting Meg's arrival. Soon, she was drawn into analyzing the events across the street when a car pulled into the driveway. In the darkness, she couldn't tell if it was the neighbors' gray Honda. A person stepped out and went inside. Kate recalled the first day she witnessed the young couple arguing. *Maybe the young man is returning?* Kate rooted for the couple to fall in love again. After there wasn't anything more to discover, she crawled into the kitchen to join Liz.

Over the aroma of raw carrots and potatoes, Liz and Kate reminisced about past Thanksgivings. Kate told about how Brian used to hurl olives into her mouth from across the table. Most landed on the floor. She was going to miss Brian this Thanksgiving.

Liz told one of her childhood stories; about the time she and her sister volunteered to make dessert. The fire department came to put out a small fire in the oven. Liz assured Kate that her cooking skills had improved.

Meg rang the doorbell. A rush of cool air freshened the apartment, as Liz opened the door.

"It's wicked cold up here," Meg said, dropping her duffel bag.

"It's November, you know," Kate said, excited to see her best friend.

Meg removed her coat, knelt down and hugged Kate. "How the hell are ya?"

"Good!" Kate exclaimed. "How are you?"

"Happy to be on the ground. The flight was really bumpy."

"I'm sorry." In the excitement in seeing her friend, Kate had forgotten to greet Roberta, who brought Meg from the airport. "Oh God, Roberta, I'm sorry. Please take a seat. Want a beer?"

"Oh, thanks, Kate," Roberta said heartily, "but I have to get going—we've got the in-laws at the house."

"Thank you very much for picking up Meg," said Kate. Meg echoed her thanks.

"No problem at all—happy to do it. See you guys tomorrow night at Ray's," said Roberta in parting.

"Meg, this is Liz Young," announced Kate. "Liz, Meg."

"Kate has told me a lot about you," said Meg.

"Same here," Liz said. "I'm going home. Do you need anything before I leave?"

Kate shook her head. "Thank you for staying. Have a good Thanksgiving, Liz."

"I will," Liz said, with a big smile. "See you on Monday."

Kate and Meg settled in the living room and enjoyed a cold beer, while they caught up on the latest news.

"I love the apartment," Meg said. "I especially like the picture of the barn."

"Me, too," said Kate.

"Come up and stay at the barn over Christmas, if you want," Meg said.

"That would be great, if we have time."

"Are things any better?" Meg asked.

"Somewhat," Kate said. "We haven't had a fight in a week, so that's something."

"When was the last time?"

"Saturday," Kate said. "It was the first time in over a month."

"Over a month?!" Meg said with astonishment. "Why the hell didn't you tell me this?"

"I'm not in the habit of talking about my sex life over the phone," said Kate, with a smirk.

"Since when?" Meg asked, chuckling. "You always used to."

"Yeah well, I guess there hasn't been too much to talk about lately."

"So, what time can we expect the young chap home?"

"Around 9:30."

"No wonder you're not getting any. The poor boy is tired," Meg said. "He works his little butt off."

"Yes, that he does," Kate said. She felt relaxed in Meg's company and the words flowed freely.

Meg's stories transported Kate back to their days at the Miller School—carefree days filled with friends and good times. Kate wouldn't trade those memories for all the dollars in the world. It was a wondrous atmosphere, that school atop a mountain, where she spent the bulk of her childhood and teenage years, and where Meg still worked. It was like being part of a big family; some of whom Kate knew well, some of whom were just acquaintances, and some of whom she avoided like the plague.

The school, a mini civilization, was high above the surrounding valley. Only much later did Kate grasp how isolated they all were on top of that mountain. If she was ever faced with putting her own child into a residential school, she would instantly decide upon the Miller School. For a second or two, Kate wished she could relive her younger years, just to experience the good times all over again. Then she reflected on the past seven years, so satisfying and loving with Eric. These years far outshined her youth.

Kate told Meg about Wilcox, not leaving out a detail. She grew intense, as she derided Wilcox's pig-headedness, his hideous plaid suits, and the patronizing tone that had pierced her to the core. Her frustration with Wilcox showed all over her recoiling body, but her words flowed easy. Whether from the beer, or the repulsion she felt for Wilcox, she grew animated. She confessed she was terrified about presenting her case to the academic board. Meg reassured her of her abilities, jokingly suggesting drinking a beer or two before the presentation. Amid their laughter came the sound of Eric's keys at the door.

He greeted the two giggling women: "Oh, God, don't tell me you two are drunk already?"

"There he is," Meg said and rose to hug and kiss him. "How the hell are ya?"

"I'm fine," he said.

"Kate tells me you're working your little butt off." She pinched the area in question.

"Yeah, I am," he said. "I hear the sound of a beer calling me from the fridge."

"We were just saying maybe you guys can come up to the barn over Christmas," Meg said. "You think you can make it?"

"I think so. I think so," he answered. "So, how the hell have you been?" Eric leaned over and kissed Kate.

"I've been fine," Meg said. "Let me get you that beer."

"You're an angel," he said and sat down behind Kate to rub her neck. "How was your day?"

Cocking her head back, she peered into his eyes as if viewing stars in the sky. "It was good," she said. "How was yours?" The tension in her neck melted away under his strong touch.

"Pretty calm today. Most of the kids have gone home. Ray invited some of the kids from far away to come over to his place for Thanksgiving." He took the beer from Meg. "And how was the flight in from Manchester?"

"I consider it a good flight when nobody pukes, and luckily nobody puked. I give it a score of ten."

"So, what's new in your life?" he asked.

"Do you notice anything different?" Meg asked, as she sipped her beer.

Both Kate and Eric studied her carefully. "We're clueless. Give us a hint," Eric urged.

"What dirty, white thing is missing between my two fingers?" Meg helped them along by putting her two bare fingers to her lips.

"You stopped smoking!" exclaimed Kate.

"Congratulations to you!" Eric said, happily. "I've never thought I would see this day."

"Yeah, well, I cried my first nicotine-free day. That was over a month ago."

"What else have you been keeping from us?" Kate asked, excitedly.

"I've been seeing somebody," she answered.

"Who is it?" Kate desired an answer quickly.

"His name is Jeff and he's a very nice guy."

"How old is he?"

Meg grimaced. "24."

Eric choked on his beer. "24?" The girls chuckled at his antics.

"Where did you meet him?" Kate asked.

"At the mountain," Meg answered. "We met just by coincidence one day and boom, here we are two months later." She gauged the reaction of her two good friends. "He was supposed to come with me, but he seems to be still attached to the umbilical cord."

"Maybe he's younger than you think?" Eric teased.

"Shut up over there," said Meg. "I know I'm an old hag at 36—so what."

"I'm happy for you," Kate said.

"Only you, Meg. Only you," Eric said with a grin.

"Be happy for her," Kate said to Eric.

"I am," he said. "It's about damn time you met someone. May it last a long time."

"Cheers!" Kate exclaimed.

Eric raised his bottle.

"Thanks," Meg said and they clinked bottles in a spontaneous toast. Eric raised Kate's glass for her and the three of them all clinked again.

The three friends chatted away for two hours. Eric was the first to succumb to exhaustion, retiring for the night. Kate and Meg talked on long into the night, sharing news about mutual friends. Some were doing well, and others, not so well.

Thanksgiving morning brought cold, gray skies. Snow was in the forecast. Eric rose first and fixed breakfast. Meg awoke to the smell of fresh-brewed coffee. She and Eric watched the Macy's Thanksgiving Parade on TV, as they skimmed through the morning paper.

"I would kill for a drag—just one drag," Meg said with humor.

A month without a cigarette hadn't lessened her craving for nicotine with her morning coffee. It was still ingrained in her psyche, putting a cigarette between her lips and then lighting it up with a flicker of a flame—all without a thought. Like putting a key into a car's ignition or dialing a familiar phone number, smoking was just another automatic task. Now, Meg had to reprogram her brain.

"How's work going?"

"Fine," she said. "How's work for you?"

"Tough. I've never worked so hard in my entire life."

"Yeah, Kate told me you work long hours."

"I rarely get home before ten. I hardly see Katie," he said. "It sucks."

"Are you two doing okay?"

"I guess," he said, hesitating briefly. "We argue a lot more than we used to."

"Yeah? It's been an adjustment period."

"Yeah, I guess."

"It will probably make your relationship stronger," said Meg.

Eric glanced at the television. "Here comes Santa." The parade was winding down.

Minutes later, Kate crawled into the living room. "You missed Santa Claus, Sweetie," Eric said.

"Oh no, did I?" Kate said jokingly. She smiled at Meg. "How did you sleep?"

"Very well," Meg said.

"I'm sorry I slept so long," said Kate. She caught a glimpse of the gray Honda parked across the street.

"What the hell are you looking at?" Meg asked.

Eric answered for her: "She has this curiosity with the people across the street."

"They are just a couple of young people who seem to be having trouble."

"You watch them through the window?" Meg asked.

"Yeah—I'm good like that."

"Columbo should hire you as his sidekick," Meg joked.

"Sounds more like *Rear Window* to me," Eric added.

"Are you making fun of me?" Kate asked Eric, leaning over for a kiss.

"No," he said, "but your friend is."

"Yeah, I'm used to her." Kate wedged herself between his knees and rested her head on his stomach. This was her favorite pillow of all time. Her head rose and fell with his every breath, like a ship drifting upon calm seas. She was content to spend the entire day on his ocean.

The coffee table was cluttered with empty dishes and glasses. Eric cleared, while Meg dressed Kate and herself for Colberg's party. Kate briefed Meg about all the people who she thought would be there, celebrating the start of basketball season. It was an annual ritual.

Being in the company of mostly strangers worried Kate. Meg reassured her that everything would go smoothly. She reminded Kate of the day she met Eric, and the uncertainty she felt, dumbfounded that Eric could fall in love with someone like her. Kate remembered it all with a sense of embarrassment followed by awe. She was one of the lucky ones.

The ten-minute drive to Colberg's was punctuated with idle chitchat. Colberg's street was lined with parked cars. Kate felt a twinge of nervousness, as she anticipated the looks she would receive from curious guests. At least she had Meg to talk to.

Eric pulled into the spot Colberg had saved for them. He led Kate indoors and through the maze of people, stopping to shake hands and conversing with his colleagues and their spouses. Kate imagined people thinking Meg was her nursemaid. Kate held out her flailing arm to people in hopes that they would shake her hand. Most readily did. Others stared vacantly at her arm, perhaps concluding the gesture was involuntary.

Roberta came within sight. Kate was relieved. The three women found a spot for themselves. Champagne was the drink of choice for the night and they welcomed a glass of the bubbly. Glimmers from the crystal chandelier danced on the ornate wallpaper in the foyer. Not a thing was out of place. Every painting hung perfectly straight. Not a streak could be seen on a window.

"This house is beautiful," Roberta said.

"You should see the bathroom," Meg said. "I was expecting a valet in a tuxedo to pop out of the closet and hand me a finger towel."

"The boys are in the kitchen, talking sports," said Roberta. "We won't see them all night."

Kate grinned. Realizing the room was too noisy for her to be heard, she resolved to listen to Meg and Roberta. The Champagne took charge of her system and she began to talk more, no matter if anyone heard her or not. Again, the doorbell rang and moments later Dianne appeared.

"She's here," said Kate.

"Who?" Meg asked.

"Psycho."

"The woman with the frizzy red hair?" asked Meg. "I thought Eric said she wasn't coming."

"I guess she changed her mind," said Kate.

"Talking about Dianne?" asked Roberta.

Kate and Meg nodded.

"We had her over for dinner last week," Roberta said. "She's very—different."

They watched Dianne, as if a Hollywood actress were entering a party after a screening of her latest film. They agreed Dianne was overdressed for the occasion. Her black satin dress barely covered her thighs—apparel not well adapted to the cold Syracuse winds.

"She must be cold," said Kate, stating the obvious.

"I think that's her motive—to show everyone she's cold,"

Meg said.

Behind Dianne, no husband followed.

Kate's curiosity started to rise. "Where's Mark?"

"Who's Mark?" Meg asked.

"Her husband," answered Kate.

"She's married?" Roberta asked. "John didn't mention that."

"Eric says it's not a good relationship," Kate said.

"What was that last word?" asked Roberta.

"Relationship," Meg said. She had heard Kate say that one enough times.

"They have been separated for a month," Kate said. "Dianne wanted to have Thanksgiving with him, but from what Eric tells me the husband sounds a little whacked himself."

Meg repeated the sentence to Roberta. Their nervous giggles drew looks from the others. Kate told Meg that a trip to the bathroom was necessary and they maneuvered through the forest of people.

The bathroom was as elegant, as Meg had described. Kate had only seen this type of bathroom in magazines. Then, they went to the kitchen.

"Are you looking for Eric, Katie?" asked Colberg.

Kate smiled at him. "Yeah."

"He went out front to check on Dianne's car," said Colberg. "Do you want me to go out and get him for you?"

Hearing that Eric had suddenly been blessed with mechanic skills stunned Kate. "No, no, thank you. Just tell him to find me when he gets back, please."

The noise in the kitchen hampered their communication. Meg interpreted for Colberg.

"Okay, I'll be sure to tell him."

"Thank you very much," Kate said. Again, Meg repeated for her.

"Are you two enjoying the party?" Colberg asked.

"Yes, this is a great house you have here," said Meg.

"Thanks. Oops, I think I hear my wife calling. See you two later." Colberg retreated into the crowd.

Meg wheeled Kate back into the living room to rejoin Roberta.

The idea of Eric looking under the hood of a car was almost humorous to Kate. Knowing that Dianne was the beneficiary of his newfound talents bothered Kate like a faucet dripping during the night—not letting her rest. She couldn't do much about it and Kate welcomed a second glass of Champagne. "I would like to know when Eric started fixing cars. He can't even change the damn windshield wipers on the truck," said Kate.

"Will you calm down," Meg softly demanded. "He'll be back in a minute. Drink your Champagne."

Within minutes, Eric walked in. The cold air had reddened his cheeks. "Doing okay?" he asked as he leaned over Kate's shoulder.

"Yeah," she answered. "Did you fix her car?" Her tone was condescending.

"Dammit, Kate, I was just trying to help," he said at a low volume, but his eyes screamed. He went back into the kitchen.

Kate struggled to keep her composure. "That went well," she said sarcastically, trying to get the spotlight off of her. Embarrassment kept her silent for several minutes.

If time moved any slower, Kate imagined she could reverse the minute hand to withdraw her earlier comments to Eric, but to her discouragement time slowed only to a crawl.

Minutes before midnight, most of the guests had left. Kate went into the kitchen to find Eric. He was conversing with Ray, John, and Dianne. The dialogue between them stopped and all eyes were on her. Eric asked if she wanted to leave. Only Kate noticed his curt tone. Meg put on Kate's jacket as Eric continued to talk. Kate had an opportunity to observe Dianne. She was still bare-shouldered. *The blood in her veins must be as hot as the lava,* Kate mused. *Maybe her skin is made of leather.* Though she sat five feet away, Dianne never looked at Kate.

The ride home was quiet. Eric concentrated on the road. Kate looked at the passing cars. Meg sat in the backseat and struggled to keep her mouth shut. "You guys are driving me nuts," Meg finally said, as they neared their driveway. "Please talk to each other!"

Eric looked in the rearview mirror. "I've got nothing to say."

"You haven't said a word to each other for two hours."

Kate spoke up. "I'm sorry, Eric. I'm sorry for what I said."

"You're not sorry! You can't stand Dianne," he said. "Whenever you see me with her, you freak out."

"I don't trust her, Eric," Kate tried to say calmly.

"Is it Dianne you don't trust, or me?"

"I don't trust Dianne!" she exclaimed, glaring at her husband.

"What the hell is she gonna do, Katie?"

Kate answered with a vacant stare.

"Please don't worry," Eric said.

Kate had no response. She watched him exit the truck.

"He's right, you know," Meg said.

"I know," said Kate.

Chapter 7

Three games, three wins for Syracuse.

The Carrier Dome was packed with screaming fans. Loud buzzers startled Kate. She sat with Roberta and Carl. They did all the talking. Her words would be drowned out by the roar of the crowd. They sat near the Syracuse bench. In their attire, the players and coaches sat up front. Behind them sat Eric, John, and Dianne. Kate missed Eric. She wished things could return to the way they once were. Four months earlier, she could hardly wait for the basketball season to begin. Now, she wished it could be over in 17 minutes and 43 seconds.

With less than five minutes left, Syracuse was up by seven points. Bobby James went down, grimacing and grabbing his ankle. Eric rushed onto the court. Dianne followed, and together they helped Bobby off the court. The crowds were suddenly quiet.

Despite the loss of Bobby, Syracuse went on to win it. Students left their seats quickly, no doubt headed for the nearest campus party. Roberta rushed home. She was expecting company. Carl sat with Kate.

"You don't have to stay," Kate said. As expected, Carl was unable to decipher her words.

"I'm gonna get this, I swear I am," he said with determination. "Say it again."

"You…" Kate said.

"You?"

Kate nodded with enthusiasm.

"I what?" Carl asked.

"Don't..."

"Door?" guessed Carl.

Undaunted, Kate repeated the word.

"Does it start with a D?" he asked.

She nodded.

"Say it again," he said, and she did.

"Don't!" he exclaimed.

Kate beamed. Her body showed her excitement, regaining control of her flailing arms. "Have to…"

"I don't have to what?"

"Stay," Kate said.

"I don't have to stay?" said Carl, repeating her sentence.

"Yeah," she answered.

"I got nothing else to do and I just can't leave you here by yourself," he said. "You never know if some crazy, deranged person is going to pop out of the stands and have their way with you, especially when you're not in your power chair."

His words embarrassed her slightly and she tried in vain not to smile. "Good point."

"Was that 'Good point'?"

She nodded.

"See, I'm getting it," he said, confidently. He and Kate rested for a moment, as if they had just climbed ten flights of stairs and were preparing to climb another two flights. Janitors were already at work in cleaning the stands.

"It must suck having to sit here and wait for Eric after every game."

"Sometimes," she said, keeping her answer short.

"'Sometimes,' right?"

She smiled.

"I mean, what if you have to take a leak or something—what do you then?"

"Hold it," she answered.

Carl's laughter filled the Carrier Dome. The janitors looked over at him.

"Are you serious?"

"Yeah."

"Man, oh man!" he said. "You're amazing, you know that."

"No, I'm not. I just do what I have to do."

As time went on, her words became easier for Carl to understand. He watched her lips, as she slurred the words like a career drunk.

"So, how did you and Eric meet?" he asked. "That *is*, if you don't mind me asking."

"No, no, I don't mind," she said. The question prompted the memories to surface. "I will tell you sometime next week when I have my computer."

Carl stared at her for a moment. "The last word was 'computer,' right?"

She nodded and repeated the sentence until he understood.

"Oh, okay—the story's that long, uh?"

"What day is good for you?" she asked

"Thursday's good," he answered. "My finals will be over. Should I stop by around four?"

"Yeah, four will be good," said Kate.

Carl continued to ask Kate easy questions, focusing on she and Eric's life together. Memories came rushing back. She remembered the gym was filled with kids in wheelchairs, filled with noise and excitement, and amongst the flocks of people were Kate and Eric, on opposite sides of the gymnasium. She noticed him in the crowds. He went over and introduced himself. When she didn't notice him approaching, she jumped when she saw him. He apologized and proceeded to talk to her. She had a portable typewriter on her lap table. The piece of paper in the typewriter was filled with one-line sentences. Eric read the last line. She was mystified by his interest in her during that first encounter.

"I didn't know where you were all this time," Eric said, walking toward Kate and Carl—jolting Kate from her reverie. "Hey, Carl, how are you doing? I haven't seen you in a while."

"Oh, fine," he answered. "I was just here keeping your wife company, while she waited."

"I appreciate that, Carl—thank you."

"How's his ankle?" Kate asked. All she wanted was to go home.

"A bad sprain. Nothing's broken. He'll be out for a good four weeks or so," Eric said. "I wish we could give you a ride back to the dorm, Carl, but there are only two seats in the truck."

"Oh, that's okay. The dorm is five minutes from here. I can make it in four."

They all laughed.

The air outside enlivened Kate. A light snowfall was illuminated by the building's floodlights. Eric helped Kate into the truck. "You're quiet tonight," he said.

"Yeah, well, I'm a little tired," she said. Eric struggled to start the engine, but it wouldn't turn over. "You know, someday you are gonna get stuck in the middle of nowhere and you're gonna freeze to death waiting for someone to pull you out of a snow bank," Kate said.

Eric looked at her, bewildered. "Where is that coming from?"

"I just want to get home, Eric," she said.

"I told you that I was sorry," he said. "We had to wait for Dr. Freham to show up. We waited an hour for that jerk just so he could tell us something we already knew. And then he has the nerve to rip us apart because we called him in. What was I supposed to do?"

"Forget it," she said.

"No, no—don't hand me that 'forget it' crap," he said, vehemently.

"I really would just like to go home and go to the bathroom, if you don't mind."

Eric tried the engine. By the grace of God, it started. "I wouldn't mind at all, dear." His patronizing words demanded a scornful glare. It was colder inside the truck than outside. It was another silent and colorless ride home.

Going to the mall meant playing chicken with the crowds. With Christmas approaching, Kate struggled to bring herself into the holiday spirit. At every corner, gigantic Christmas trees reminded her of the impending celebration. Liz walked with her through the commercial pageantry.

This was the first year Eric wasn't with her to do Christmas shopping. She was in no mood to spend the day at the mall. This year felt different, lonely. She looked forward to flying to Boston Friday, ever so grateful that Syracuse was scheduled to play Boston College on Christmas Eve. Memories of Christmases past filled her head, as Kate reminisced with Liz. Kate spotted a black leather jacket and bought it for Brian.

The crowds dispersed when they saw Kate on wheels coming toward them. Coming out of a store felt like coming onto a four-lane highway. Kate merged. Darting in and out of crowds unraveled her nerves.

Finals week was going to be brutal. The idea of rearranging classrooms, dealing with cranky students and the overall stress she was about to endure made her wish she was at Club Med. She just had to survive until Friday.

Like the previous night, tensions were high between husband

and wife. On the ride home, the rented van was as silent as a monastery. As they pulled into the driveway, Eric abruptly broke the silence: "Do you want me to pick up dinner on the way home from dropping off the van?"

"Sure," Kate said.

"What do you want?"

"Whatever you want," she said.

Liz excused herself for the night, and Kate thanked her for going to the mall. Liz took a bag full of presents home to wrap for Kate.

"Just tell me what you want for dinner, Kate," Eric said after Liz got into her car.

"Why are you yelling?"

"I wasn't yelling," he said sharply. "Just give me an idea what I can pick up."

"How about pizza."

"Thank you very much," he said mockingly and took her inside. He slammed the door on his way out.

The evening news was, on but offered little consolation to Kate. Reading wouldn't soothe her nerves and watching the news brought only more anxiety. Above the television was the picture of the barn, their barn. More than anything, she wanted to go there. Being there would get things back to where they were supposed to be. A week was too long to wait, but she had to wait. As her arm wiggled back and forth, crunching her elbow against the coffee table, she rested her head on her arm, scolding herself for the recent problems with Eric. She wanted to fast-forward to next Sunday when they would be at the barn.

Eric returned, and dropped his keys and the pizza box on the coffee table. He went to fetch some plates and drinks. His pace was sluggish. Kate realized just how tired they both were and how much they needed time together.

"Anything different on the news tonight?" Eric asked to break the silence.

She didn't expect his question. "No, not really." They ate, as they watched television.

A commercial break came. "Would you mind picking up something for Liz for Christmas?"

"Sure," he said evenly. "Any ideas for what I could get?"

She suggested a few things.

"Hopefully, I will get a few hours off. It's going to be a busy week."

"Yeah, I know," she said. He got up to clean the dishes. Weighing the pros and cons of getting into deeper issues with her husband, she crawled to her usual spot in the kitchen. "You look tired," she said.

"So do you," he said.

"What is wrong with us?"

"Oh, Katie, there's nothing wrong with us."

"We fight all the time, Eric."

"Do we have to get into this now?" he asked, with his back was turned to her.

"Can you think of a better time to talk about this?" she asked. "You seem to work all the time, so it's kind of difficult to do anything with you."

"Uh, here we go again," he said.

"What? What did I say?!" Kate exclaimed.

"Tomorrow I'll go into Colberg's and tell him that I can only work four hours a day because my wife misses me. Is that what you want, Kate?!" he yelled. His entire body was rigid.

"Why the hell are you getting so mad?" she asked. "Why do you always throw the threat of quitting in my face? Would you like to quit, Eric?"

"I think you would like me to quit."

"No, I don't want you to quit!" she said, forcefully. "I just want us to be civil to each other."

"Well, ditto to that!" he shouted. "You should go first!"

"You know what. I might stay in Boston for a few days after you leave on Wednesday."

"An extra few days with Dot—sounds like one hell of a good time," he said, with a sarcastic tone.

"Screw you," she said under her breath but loud enough so he understood. She crawled back into the living room and stewed. She heard his fingers tapping on the computer in the den. She wanted to leave for a while, take a walk like normal people do after a fight, but there was no way. It was too cold. Even if she could get herself in the wheelchair, get her jacket on and open the door to go out, she was trapped like a soldier in a foxhole, waiting for the battle lines to be drawn in their dirty little war. She needed Eric's help to get ready for bed. This fact distressed her. She wished that just this once she had the ability to change and put herself to bed. Bidding to regain some control, she told Eric that she planned to sleep in the den. He did not protest. She slept in the den for the next four nights.

As Kate had predicted, finals week was chaotic on campus for students and instructors alike. Her office, usually quiet, was transformed into Grand Central as disorganized students filed in and out, hoping to cram a semester's worth of lectures into an hour long visit with a tutor. Trying to move five feet was almost impossible in the crowded office. She was trapped behind her desk, just as she was trapped at home. She traveled from building to building, setting up extra classrooms for finals and angering faculty who disliked the changes. She sensed they didn't like being told what to do by a nonverbal crip in a wheelchair. The paperwork piled up on her desk. By the end of finals, she knew every hallway, every room, and every elevator on campus. Her mind rarely drifted to Eric. The only time she thought about him was when she saw him walking on campus with Dianne. They laughed and chatted nonstop, as they walked at a distance. As the winter sun set, the cold wind blew in her face and tears clouded her vision. She couldn't feel anything but her heart plunging into her stomach.

When she returned to the office, Emily was waiting. She opened her laptop and said hello to Emily.

"You wanted to see me?" Emily asked.

"Yes," Kate said in her natural voice and hurriedly typed: "How are finals going?"

"Oh, they went very well," Emily said. "Thanks for asking."

Kate was already typing her next sentence. "Would you mind if I contacted your state counselor to see if we can get you some new equipment? If you had a computer of your own, we could set up some programs to help you with your reading so you'll be more independent."

"I haven't had much luck in getting my state counselor to do anything for me, except to buy me a tape recorder," said Emily. "But be my guest."

"I seem to be lining up all kinds of arguments for myself," Kate typed. Her thoughts turned to her recent argument with Eric. She would have given anything to go back and make

things right. "I'll contact her after the holidays."
"Great. Keep me posted," Emily said.
Kate's exhaustion was actually helping her type: "I've been all over campus making sure that finals are held in accessible rooms, and those kinds of things."
"Haven't the professors figured that out by now?" Emily asked.
"You wouldn't believe how many instructors neglect things like this," Kate said.
Emily's friend walked into the office. Emily introduced her to Kate and rose to leave.
"You two have a nice holiday," said the computer.
"You too, Kate," Emily said and was gone.
Kate was too tired to get any paperwork done. She went home and ate dinner with Liz. All she wanted to do was sleep. She lay down on the futon in the den, and didn't wake up when Eric came home. In the morning, she awoke after he'd left for work. They never saw each other, or even talked on the phone for four days. The only communication was a note he'd left on the refrigerator, reminding her what time the flight left on Friday.
Thursday was a light workday. Finals were over, and by lunchtime the students and faculty had smiles upon their faces. The campus was a ghost town. Mr. Leonard had already left. Kate and Sue shared stories of past Christmases: memories of waiting for Santa, and later on discovering he was just a figment of their imagination. Kate recalled how she and Brian used to search the entire house for presents when their mother left for work. The memory brought an overdue smile to her weary face.
Carl rolled into the office. Kate had totally forgotten about their appointment.
"I hope you don't mind I'm here a little early," he said. "My dad is picking me up at 4:30."
"No, no, this is a good time," she said in her natural voice and then typed: "How did finals go?"
"I think they went okay," Carl said confidently.
"Good," she said and then typed: "Do you still want to hear how Eric and I met?"
"Yeah. I was hoping you'd remember."

As Kate typed, her arms were composed by her side.

"I have never seen you so still. You must be tired," said Carl.

She looked up and agreed. "We met at a sports event down on Long Island in 1987. We were in a gym and he came over and introduced himself. We ran into each other again and had a couple of drinks together with some friends. He told me he was a junior at Springfield College, where I was heading the next fall. We kept in touch and he came to visit me in New Hampshire. That's when we started seeing each other."

"Was it love at first sight?" asked Carl.

"Not really. It took a while," she said.

"Were you nervous when Eric came to visit you the first time?"

"I guess, a little. I wasn't sure of his intentions. I figured if he had the courage to approach me, then I should have the courage to respect him."

Kate's candor prompted Carl to share a little bit of himself. "Last week, some girl came up and started talking to me and not understanding why..." he said, nervously, "I clammed up. I was afraid people might harass her because she was talking to me. I didn't want that."

Kate was hit with a tidal wave of memories of Eric. As she typed, she reflected on the past week at home. She became upset without displaying it. "You have to be confident about who you are," she typed. "That wheelchair doesn't show what's in your heart, or how you think."

"It shouldn't, but it sometimes feels like it does," Carl said.

"I've always believed there's somebody out there for each of us. Be patient, love will come to you. When you come back next month, don't be afraid to talk to this girl," she said.

"Alright, I won't clam up next time. It's my New Year's resolution. Thanks for the advice. I know why Eric loves you so much."

"Thanks, Carl," she typed. "Please tell your dad that he can attend the academic board meeting. I'll let him know the date as soon as it's set."

"He'll be glad to hear that," Carl said. "See you after the break."

"You have a good vacation," she said in her natural voice.

"Hey, I understood that!" he exclaimed. "Get a good rest.

Good luck on nailing Wilcox."

She'd survived the long, trying week. Sleep was just around the corner.

Holiday travelers swarmed the airport. A big northeaster storm off the coast of New England was playing havoc with arrivals and departures. More delays piled on the screen. Kate grew increasingly anxious.

With a clipboard in his hand and a pen behind his ear, Eric was in his take-charge mode. Kate observed him, as he corralled the players like a drill sergeant. She knew to stay clear: don't ask Eric any questions and don't look at him funny. This was the first time she'd accompanied him on a road trip. Dianne walked in and Kate followed her every move. Dianne planted herself next to Eric. Kate's heart sank. A smile appeared on Eric's face—something Kate hadn't seen for a long time, and now, it was aimed at someone else. She wanted to be the one who made him smile. She wanted to make him laugh like she used to do.

More flight delays multiplied on the monitor, but their flight was unaffected. Kate had Eric take her to the bathroom before boarding. She feared being sucked out of a plane's lavatory at 30,000 feet, as in a scene from a seventies movie.

As they boarded the plane, she felt like an extra piece of luggage. All eyes were on her, as Eric carried her down the aisle. He and Kate talked very little. She fretted about the storm in Boston and just wanted to get there safely, as quickly as possible.

As soon as the *fasten seatbelts* sign went off, Eric turned to Dianne, seated one row behind them. Kate leaned forward, hoping to catch a piece of their conversation, but the din of the engines was too loud. She sensed that Dianne was in distress. Eric went and sat next to Dianne.

Stuart King sat in front of Kate and another member of the Syracuse team, Tim Londey. Eric went up and conferred with them. Kate watched their interaction. It was like they had known each other for ten years. She smiled. Eric introduced her to the young men. She recognized them from practice and raised her fist for them to shake. They extended their hands and Eric encouraged them to grab her hand. They wanted to know everything about Kate, especially how she got to be the way she was. For the first time in a week, she and Eric were communicating, if indirectly.

Eric explained Kate's story to Stuart and Tim, starting at the beginning: the summer of 1967. It was an incredibly hot summer. Her parents, Doug and Dot, were working hard to meet a deadline. They had recently started their own architectural firm. Dot was stretching herself thin, between working and taking care of a rambunctious 16-month-old boy. Eight months pregnant with their second child, Dot passed out from dehydration and fatigue. She was hospitalized for two days. Days later, she returned to the hospital and was in labor for 26 hours.

Back in the 60's, there were no fetal monitors or ultrasound machines. Kate's umbilical cord had become knotted around her neck, restricting the flow of oxygen to the brain. She was placed in an incubator for several days.

Stuart and Tim stared at Kate like she was one of the Seven Wonders of the World. Eric resumed his conversation with Dianne. Kate's heart sank. She didn't let her disappointment show, continuing to amuse Stuart and Tim by head-spelling words. Letter by letter, she drew in the air with her nose, while Stuart and Tim tried to guess the word first. She enjoyed herself. Eric was still talking to Dianne, who was crying into her trembling hands. Kate felt nothing, not even a speck of compassion. She wasn't happy with herself.

Eric returned to his seat for the final descent into Boston. His hands were clasped in his lap. Three months ago, her hand would have been holding his. Kate blamed herself.

The landing was surprisingly gentle, considering the brutal winds. She breathed a sigh of relief.

Chapter 8

The main terminal of Logan Airport was jammed, testing everyone's patience. Eric searched for his mother-in-law, while being careful not to bump Kate into any strangers' legs.

Mrs. Reed was near the entrance to the concourse, looking as if she had to be somewhere else. They exchanged hugs and kisses and then she rushed them along to her car, which was double-parked in front of the terminal.

She drove like a stunt driver, wasting no time getting to the Avis building to drop Eric off. He would pick up the rental car and meet them at her house. Mrs. Reed darted into the traffic. Kate felt safer at 30,000 feet in the middle of the rainstorm.

"Why the hell are you jumping so much?" Mrs. Reed asked, nervously.

Kate heard this complaints countless times. It dismayed her that after 27 years, her mother still did not get it.

"You're driving a bit fast, that's why," she replied, trying so desperately to sit still. "This is what I do. I jump at everything."

"Did we wake up on the wrong side of the bed this morning or what?" Mrs. Reed asked.

"I'm sorry," Kate said. "It's been a very busy week."

Mrs. Reed glanced over at Kate. "You look tired. Are you tired? Maybe it would be a good idea if you went to bed early tonight."

Another thing Kate failed to understand was why her mother still treated her as if she was ten years old. "Maybe," Kate answered, not wanting to squabble.

"Eric looks tired, too."

"Yeah, he is tired," said Kate. She reacquainted herself with the landmarks of the old neighborhood: the brownstones, the street signs she had known for so long. Here and there a house had been painted a different color, expanded up or out, or completely disappeared from its foundation. Everything was mainly the same, but to Kate things that had previously seemed so comfortable and so familiar were now very strange.

"Does Eric like his job?" Mrs. Reed asked.

"Yeah, he likes it."

"Brian tells me he works long hours," said Mrs. Reed.

"Yes, he does work a lot."

"What?"

Kate repeated her sentence in a louder voice.

"Poor guy. He looks like he's being run ragged."

Kate wanted the conversation to end. The questions about Eric were draining. She had no idea how he was, even though she had just spent two hours on a plane with him. All she wanted to do was sleep.

Mrs. Reed pulled into the driveway. The garage door opened to reveal Brian's car, exhilarating her spirits. Mrs. Reed unloaded the wheelchair from the trunk. Brian appeared, wearing a worn pair of blue jeans and a T-shirt. He picked up Kate in his arms, brought her inside and sat her down on the rug in the den.

In the distance, Mrs. Reed could be heard yelling for Brian. The screech of her voice brought Brian to his feet. He took Kate's jacket off. Mrs. Reed yelled for him again.

Kate crawled around and looked for details that she knew would please her eye. The Christmas tree was trimmed with white lights, just like many Christmases before. Underneath, a drift of presents appeared to be holding the tree upright. She was careful not to disturb any of the boxes. In the dim lighting, she read the tags on the gifts. The smell of Scotch tape confirmed that it was indeed Christmas. Many of the presents were addressed to her from Brian, sheathed in cheerful wrappings that depicted Old Saint Nick. She felt like a kid again.

Brian found Kate in the living room and offered her a beer. She accepted and crawled back to the den. An L-shaped couch afforded her the most comfort and she sat in the corner on the floor. Brian returned with a glass of beer and a dishtowel, and set them down on the coffee table. She looked at all of the books on the shelves, feeling quite at home. The beer calmed her nerves even more.

Mrs. Reed walked into the den, hyper as a child on sugar. She picked up Kate's jacket from the couch and straightened the pillows. She shot Kate a look—if one drop of beer fell on the table, Kate would own it. Kate gave her mother a smile, which was not returned. Mrs. Reed left.

Kate and Brian talked over the last five months. It reminded her of the countless weekends they had spent alone as children while their mother worked. Memories of Saturday mornings sitting in front of the television, watching cartoons, hadn't faded. Brian was the only one she could depend on. They were a team. They never disappointed each other. He was always there for her and she was always there to help him with his homework. Though sixteen months older, Brian was slightly behind in his learning skills. Peanut butter and jelly sandwiches were the weekend cuisine for breakfast, lunch and occasionally dinner when Mrs. Reed failed to make it home in time to cook.

As their beer disappeared, they talked for an hour. Mrs. Reed ducked in every 20 minutes into the den, saying a quick word and then returning to her duties in the kitchen.

Kate was concerned that Eric still hadn't arrived. The wind had its way with the awnings on the back of the house, trying relentlessly to rip them from their brackets. The rain beat down against the windows.

"What a day to fly," Brian said.

"You didn't drive home with Mario Andretti in there," Kate said, gesturing in the direction of the kitchen.

"It's a good thing she has a tank for a car," Brian said.

"Yeah."

"Eric should be here any minute," said Brian, noticing that his sister was looking at the clock.

"Yeah," she said.

Mrs. Reed popped in again. "If Eric doesn't get here soon, dinner is going to be dried out."

"He'll be here soon, don't worry," Kate said. Mrs. Reed let out a long, drawn-out sigh that had lost its effect on her children. Kate remembered how that exact sigh used to make her crumble, as if she was a standing wall at the mercy of a wrecking ball. Occasionally, the same wrecking ball demolished Brian. Together, they learned how the wrecking ball swung, avoiding the direct strike.

"I think I hear a car," Brian said.

Eric sprinted into the garage from the pouring rain. "Those jackasses didn't have a car for me," he said, as he entered the den. "I had to run all over the airport, begging for someone to give me a car."

"You should have called," Brian said. "I would have picked

you up."

"Oh, thanks, but we need our own car this weekend," Eric said. He peeled off his wet socks.

Eric turned to Kate. "Is Dot having a bird?"

They all laughed. "Yeah, kind of."

Eric went into the kitchen to apologize to Mrs. Reed.

Mrs. Reed accepted his apology. For a moment, Eric thought he was back in grade school, pleading for leniency from the principal.

They took their familiar places around the dining room table. Brian sat on Kate's right side, so he could feed her. Eric had no objection. The conversation flowed. Brian talked about the lack of work. Eric talked about his crazy schedule at Syracuse. Mrs. Reed chatted about her big new project in East Boston. Kate remained quiet, well aware that if she entered the conversation Mrs. Reed would remind her that her food was getting cold and would criticize Brian for not feeding her fast enough.

With dinner finished, all but Mrs. Reed stayed in the conversation. Kate joined the dialogue, though seldom speaking directly to Eric. Kate told Brian things about work. Eric sat and listened to things he should have known, feeling a bit out of touch with his wife. When he spoke, Kate discovered things about him. It wasn't long before Brian sensed some uneasiness. He also detected the lack of tenderness between them. It scared him to see their distance. It scared him to see his sister so somber.

"Kate tells me the plane ride was a little bumpy," Brian said to Eric.

"Yeah, it was."

By a little alcohol flowing in her bloodstream, Kate felt emboldened. "So, what was the matter with Dianne?"

Eric glared at Kate, but saw no choice but to explain. "She is planning to leave her husband. Is that all right with you, Kate?" He stood. "Excuse me, while I get another beer."

Kate blushed with embarrassment. "Do you think you can get me ready for bed?" she asked her brother.

"Sure," Brian said. "What was that all about?"

"Not now—I can't talk now," she said and looked away to hide her sad eyes.

"Did you want to go to bed now?" Brian asked.

"Yeah," she said, searching for a way to hold herself together.

Christmas Eve dawned with rain and wind. Kate felt odd waking up in such a familiar but strange space. The futon was still warm where Eric had been sleeping. She rolled over into the middle of the bed and heard the shower. When he emerged, she waited for him to speak. He suggested she go back to sleep. His tone was gentle, not hostile as she had suspected it might be. He was off to practice with the team at Boston College. She turned and stared at the wall. A lot went through her mind. Hypnotized by the sound of driving rain, she searched for some way to repair their relationship. She planned what she wanted to say to him on the drive up to Meg's on Christmas night. She would tell him how much she loved him. She would reconcile all of their issues and would remind him of their past.

It all seemed simple in her imagination, but she realized that situations unfolded very differently in reality. She had no control over Eric's words and reactions. She envisioned an end to their arguments and a new beginning. The white wall served as her blank canvas.

Eric entered the Boston College locker room, carrying a Dunkin' Donuts bag. Colberg and Dianne were sitting on a bench and he handed each of them a cup of coffee. "So, how did the night go?" he asked.

"Stuart is spiking a temp of 102 and he has some lung congestion," explained Dianne. "No chance he can play today."

"Why didn't anyone call me?" he asked, very alarmed.

"It developed overnight. He seemed fine last night."

"Oh, man," he said. Eric thought of the irregular jog, ever so slight, on Stuart's electrocardiogram. He prayed that Dr. Freham was right to dismiss it. "How are the rest of the guys?"

"Pretty good," said Colberg. He stood and patted Eric on the shoulder. "I'll be back in a minute."

"I have this feeling that something's wrong with Stuart," Eric said quietly to Dianne.

"Like what?" she asked.

"During his stress test, I saw this irregularity on the ECG."

"Did you bring it to Freham's attention?"

"Of course, but he said it was nothing."

"So, what's the problem?"

"I don't know. I don't know," he said. "My gut tells me something's not right. After the test, I went looking for last year's ECG, but it wasn't in his file."

"Did you tell Ray any of this?" she asked.

"Yeah," he answered. "He called me into his office because I second-guessed Freham. I didn't really have time to check all the records."

"Do you want me to look?" she asked. "I'm always in there."

"Yes, I need your help."

"Okay."

Soon, the team arrived, ready to be taped up and iced down. Eric's first concern was Stuart. He confirmed the diagnosis of fever and lung congestion. With nothing left more to do for him, he sent him back to the hotel.

Twenty minutes until tip-off and County Forum was filling up with anxious fans and spectators, a few of whom were dressed in festive holiday colors. Christmas music played in the background. Brian and Kate waited by the door for Eric to situate them in the most favorable spot for Kate to watch the game. She prepared herself to jump a lot at the loud noises. She kept an eye on the clock counting down to tip-off, knowing that if she didn't she would pay the price. Her left arm was securely restrained under the wheelchair's armrest. She was content to leave it there for the entire game, even though she would feel the soreness later. Eric came by and hastily ushered them to the Syracuse bench. His eyes were directed everywhere but at Kate. Only once or twice did their eyes meet.

He left to take his seat behind the Syracuse bench. Kate was surrounded by two 2,000 people, but she felt alone. She forgot all about the clock and the buzzer practically jolted her out of her wheelchair.

Brian noticed Kate's low spirits. Eric sat next to Dianne, chatting as they cheered for Syracuse. During halftime, Brian asked Kate if the redhead was the same woman she'd mentioned the previous night. Kate said it was. Brian wanted more information, but Kate wasn't in the mood to talk. She kept an eye on the clock, as it counted down the seconds to halftime. She anchored herself against startling. This time, she succeeded.

In the second half, Syracuse lost its nine-point advantage over Boston College. The home crowd was getting louder and louder, as Boston College made shot after shot. Frustration started to show on the Syracuse bench. Kate caught a glimpse of Eric, on his feet, looking anguished as he watched his team collapse. She was relieved that he had stopped conversing with Dianne, if only for a few minutes. Time ticked down and the crowd roared unmercifully. In minutes, the game was over and the jubilant crowd began to disperse. Eric jogged over and said he'd be home in about an hour. It pained Brian to see that he didn't kiss Kate goodbye. In the car, Brian pressed Kate to explain the situation. Again, she didn't want to discuss it.

Kate saw a familiar car parked in the driveway. Inside, hugs and kisses greeted her from her Aunt Fran and Uncle Bob. They all sat around the kitchen table, mostly discussing the Boston College victory. Kate found it hard to get enthusiastic over the win. The conversation turned to topics she had no clue about. Soon, that one-way mirror went up. Kate saw them, but was herself invisible. Fran talked fast, like a parrot on speed, and in the same high-pitched voice. The smell of cigarette smoke overpowered her sweet perfume. To alert the others that an actual person was in their presence, Kate banged her leg against the table; *I'm still here!* At once, Brian recognized her isolation and made an excuse to take her into the den. He whispered an apology and hugged her tight. Uncle Bob joined them and they watched television, while Aunt Fran prepared dinner. An hour later, Mrs. Reed came home with a dozen presents she had put off buying until Christmas Eve. Mrs. Reed warned Kate not to get any beer on the white carpet, and then ordered Brian to help her wrap her gifts. Brian rolled his eyes and promised Kate they'd return soon. Kate drank a second beer.

Uncle Bob's brown polyester pants and brown-and-beige-striped shirt exaggerated his pear-shaped body. His remaining hair was combed over to disguise his baldness. Soon, he was fast asleep and Kate had the green light to search the channels for something more exciting than golf. Using her knuckle, she finally came across an old version of *A Christmas Carol*. She loved the classic story. Once it was over, she crawled into the living room and gazed at the Christmas tree, examining each ornament as if it might convey the Christmas spirit she lacked within her heart. The only comfort she found was in a tiny sled dangling from a branch—a perfect replica with wooden slats on metal runners. It reminded her of sledding adventures with Brian.

All the Christmas presents were wrapped in time to be torn open the next morning. Brian came downstairs with a stack of boxes. He tried once more to get her to open up to him, but Kate diverted his attention by recalling their sledding escapades. He was pleased by the memories, but continued to worry about her.

They heard Eric's voice and Kate grew visibly tense. Brian tried to imagine what was troubling them. Eric said hello to Aunt Fran in the hallway, while Kate and Brian listened to their depthless exchange. She grew angry. After seven years, almost nobody in her family could talk to Eric like he was part of the family. Maybe they suspected Eric would leave her—so why get so attached to him? In her fragile state, every possible reason for Eric to leave her entered her mind.

Eric made his presence known and apologized for being late. As though waiting for a shootout to commence, Brian sat awkwardly next to Kate. He desperately wanted to leave the room. Eric asked where Uncle Bob was and went to greet him.

Through Christmas Eve dinner and after, when most of the presents were opened, the air between Kate and Eric was noticeably cool, puzzling Brian and no one else. The dinner conversation once again excluded Kate, and Eric spoke for her. Kate listened carefully, ready to pounce on him for the slightest mistakes. As he described Kate's activities in Syracuse, she felt like a trained monkey doing tricks at the zoo. The people on the other side of the fence stared and wanted more tricks. Kate ran out of antics to dazzle her audience. She wished the crowd would move on to the next exhibit. She hated the zoo. Oh God, she wanted to talk for herself, in her own tone, displaying her own personality. *Maybe next time?* she concluded.

She didn't eat much, but Brian cleared the dishes without questions. Dessert was apple pie, pumpkin pie, ice cream, cakes, and cookies. Brian was able to convince Kate to eat some butter cookies. The family retreated to the living room to open gifts. Soon, wrapping paper cluttered the floor like newspaper strewn on a New York City subway. Mrs. Reed directed Brian to pick it up. Already on the edge of breaking, Kate thought seriously about telling her mother to pick up the paper herself and stop making Brian her personal servant. As always, rationale won out. Her entire body tensed up at her lack of confidence, calling herself a coward. Being home transformed her into a timid little child, afraid of the consequences if she spoke her mind. She wasn't about to ruin Christmas Eve for everyone.

Eric was on his fourth beer of the night, twirling an empty bottle on the rug. Now, Kate had something to observe. A voice calling her name broke her out of her trance. Aunt Fran held a present for Kate to open. Every eye in the room was upon Kate, as she struggled to remove the ribbon. It bewildered Kate why Fran insisted on putting ribbon around her gifts. Maybe Fran figured she would get the ribbon off one of these years—another reason to clap for the monkey. Eric reached to help her. She responded with an appreciative gaze. He did the rest, unveiling a gray sweatshirt with "Cape Cod" embroidered in purple. The sweatshirt brought back memories of their honeymoon. Gladdened by the gift, she crawled to Fran and gave her a hug. Bob had nodded off and Kate decided not to disturb him. She pushed a gift over to Brian and looked more excited than she had been for some time. He opened the box, pulled out the black leather jacket and fell in love with it. He put it on and Kate's laughter warmed him like no leather jacket could. It had been too long since he had heard that laugh—Brian got his Christmas present.

It was getting late, so Fran roused Bob and they went home. Mrs. Reed retired for the night after making sure Brian would clean up. Eric promised the kitchen would be spotless by morning.

"Go to bed, Brian. I'll get the kitchen."

"I can't let you do it alone," Brian said.

"Go to bed," Eric repeated.

"I'll get Kate ready for bed," Brian said.

"I can take care of Katie," Eric said. "Please go to bed."

"Brian, go to bed," echoed Kate.

"Okay," Brian said and kissed her forehead. "See you in the

morning."

"G'night Brian," Eric said and got started with the dishes, breaking the painful silence. "You look tired," he said.

"I am tired," Kate said.

"Why don't you head into the room. I'll join you in a second."

Without objection, she crawled into the room, too tired to even contemplate a discussion with him. When he came in, she asked about his day.

"The kids were a little disappointed, but that's to be expected," he said, as he began undressing her. "Stuart has some kind of a chest cold."

"Oh, no—really?"

"Yeah, but he should be okay in a few days with some antibiotics," he said. "Oh, guess who I met after the game?"

"Who?"

"Sandy and Taylor. They were asking for you. I told them you're kicking some faculty butt at Syracuse."

She smiled. "How are they doing?"

"They're fine. They're fine," he said.

"You should have invited them over tomorrow, before we go to Meg's."

He heaved a sigh.

"What?" she asked. Her stomach told her she didn't want to hear his next words.

"Colberg wants us back on Monday instead of Wednesday."

"You have got to be kidding?"

"No, I'm not kidding, Kate."

"Couldn't you have said no?"

"Kate, he's my boss! What the hell do you want me to do?!"

Words raced around inside her head. Her chest felt like an over-inflated balloon about to burst. "We had plans…"

"I know, but things come up."

"Do I matter to you?" she asked.

"What the hell kind of question is that? Of course you matter to me," he said. "I'm sorry that we are not handling this so well. I'm going to finish up in the kitchen."

Struggled not to cry, she collapsed onto the futon, feeling the tears about to stream down. She studied the circle of light the lamp cast upon the ceiling. The circle was divided into three perfect parts—a peace sign. *It is time for peace between them,* she concluded. The peace talks which she had scheduled for Christmas night were now postponed indefinitely. She and Eric would be apart for another week. The tears came. She wanted peace and she wanted it very soon.

The shower woke Kate from a restless night's sleep. She wanted it to be any other day but Christmas.

The rains settled to a gentle mist. She tried to pretend to be asleep—not an easy task for a person with cerebral palsy. The more she tried to be still, the more she moved. Her left wrist wiggled back and forth, as if she was trying to balance a marble on the back of her hand, hiding it under the covers. The bathroom door slid open and she lay still. What compelled her not to say anything to Eric—not good morning, not Merry Christmas—she did not know. She would have to agonize through this day, putting on a show for everyone.

Minutes later, Brian knocked on the door. "Eric said he's going over to Joe's for a while." Kate's face grew sullen and pale. "What the hell is going on with you guys?"

Her final nerve, frayed she was overcome by sadness. All the frustrations she kept inside flowed out with her tears.

Brian helped her sit up. Her body was like a rag doll. "Talk to me," he said.

She wanted to answer, but couldn't stop the tears.

"What's going on?" he asked, wiping away her tears.

She could only shrug her shoulders and look down at the wrinkled sheets. "Tomorrow..."

"Tomorrow?" he repeated. "What about tomorrow?"

"He has to go back."

"I thought he was here until Wednesday?"

"I thought so, too," she managed to say. "I don't see him anymore."

"You knew at the beginning that his job was going to involve long hours."

"I didn't think it would be so hard."

"I know, I know, Katie," he said and kissed her on the forehead. "But you know, there's only three more months to the season. After that, he'll have much more time."

"I know." She used her wrist to clear her eyes. "I just miss him."

"I know, honey."

"I was hoping we could talk tonight, going up to New Hampshire," she said. "Sorry for ruining your Christmas."

"You're not ruining my Christmas," said Brian.

Mrs. Reed knocked on the door.

"Please don't say anything to Mom," Kate whispered.

"Don't worry."

Kate turned away when she saw her mother's face. She didn't want her mother to gloat over the problems in her marriage. Mrs. Reed's persistence in trying to talk Kate out of marrying Eric two years ago shook Kate to the core. She didn't want her mother to think she had been right all along.

Brian diverted Mrs. Reed and returned to find Kate almost mended from her tears. "Everything's cool with Mom," he said.

"Thank you," she said, kissing him on the cheek.

"So, you guys need some time alone?" he asked.

"Yeah, very much so."

"How about I get rid of the Three Amigos for a while later?" She chuckled, which pleased him. "That would give you and Eric some time alone."

"I couldn't let you do that. It's Christmas, for God sakes."

"C'mon," he said. "I gotta pay you back for my jacket."

"What are they gonna think?"

"Who cares what they think. They still think you're ten years old," Brian said, with fervor. "I'll make up some story that watching *Christmas Vacation* could be the start of a family tradition on Bob's brand-new big-screen television. Maybe we can watch some other movies."

"You don't mind?"

"Not at all," he said. "As soon as Eric comes back, we're outta here."

"Why aren't you married yet?" she asked.

"Because I still live with my mother. How 'bout I give you a shower and then we go open the rest of the presents? What do you say?"

"Sounds good," she answered, cheerfully.

The shower washed away all of her tears. Brian kept the conversation positive, trying to buoy her spirits by telling her about his new girlfriend. Kate had a million questions.

Eric pulled up to Joe's apartment, remembering when he climbed up the dilapidated staircase. He feared climbing it again. New pieces of wood had been replaced. He breathed a little easier climbing but used caution. The railing felt like it was attached by two nails. He stayed close to the wall, opened the unlocked door and entered.

Beer cans, clothes, and food were strewn about the filthy carpet. The smell of alcohol permeated the apartment. In the bedroom, Joe was asleep, dressed in his ragged jeans. Eric tried to rouse him by calling out his name. Eric resorted to shaking his shoulder until he awoke.

"What the hell are you doing here?" Joe yelled.

"It's Christmas!"

"You scared the crap outta me!"

"Were you expecting somebody else?" Eric asked, snidely. "A cop, by any chance?"

"Shut the hell up," Joe said. "Don't be smart."

"C'mon, let me buy you breakfast," Eric offered.

"Is that all I get for Christmas? A stupid breakfast?" Joe impishly asked.

"I think you got more than your share of presents from me this year, Joe," Eric said. "I'm already saving up for next year."

"Shut up, alright." Joe headed for the shower.

Eric began the harrowing job of cleaning up. He approached the mess with caution, anticipating a rodent would come scurrying out at any moment. Sadness came over him, as he witnessed how his brother lived. His energy decreased with every empty bottle and soiled shirt he picked up. He opened a window and debated whether to open the refrigerator, remembering the last time he looked inside. He decided not to spoil his appetite.

Most of the restaurants were closed. Joe suggested a diner he frequented. The sign in front was cracked, exposing the fluorescent bulb. Picture windows framed the lonely people inside. As if they had been sitting there for a century, Eric was struck by their desolate expressions. The notion hit him hard in the stomach. He wanted to go home to Kate. She could cure his despair. He had to bear sitting through breakfast with his brother. Joe walked over to the counter and started chatting

with the waitress.
"Eric, meet Rita; Rita, this is my highly successful brother, Eric."
"Nice to meet you," Eric said, shaking Rita's hand. "He exaggerates."
"Okay, so he's a no-good loser like his brother," said Joe.
"Nice to meet you," Rita said, laying out menus.
Rita attended to her adopted family on Christmas. Eric was struck—Rita reminded him of a saint, feeling great reverence for her station in life. Looking like any ordinary person, Rita had a kind hand and a big heart, Eric speculated.
"What the hell are you looking at?" Joe whispered, conspiratorially. "She's ugly."
"Oh, that's a real nice thing to say on Christmas," Eric replied.
"Well, she is." Joe turned to Eric. "So, why ain't you home with your wife?"
"I wanted to see you," Eric answered, flatly.
"You are giving me a line of crap."
Eric looked up from his menu. "Would I give you a line of crap on Christmas Day?" Eric asked with sarcasm
"Shut up," Joe said. "If you just came here to humiliate me, you can leave."
"Alright, I'll shut up—you big baby."
"Thank you," said Joe.
They ordered breakfast and handed the menus back to Rita.
"So, why ain't you home with your wife? Why are you hanging out with me?" Joe asked.
"I must say, you are very observant when you're not loaded." Eric fiddled with his coffee cup. "We're just having some minor problems adjusting, that's all."
"Is she holding back?" Joe asked childishly.
Eric looked away.
"What?! That was a serious question."
"Just when you're on the verge of convincing me you have a brain, you go and say something idiotic." Seconds went by with no words being said. Rita brought their orders, breaking the impasse. Eric ate as fast as he could, wanting to remove himself from the gloomy surroundings.
"Hey, listen," Joe said. "I want to say thanks for coming and

bailing me out of jail."

"You're welcome. The pleasure was all mine," Eric said in a sarcastic tone. "But I warn you, I'm running low on money. We need a van soon, so stay out of jail."

"It was only a little pot," Joe said.

"Next time, you won't be so lucky."

"My little brother, Mr. Goody-Two-Shoes, would never do anything illegal." He smirked at Eric. "But you're gonna screw up sooner or later, I just know it."

Eric raised his coffee cup. "Here's to that day. I'll make sure you're on hand when I screw up."

"What a sarcastic jerk you are," said Joe. "You think I can't function in the real world, don't you?"

"You never tried," Eric said. "It might surprise you just how easy it is to straighten up and be somebody."

"Like who? Dad?" asked Joe. "No, thank you. I don't even want to be a 'successful' business man with a wife and 2.5 kids, who travels eleven months out of the year, screwing every woman he meets. I should've strangled him when I had the chance."

Eric gained a fresh insight into his brother. "No one said you had to be like Dad."

"You know what I did with the money he left me?"

"No."

"After Mom died, I threw what was left of it off the Tobin Bridge," Joe said. "I didn't want his money." He stared vacantly out the window.

"You didn't do that," Eric bluntly said. "That's bull."

"It's not bull!" Joe exclaimed. "I threw it off the bridge. After Mom got sick, there wasn't much left, paying for all her care."

Eric was bewildered that Joe would do such a thing. At the same time, he was touched that he had honored their mother that way.

"Now, I think back and kick myself," Joe said. "I could have bought a brewery and sat back, drinking beer all day long."

It was too good to last—a brother with a brain and a heart, concurrently. "You're unbelievable, you know that," Eric said, deflated.

"Are you finished yet, 'cause I need to go do something?"

"What—rob a bank?"

"Very funny, little brother, but no," Joe said and drained the last of his coffee. "None of your business."

"I don't want to catch you on an episode of *Cops*—do you hear me?" Eric said. He put some cash on the counter and wished Rita a Merry Christmas.

"Same to you," said his saintly host.

"Later, Rita," Joe said.

Eric hoped that Joe had gotten something out of his visit. Feeling like a failure, Eric couldn't find a way to help his brother. He dropped Joe off at his apartment. As he thought about his brother, he kept reminding himself that it was Christmas, even if it felt like any average Monday in April. Home, with Kate, was where he wanted to be.

Kate heard Eric slam the car door. She prepared herself for the worst. She wanted to be in a different room when Eric walked in, but time didn't allow her to move. She felt nervous and exposed. Mrs. Reed and Fran greeted Eric in the kitchen. His energetic voice calmed Kate a little.

"Merry Christmas, everyone," said Eric.

In awe and with incredible joy, Kate felt Eric's arms encircling her shoulders from behind.

"I thought we were gonna have to send out a search party for you," said Bob, who was sitting on the couch.

"No, I just needed to see my brother before his twelve o'clock happy hour," Eric said.

She loved how his warm body surrounded her. "You're okay?" she asked softly, reaching up to touch his shoulder.

"Yeah, I'm better now," he said and tightened his embrace.

Kate could barely catch her breath being cloaked in his love.

"You know," Brian said, "we better get going if we're going to catch the movie at one." He winked at Kate.

"For God sakes, Brian, we almost have an hour and it takes two minutes to get to our house," Bob said.

"*We're* not going, are we?" Eric whispered in Kate's ear.

She shook her head.

"C'mon, we need to pop the popcorn and all that other good stuff before the movie starts," Brian said.

"Okay, okay," Bob said and hoisted himself up from the couch.

"Kate and I will stay here and clean up a little for Dot," Eric said.

"I guess we'll see you later," Bob said.

"Have fun cleaning the house," said Brian, smiling.

"Thanks, buddy," Eric said to Brian, with a quick raise of the eyebrows as if to say, *I owe you one*.

"I'm sorry." She immediately burst into tears.

"Hey, hey," Eric said, as he held her. "It's okay, Sweetie—I'm sorry, too. I miss you, you know."

Getting the words out was a struggle. "I miss you so much," she said.

"I know you do, Sweetie," he said and kissed her forehead. "In a few years, I'll get a promotion and when I do, I can order people around. When five o'clock rolls around, I can tell people to take off, I'm going home to my beautiful wife."

"Take off?"

"Yeah," Eric said. "I'm gonna tell them to take off."

She tried to settle down. "I had tonight all planned out, you know."

"Like what?" he asked.

"I was hoping we could've talked in the car. I just wanted to have some time with you when we didn't fight," she said, bursting into tears again.

"I don't wanna fight anymore, Katie. I really don't, Sweetie," he said and held his wife close, as she drained the tears and emotions from her body. "Can I hold you like this for the rest of the day?"

She nodded. "I love you."

"I love you," he said tenderly and kissed her. He carried her to the couch and sat her on his lap. The room was very quiet. The only sound was the intermittent hum of the refrigerator.

She listened to him breathe and felt his heartbeat, sitting perfectly still across his lap. They had reached peace. "What are you thinking about?" she asked.

"This morning," he said. "I saw some lonely people today—at the diner where Joe and I ate. There were eight or nine people, all sitting at different tables. And on Christmas. And my brother was one of them. It depressed me."

She sensed the hurt on Eric's face. "Joe has a brother who cares."

"Yeah, but I don't think it's enough," he said.

"Tell me, what more can you do for him?" she asked. "You put him in detox twice and that didn't work. You tried to get him into a work program. He didn't like that. You post bail every time he gets arrested."

"He says he threw all the money Dad left him in the Boston Harbor."

"He's lying," she said quickly. "He buried it somewhere."

"Yeah, I know," he said. "I wish he'd give me some of it, so I can pay off his stinkin' debts." He sighed. "So you think I'm doing enough for him?"

"Yes, you are," she answered. "You've done all you could."

His tender gaze was followed by a hug and a passionate kiss. "I love you so much," he said. His sadness was dissipating with each minute that she was in his arms. Christmas had come without having to open any gifts. The smell of her hair delighted him. Her soft skin enchanted him. Kissing her exhilarated him.

"You know what?" she asked, devilishly.

"What?" he asked, knowing her intention.

"We have the house until five. I say we make the most of our time and go get naked."

"Get naked, huh?" he asked, rhetorically. "I told Dot I'd clean up the house," he said without conviction.

"I'll make it worth your while," she said and kissed him with every ounce of her love.

"When you put it that way, how can I resist?" Their passion was all they felt. "I can't think of a better Christmas present."

Before leaving the couch, they shared another enthusiastic kiss. With Kate already in his arms, he stood and carried her to the bedroom.

Chapter 9

The air turned cold and winter had finally arrived. Saying goodbye to Eric was a test of Kate's will, but she realized the time apart would make them stronger. He packed his duffel bag, as he recited his schedule for the upcoming week. She etched every date, time, and place into her brain. She imagined locking him in the bedroom, so he couldn't escape.

It was time to say goodbye. Eric kissed her and promised to call every night. They would miss New Year's Eve together. Six days seemed like twelve months to Kate. She assured Eric she would be fine, all along feeling sadness.

He handed her plane tickets to Brian and went over departure times and other details. It pleased Brian to see them acting like husband and wife again. He shook Eric's hand and walked him out to the garage. The rush of cold air made the moment almost unbearable. By the time Brian closed the garage door, Kate began to miss Eric.

It had been a long while since Kate had seen the sights of Boston. The familiar skyline reached up, entering heaven as low clouds veiled the top floors of buildings. Traffic was lighter than normal on Storrow Drive, as they cruised along the banks of the Charles River. The pathways were devoid of the usual joggers, walkers and cyclists. Kate had expected to see a few hardy souls, but she spotted no one.

Brian steered his way through downtown Boston, driving in and out of undesignated streets only a few people knew about. He drove past the Boston Garden and pointed out the new facility, which neared completion. She recalled the games she saw with Brian in the old Garden.

Brian talked about his new girlfriend and how he had kept their relationship a secret until he knew it was serious. He confessed he had sneaked out to see her on Christmas Day. Kate's excitement lit up the cloudiest of days. He told Kate he wanted to introduce her to Allison the next day. Kate looked forward to meeting Allison. She wanted to make a good first impression. *What should I wear?* As Brian described Allison, Kate's uneasiness passed. Brian parked and wheeled she into the entrance of the new Garden. The vast space doubled as

Boston's North Station. They went over to the Boston Sports Market, which Brian managed.

Brian introduced Kate to a few of his coworkers. His flattering words caused her to shake her head in disagreement, uncomfortable with praise and adulation. She looked around at the merchandise. Bruins and Celtics baseball caps and pendants lined the walls. Applications were being accepted for the purchase of items from the old Garden after its demolition. She thought Eric would appreciate a Garden keepsake as next year's Christmas gift. Brian assured her that he would get her a souvenir at minimal cost.

Spending the day with Brian made Kate feel like she was playing hooky from school. They exchanged news of friends they both had known from years ago. A few had gotten messed up on drugs or alcohol. Some had managed to go straight, while others didn't try at all. Kate grew sad, frustrated, and angry, as she thought of these people out of control.

"You mind if I ask you a personal question?" Brian asked.

"No, I don't mind."

"Do you and Eric plan to have kids someday?"

The question surprised her. "I guess," she answered honestly. "We haven't talked about it in a while."

"Do you want kids?" he asked.

"I thought I did," she said, "but…"

Brian waited for her to finish her sentence. "But…?" he asked.

"How would I hold the baby without hurting it?"

Her candid reply rendered Brian speechless. "Have you talked to Eric about this?" he asked.

"We don't have time to talk about anything these days," she said.

He glanced at his sister and was seized with sympathy for her burden. "I'm sorry I brought it up."

"Don't be sorry," she said. "You're the only one brave enough to ask me that question. I appreciate it. Do you think Mom would ever consider asking me that?"

"No, not in a million years," he said.

"Also, the thought of having to pee every five minutes for nine months makes me crazy," she said.

Brian chuckled. "Wait a minute," he said, "are you telling me that you're more worried about having to pee frequently than you are about the pain of labor?"

"Yeah," she said. "I'll probably have to have a C-section anyway and they knock you out for that."

"You are too much," he said, laughing. "You crack me up."

"What? Just because I worry about having to go to the bathroom more often doesn't make me crazy," she said. "What if I have to go when nobody is around?"

"I guess you'll need to work out a plan, so there's someone with you all the time—in case you do need anything. It can be worked out, you know."

"Yeah, I guess," she said. "I'll be so tired."

"True, but pregnant women are always exhausted."

"When did you become Mr. Obstetrician?"

"I just think it would be very exciting if you had a baby." His words eased Kate's uncertainty, but her apprehension lingered. He grabbed her hand.

"What brought this on about kids and all that?" she asked.

"Oh, the other night Allison and I were just talking about it."

"You're already talking about kids?"

"Yeah, I can talk to Alli about anything," he said.

"You really love her, don't you?"

"Yeah, I do."

Her spine tingled, sensing the joy pouring out of him. "You'd be a terrific father."

"Thanks, Katie," he said. "Hey, by the way, Dad wants to see you."

"I bet you told him we would come over?"

"Well, you haven't seen him since June," he said, "and he really wants to see you."

"I bet *he* won't ask me if I want kids," she said. "Dad never calls or writes."

"I told him we'd stop by on Thursday."

"Do I have a choice?" she asked.

"No, not really," he said. "You could just stay home with Mom, I guess—if she's there, that is."

"No, that's okay," she said. "Is Allison coming?"

"I don't know, I haven't asked her yet."

"Well, tell her she needs to come, too."

They fell into a comfortable silence for the short ride home.

Kate had to be patient with her dad, as he struggled to understand her words. Simple, short sentences pleased him. She thought about typing out a few questions for him: *How's the job? How's the new car? How's the dog?* Having Brian at her side would relieve her apprehension.

Eric called that night, but it didn't ease Kate's longing to see him. Hearing his voice calmed her for 24 hours until he called again. The countdown was on; five more days until she would see him. She stayed up nights thinking about their future, the children they might raise. It frightened her to think she would not be able to bond with her children, physically and emotionally. *Would they know my touch? Would they understand my words?* The hours trickled by, but the answers to these inescapable questions did not come. The movement of her hand kept pace with the ticking of the clock. In the dark, she wrestled with her doubts until she was exhausted.

In summertime, Faneuil Hall is filled with people, shopping and eating. On this day, few people braved the cold. Kate resisted the tempting treats, as Brian pushed her down the never-ending corridor of food. She felt self-conscious about eating in front of Allison, whom she was about to meet.

They waited for Allison in the large rotunda of Quincy Market. Kate searched for a slender woman, with shoulder-length blond hair. Her nerves showed in her extra movements. She wanted to make a good impression for the sake of her brother. Calming her, Brian put his hand upon her shoulder.

Brian rose to his feet to embrace Allison. Kate noticed right away that they were deeply in love. Her fears subsided.

Kate extended her arm, as steadily as possible. Allison reached forward with both hands, grabbing Kate's hand and arm. Kate smiled in appreciation. Allison was prettier than Brian had described. Her golden hair enhanced her electric-blue eyes. She spoke eloquently and had an exquisite presence. When her gaze fell upon Brian, it could remain on him for her entire existence.

"I'm sorry Eric couldn't be here to meet you," Kate said, struggling to speak clearly.

Allison listened closely, but failed to understand. Brian

interpreted for her.

"Oh, I'm sorry, too," Allison said. "Brian tells me he's a nice guy."

Kate smiled brightly and nodded.

"Where is he now?" asked Allison.

Allison's confidence put Kate at ease. "He's in Syracuse, working hard."

Again, Allison needed Brian's assistance in deciphering Kate's speech.

"Katie wants to know if you'd like to come to dinner at Dad's tomorrow night," Brian said. "She's a little scared of not having anyone to talk to. Isn't that right?"

"I'm not afraid," said Kate, "I just don't want to get stuck looking at the wall all night long."

Brian translated again.

"Have you met Dad yet?" Kate asked Allison.

"Yes, but only once," Brian answered.

"What have I done only once?" Allison asked Brian.

"Met Dad," he said.

"Oh, yes," Allison said. "He's a very nice man."

Kate kept her opinion of her father to herself.

"Brian tells me you work for Fleet Bank—how is that?" asked Kate.

Again, Brian acted as interpreter.

"Oh, it's great, although working with numbers all day can be cumbersome," she answered. "Brian is a good detour away from all that."

"She loves me because I'm simple," he said, smiling. They all laughed. "Can I get you girls anything to eat?"

"I'm fine," Kate answered.

"A cup of coffee would be great, hon," said Allison.

"Sure you don't want anything, Katie?"

"Positive," she said. He walked away and Kate felt awkward not being able to converse freely.

"How was your Christmas?" asked Allison.

"Good!" Kate kept her answer short.

"Good?" guessed Allison.

Kate nodded. "How was yours?"

"Great," Allison answered. They were both relieved that Allison understood the question. "When are you going back to

Syracuse?"

"Monday." Kate was thankful there are only seven days in a week.

"Did you say 'Monday'?" Allison conjectured.

Kate nodded, exuberantly.

"Great!" Allison exclaimed. "I'm having a New Year's party at my place. Can you come?"

"Umm, I don't know."

"I didn't catch that," said Allison. "Would you mind saying it again, please?"

Allison saw Brian approaching. "Help me out, hon."

"What was the question?" he asked.

"I invited Kate to the party."

"You want to come with us?" he asked Kate.

"Sure," she said, "If you don't mind me tagging along."

"Don't worry," Brian said, "Alli and I can stand not sleeping together for one night."

Allison slapped him on the arm. "Stop. How do you know that was what she was thinking?"

"Because I know my sister," Brian said. "Isn't that right, Katie?"

"You caught me," admitted Kate. "I just don't want to spoil your good time."

Brian laughed and relayed her words to Allison.

"We'll have a great time—don't worry about it," said Allison. "We'll enjoy having you with us."

Kate smiled. "Thank you."

"Did you think we would leave you home on New Year's Eve?" Brian said. "No way, baby!"

"You have a good guy, Allison," said Kate.

Brian happily translated.

"I know I do," Allison said. She squeezed Brian like he was an oversized teddy bear.

Kate had never seen Brian so happy. She felt Allison was the right woman for him and spirits soared.

On Thursday morning, the office looked like a small garbage dump. Colberg and Dianne were returning after four days off. As soon as he arrived, Eric began to clean up. He dismantled the tower of Styrofoam cups he had built. As a kid, he spent the days after Christmas building towers. Previous towers consisted of Lincoln Logs or Legos.

He'd spent the previous evening at Griffys', recalling the jokes told. He looked forward to passing the jokes onto Kate when she got home. As he cleaned, he watched TV. Hearing about an infant being left in a car while the mother partied at a local bar sickened him. He couldn't comprehend how a mother could leave her five-month-old child for hours in a freezing car. He struck the dustpan against the garbage can, as though he was beating some common sense into the drunken mother.

He was the only one who was putting in a full eight hours a day. Even Colberg had dodged in and out of the office. He swore that he wouldn't get stuck working next Christmas. The thought of Kate being so upset returned to him. He wished he stayed in Boston with her. His head was heavy with his thoughts when Dianne arrived.

"Hey, you're here early."

"I figured I'd get some petty stuff done before nine," he said, pointing to the papers on his desk.

"How's Stuart doing?" she asked.

"He's doing okay. The antibiotics cleared up the virus, but he still has a little congestion," he said. "He was a little bummed he couldn't go home for Christmas, so I spent Monday night and Tuesday with him."

"Do you think he'll play Saturday?" she asked.

"I wouldn't play him, but that's up to Freham."

"So, how was your Christmas?" she asked.

"It was good. Short, but good," he answered. "And yours?"

"I spent Christmas with a few friends over in the next town," she said. "And Monday I moved out."

Eric nodded. "Did everything go all right?"

Tears streamed down Dianne's face. "Yeah, as well as could be expected." She grabbed a tissue from the desk. "It's going to help, getting back to work."

"Let me know if there's anything I can do, okay?" he said.

"Thanks, I will," she said. "Oh, Eric, before I forget." She pulled a small Christmas gift from her bag. "This is for you."

"Oh, Dianne, I didn't get you anything," he said, walking toward her.

"You didn't have to get me anything," she said. "Don't

worry about it." She handed him the small red box.

"Thank you." He opened the box. "Holy cow, Dianne!" Eric exclaimed when he saw what was inside.

"It's one of the original pins from the 1955 NBA Championship, when Syracuse had a pro team," she gushed. "They finally won that year."

"Where did you find this?" he asked, holding the pin with tremendous care.

"My Dad worked for the team, so we always had extra pins lying around the house," she said. Her smile grew when she saw the excitement.

"Now I really feel bad I didn't get you anything," he said and put the pin back into the box. "I don't want to lose it," he added, putting it into his pocket. "Thanks, Dianne."

"Oh, you're welcome," she said. The pin changed the mood in the room. Eric forgot about the unfit mother and Dianne forgot about her unfit husband. He showed off the pin to everyone he met that day. As he showed off the gold pin, Dianne looked on, delighted.

In dress jeans, a black sweater, and black boots, Kate looked like she could take on the world. She was uneasy about the impending evening with her father. Brian knocked on the door of Mr. Reed's tenth-floor apartment. Mr. Reed soon appeared and invited his grown children in. He gave Kate a gentle hug and abruptly started taking orders for drinks. Then, he introduced his guests to Ms. Levant, whom he described as a friend. Ms. Levant approached Kate timidly, as if she crossed paths with a snake. Ms. Levant recited Kate's accomplishments one by one, like she had rehearsed them for this very moment. Kate just nodded, becoming more and more anxious. Much to her relief, Brian interrupted with some small talk.

Mr. Reed's appearance had not changed in six months observed Kate. His hair, still graying and thinning, lay perfectly on his head. As the others chatted, she remained silent. The clock on the stove reminded her that in three hours she would talk to Eric.

She finished her first beer when Mr. Reed asked about Eric. It was the first time he had inquired about Eric in seven years. Gladdened, she remarked he was fine. Brian translated. Mr.

Reed returned his attention to Ms. Levant, boasting about her achievements, as if she was the queen of her occupation. She looked at the clock again. Brian sighed. Kate discreetly nudged his leg, preventing him from creating a scene. Allison noticed Brian's irritation at his father. Brian stood and fetched two more beers.

Everyone left for the restaurant. In the parking lot, Brian blew off some steam. Kate was surprised by his simmering anger at Mr. Reed. He wanted to go home, but she and Allison managed to settle him down. Kate blamed herself for Brian's anger, as she blamed herself for a lot of things. She began to blame herself for the dysfunction in her family—the divorce most of all. *If I hadn't been born with cerebral palsy, would things have been different?*

Dinner was over in the blink of an eye. Mr. Reed did not speak to Kate until he had to say goodbye. Quietly, Brian built up anger, as his father ignored Kate. Every time he became tense, she touched Brian's side, expecting steam to start coming out of his ears. Leaving the restaurant, Brian put Kate in the car and then said he needed to go back inside. His true intent was to confront Mr. Reed. He disappeared around the corner, catching up with Mr. Reed on the other side of the parking lot. "You know what, Dad?" he said to his father's back.

Mr. Reed turned around to face his son. Ms. Levant was in the passenger seat.

"You're a hypocrite," Brian said. "You tell your girlfriend all about Katie, how much she's done, and then you turn around and hardly talk to her the whole night! Was this show-and-tell hour?!"

Something beyond Mr. Reed's control drove his hand furiously across Brian's face. He got into the car and drove off.

Brian stood there and tried to comprehend the last several seconds. The condensation from his breath expanded in the dark, cold night. Slowly, he walked back to his car. He touched his face where his father's hand connected and worried that the trauma would be displayed like a neon light. He took a deep breath before opening the car door. "Are you two warm enough in here?"

The women said they were.

"What did you forget in the restaurant?" Allison asked in a

curious tone.

"Just wanted to use the bathroom," he said.

Kate detected the change in Brian's demeanor and knew he had exchanged words with their father.

"Hey, Alli, want to go meet Mom?"

"Sure," she said, trying to sound enthusiastic.

Kate she tried to imagine what could have happened between Brian and their father. Soon, her thoughts migrated to Eric. She missed him—almost inconceivable how much. She would be hearing his voice soon.

Eric sat in front of the television finishing up the leftovers. There was a knock on the door. It was Dianne. "Hi, come in," he said.

"I don't want to stay too long," she said and walked into the living room.

"Please sit anywhere." He turned on the nearest lamp. "Can I get you something to drink?"

"No thanks, Eric," she answered. "I found Stuart's records from last year." She reached in her backpack and pulled out a manila folder. "These were all I could find."

He took the folder, looked for an ECG printout, but didn't find anything.

"The funny thing is," she said, "all the other kids' records and reports have thorough documentation. Stuart's records are extremely scant."

"Why doesn't that surprise me," Eric mumbled. "Maybe I'm grasping at straws here? I got nothing else to go on."

"I feel awful that I couldn't find anything helpful," she said. "I looked high and low in Records."

"Don't feel like that," he said, "you're only going on my assumptions. And besides, I shouldn't have involved you."

"I don't mind getting involved, Eric," she said. "I believe you."

"I'm just grasping at straws," he said and headed toward the kitchen. "I need another beer. Are you sure I can't get you anything?"

She smiled graciously. "No, thanks anyway. I gotta get going home." She put the folder back in her sack and noticed the etching of the barn. "That's beautiful," she remarked.

"Where is that?"

"We like to assume it's the barn in New Hampshire we spent some time in, but I actually don't know where it is, or if it really exists."

"It's beautiful," she said, as they made their way to the front hall. "I guess I'll see you bright and early tomorrow."

"Yes, bright and early," he said. "Good night, Dianne."

"Good night, Eric."

He looked out the front-door windowpane to make sure she got into her car safely.

At times, the roar of the crowd was almost deafening. The game was close between Syracuse and Villanova, but as the minutes drew down the crowd hushed. With nearly a minute left on the clock, it became clear that the ten-point deficit proved too much for Villanova to overcome. Syracuse scored a New Year's Eve victory.

As they waited for their plane to depart, the team celebrated. Laying his head back on the seat, Eric yawned. Dianne sat next to him. The hum of the engines lulled him to sleep. The plane rolled away from the gate.

The sky was dark, the lights from Philadelphia illuminating the purplish winter air. As the plane climbed, Eric remained sleeping. As though she was watching a newborn, Dianne gazed at him every other minute. Every time he stirred, she looked over. Her magazine only kept her attention when he was still. Conversations held across the aisle were too difficult to hear. Eric awoke an hour later and she had someone to talk to for the rest of the flight.

In the Syracuse terminal, a few of the team's staff members discussed going to a tavern near the university to ring in the New Year. Eric looked at his watch. It was an hour before midnight. They urged him to come. Dianne reminded him of his pin and how buying her a drink would even up things. He agreed.

He got a ride with Dianne and commented about the efficiency of heating in her car, comparing it favorably to his. Reaching the tavern, he needed to look at all the parked cars for any abandoned children. Inside, his eyes were drawn to the many neon signs, and his ears were bombarded by loud rock music. Above the crowd, television sets were turned to *Dick Clark's Rockin' Eve*. The crowd was boisterous and drunk, waiting for the clock to strike midnight.

"Do you believe all these people?" he asked loudly.

"They are all nuts!" Dianne said in his ear. "Hey, where did the other guys go?"

He took a gulp from his beer. "Maybe they got swallowed up by the crowd?"

"You seem to be in a good mood tonight," she said.

"I am," he said.

"Me, too," she said. "I really think this New Year is going to work out good for me, and hopefully for you, too."

"Cheers to that!" He lifted his bottle and clinked it with hers. "Do you think we have any chance of making it to the Final Four this year?" he asked.

"I really think we have a good chance."

"I hope so."

"It would be nice," she shouted over the din.

He nodded and took another gulp. "We need to stay healthy. That's the biggest obstacle.

With a quick nod, she pointed to one of the televisions. "One more minute."

Like zombies, all watched the crystal lighted ball drop in Times Square. The clock reached down to the ten-second mark and all chanted down: ten, nine, eight, seven, six, five, four, three, two, one, Happy New Year!

It was over before Eric realized what he had done. The blank look upon his face remained for several seconds. As he looked at Dianne, his fingertips touched his disloyal lips. "I'm sorry—I gotta go," he said and walked off into the crowd.

"Eric! Eric!" she yelled.

He didn't stop to answer, feeling repulsed with himself.

She caught up to him at the entrance. "Do you want a ride home? It's cold," she said.

He considered her offer. "No, no, I think I'll walk," he said. As soon as he left the tavern, the cold began to settle in his core.

As all the couples in Allison's apartment hugged and kissed, Kate suddenly felt alone. Brian kissed her cheek to celebrate the New Year. Allison did the same. Surrounded by people drinking and celebrating, she felt as if she didn't belong. Guests seemed to question who she was and her purpose for being at the party. With no rugs on the floor, she sat, uncomfortable and solemn, in her manual wheelchair. The floor-to-ceiling windows provided everyone with a spectacular view of Boston and beyond. She looked out toward the western part of the city and into the darkness, gazing in the direction of Syracuse.

Brian held her second glass of Champagne. It hit her that Eric was far away this New Year's Eve. Brian discerned her sadness, knelt down in front of her and held her close.

No muscle moved involuntarily. Her right arm hung limp around Brian's neck. Seldom had he seen her so relaxed. He attributed it to the Champagne. He carried her upstairs to Allison's bedroom loft and laid her on the bed. Within minutes, she was asleep.

Anxious to see Eric and sad to leave Brian, Kate was unsure what to feel first. Brian took her to the airport and got her seated on the plane. Brother and sister hugged and said goodbye. He promised to come to Syracuse soon. She would remember this time with her brother for many years.

Chapter 10

It felt good to be home after ten days away. It felt good having Eric close again. In two more days, Kate would go in front of the academic board to present her case against Wilcox. The butterflies started inside her stomach, as she reviewed her speech on the computer.

Eric came into the den and asked how she was doing.

"God, I'm so nervous, Eric," she said. "What if I mess up?"

"You're not going to mess up," he said and gently massaged her shoulders. "You'll do fine."

"If I do this right, Wilcox won't be teaching for a while."

"So what? Wilcox is a jerk."

"Yeah, I know," she said and sighed heavily. "Did I get any calls last week?"

"The doctor's office called confirming your appointment for the 18th, I think it was."

"Can you make it?"

"Yeah," he said.

"'Cause if you can't, I can change it."

"I can make it—I swear."

"Okay." She looked at the computer. "He's not going to have a job."

"Yeah, well," he said, "he should've thought of that before he messed with you."

She smiled at him.

"I missed you," he said, stroking her back and kissing her.

She nodded and soon forgot the words on the screen. Her eyes never left his, surrendering to his every move. The phone rang until the answering machine tended to it. Eager, Eric only needed a half of a minute to undress her. He touched every part of her, slowly and methodically, and kissed her everywhere his hands caressed. Upon her knees, she rushed to help him off with his clothes. She gazed at him with awe that he loved her enough to make love to her. She touched him. With his hand behind her neck, he guided her down to the futon.

The cold Syracuse air stirred all of Kate's senses, but failed to strip away her frenzied anticipation. Her mind picked through every word she had written and debated whether to change any paragraph, sentence, or word. The van pulled up to her office and let her off. She took a deep breath before she entered the building. It felt strange, as if she hadn't been there for six months. Everyone seemed older; everything seemed more serious. The fluorescent lights had a strange dimness. In the hallway, Mr. Leonard was walking at a swift pace, deeply engrossed in what he was reading. Kate was unnerved. She thought of ten places she would rather be. Talking to Liz eased the tension. Mr. Leonard returned at his same hurried pace and grabbed a chair next to Kate. He held a typewritten letter for Kate to read. Written by a disabled student four years earlier, it stated that she had been unfairly dismissed from a chemistry class and laboratory taught by Wilcox. Kate's worries about ousting Wilcox receded and she grew confident. Future students of Syracuse University, whether physically challenged or not, would benefit from the removal of Wilcox, who put a black mark on the reputation of the school.

Kate had only been in the Syracuse Administration Building twice before. It was a majestic building with a large wood-paneled foyer. In the elevator, everyone stayed silent. Her stomach felt like it was being pulled apart with monkey wrenches. The elevator doors slid open and she followed Mr. Leonard into a conference room. She caught the eye of Mr. Delane. He winked, conveying his confidence in her. Wilcox was on the other side of the room, sporting one of his more unsightly plaid suits—*probably purchased well before my time,* Kate mused. Liz placed her headstick on her head, turned the computer on and gave her a reassuring squeeze on the arm before she left the room.

Mr. Leonard introduced Kate to the members of the board. She nodded at each one.

It was time for her to present her case. Her heart began to beat a little faster; her headstick started moving from key to key on the computer. Muscles on the back of her legs began to twitch, fighting to hold her steady. She pressed *Enter* and the synthesizer's robotic voice boomed out sentence after sentence. She looked up to gauge the reactions around the table. She avoided making eye contact with Wilcox, for fear that his menacing gaze might unravel her.

Before the computer finished speaking, Wilcox flew into a rage and stood to defend his conduct, complaining that the investigation was a waste of time. His sudden outburst startled Kate, but not as severely as she expected. He glared straight at her and she matched his impenetrable stare, hardly quivering a muscle. The head of the academic board, Mr. Ross, politely asked Wilcox to sit back down. For a long, awkward moment, he stood motionless, looking at Mr. Ross. He finally relented and Mr. Ross prompted her to continue.

Mr. Leonard distributed copies of the newly discovered letter to the members. Solemn expressions spread over their faces. Kate recommended Professor Wilcox's tenure at Syracuse University be terminated. The emotionless voice of the computer fell silent.

Mr. Ross stood and described the procedures Wilcox would obey during his rebuttal. Kate listened to Wilcox's every word. He delivered his response with a stone-cold disposition. He was confident as he spoke to the panel of members, looking at each of them like he was selling the Bible. None seemed willing to part with their money. Wilcox explained his justification for dismissing Carl Delane. He ridiculed Kate for her unrelenting nagging during the entire semester. She chuckled to herself. After ten minutes, he sat back down in his chair and sighed loudly.

Mr. Ross rose to address the members and participants. Kate prepared to answer the questions that were to follow. The first question was directed to Kate, and she typed her response as fast as she could. Drops of sweat ran down her forehead and into the cushioned band of her headstick. The jerky motion of her arm and leg muscles made the sweat roll down her back, as she typed the last words. The computer spoke her response and she breathed normally again. The members seemed satisfied with her answer. The question-and-answer period lasted over an hour. Seldom, Wilcox looked at her. His blatant lies and smug visage made it clear to all that he had no intention of rectifying the injustice he had perpetrated against Carl Delane.

The meeting ended and Kate was relieved. Wilcox wasted little time leaving the room. Mr. Ross met with Kate, Mr. Leonard, and Mr. Delane in the hallway. His voice was positive when he promised that resolving the issue would be his priority.

A half-foot of snow fell overnight. Kate awoke to the sound of the shower running. The bedroom was dark.

"Hey," Kate said softly when Eric emerged from the bathroom.

"What are you doing awake?" he asked.

"I don't know. What time did you get home last night?"

"I guess it was a little before one."

"Honey, you must be tired," she said.

"I'll be all right. Maybe I can sneak a nap this afternoon."

"My doctor's appointment is today—remember?" She looked at him quizzically.

He bowed his head in embarrassment. "Oh, right," he said. "What time?"

"It's at one," she answered. "I need you to be there, Eric."

"I know, I know—I'll be there," he said.

"Are you sure you can make it?"

"Yeah, I'm sure. I don't know what time I'll be home tonight, though. You better ask Liz to stay late again."

"Okay, I'll tell her."

"I gotta go," he said. "Do you need to pee?"

"No, I'm okay."

He leaned and kissed her goodbye. "If you need anything, call me."

"I will," she said. On the tip of her tongue were the words "I love you," but his brisk exit caused her to tense up. She failed to get the words out. The door slammed behind him. An aura of loneliness descended upon her, feeling disconnected from him. She tried to put the feeling aside before it overwhelmed her. It would not leave her. She lay in bed, blaming herself for any problems that could arise between them. Whatever it was, inkling or forethought, it gnawed at her stomach. The bedroom became brighter as the sun rose. She stared hypnotically at their wedding picture, thinking back to that beautiful day. She would never forget that day. She drifted back to sleep.

Liz filled out Kate's medical form, as Kate sat nervously in the waiting room. She kept looking at her watch. *Where is Eric?*

Her muscles moved in every conceivable direction. Each time the door opened, she hoped it would be him. It never was. The nurse called her name and led her into one of the exam rooms. Liz followed. Liz noticed Kate's uneasiness and tried to settle her down.

As soon as Kate saw Dr. Wells, she knew her health was in good hands and felt her whole body relax a bit. Dr. Wells had a strong, reassuring presence about her.

"This is my PCA, Liz," Kate said to the doctor.

Liz repeated Kate's words for Dr. Wells.

"Nice to meet you, Liz," Dr. Wells said. "How long have you been with Kate?"

"Oh, about six months now," Liz said.

"Great," said Dr. Wells. "Kate, are you comfortable discussing things in front of Liz?"

"Oh yeah, no problem with that," she said. Liz repeated her answer.

"Her husband, Eric, will be along any minute," Liz said.

"Would you like to wait for him?"

"No," Kate said, "I don't want to hold you up."

Again, Liz repeated Kate's words for Dr. Wells.

"Okay," said Dr. Wells. Liz proceeded to undress Kate. They lifted her onto the examining table.

"Don't worry," Liz said, "I'll make sure you don't fall off."

Dr. Wells stepped on a pedal, raising the table. Liz and Dr. Wells held Kate steady, but the more she tried to relax, the more she wiggled. Sweat started to seep from her back.

"Alright, Kate?" Liz asked.

"Yeah," she answered, doing her best. She trusted Liz and Dr. Wells, but it was a long way to the floor.

Dr. Wells checked Kate's pulse, blood pressure, lymph nodes, and breasts.

"Everything seems to be excellent," the doctor said.

Kate smiled.

"Your heart rate is a little fast, but I can tell that you're nervous, which is understandable. Let me lower this table a bit," Dr. Wells said.

"She just gets a little tense in unfamiliar places," Liz said.

"Well, we're almost done," said Dr. Wells. "How long have you been on the pill, Kate?"

"Almost eight years."

Liz repeated Kate's words.

"And your periods are regular?" asked Dr. Wells.

"Yes, they are."

"Okay, great," said the doctor. Liz helped Dr. Wells get Kate into position for a gynecological exam.

"Do you think you can keep your feet in the stirrups, Kate?" asked Dr. Wells.

"I don't think so," answered Kate, relaxing her muscles as much as possible.

"Okay, we'll manage," Dr. Wells said, confidently.

Kate wanted Eric there. The puppeteer was working against her. Sweat drenched her back.

"Okay, Kate, you did great," said Dr. Wells. "Everything looks good."

There was a knock at the door. Kate recognized Eric's voice. She lacked the strength to be angry. She was just relieved.

"You have great timing," Kate said.

"I'm sorry, Katie," he said. "I had a problem getting away. Hi, Liz."

"Eric, this is Dr. Wells," Kate said.

Eric extended his right hand. "Dr. Wells, I apologize a thousand times for being late."

"Kate did fine on her own," said the doctor. "She's a trooper. You and Liz can get her dressed. I'll be back in a moment."

"I'll dress her, Liz. Why don't you go get something to drink if you like," Eric said. Liz and Dr. Wells left the room.

"How pissed off are you?" he asked.

"A few minutes ago, I hated you," she said, "but now I just want to take a nap."

"I'm so sorry, Sweetie," he said and noticed her sweaty back. "It was tough, huh?"

"A little," she said, collapsing on his shoulder.

"Oh, Katie." He lifted her into her wheelchair. "Are you okay, babe?"

"Yeah, I guess."

He held her hand until the doctor returned.

Dr. Wells returned. "Things look good. I see no problems," she said, confidently. "Do you two plan to have children?"

Kate and Eric looked at each other. He knew it was his

question to answer. "I guess so."

"We haven't talked about it in a long time," Kate said.

"That's right," he said, "we haven't talked about it in a while."

"My only concern is," Dr. Wells said, "the longer you wait, the greater the likelihood that problems may occur."

Kate and Eric were visibly alarmed.

"Obviously, you don't need to decide today, by any means, but you should be aware of the facts."

"Thank you," said Eric.

"If you want to bounce any ideas off me," offered Dr. Wells, "feel free to call me, alright?"

"Thank you very much, Dr. Wells," he said.

"When can we get the test results?" Kate asked and Eric repeated.

"Why don't you call the office in a week to ten days," she said. "Good luck."

"What do you say, Mr. Hollis?" said Kate. "Would you like to have somebody calling you Dad?"

Eric answered with a smile and kissed her. "Let's go home."

Kate and Mr. Leonard went to the Administration Building. Ten inches of snow had fallen overnight and more was forecast for the next few days. This day, Kate's stomach was only slightly less tense. She guided her wheelchair through several rough patches of snow and ice on the walkways. She was distracted by the postcard-like prettiness of the campus.

Mr. Ross greeted them in his office. His calm demeanor gave away no hint of what he was about to say. Nervousness within Kate caused more involuntary movements in her body. At last, Mr. Ross revealed his decision to dismiss Wilcox from the Syracuse faculty.

Kate and Mr. Leonard were relieved by the judgment.

Mr. Ross pressed a button on his intercom and asked his secretary to show Wilcox in. This took Kate by surprise. She hated surprises. This time, nobody noticed her uneasiness. She was confident now.

Wilcox was wearing a familiar suit. His stride was slow and hesitant. Mr. Ross wasted little time getting down to business. Wilcox immediately voiced his dissatisfaction. The loudness of his voice startled Kate. As he pointed his finger at Kate and blamed her for his situation, his eyes were bulging from behind his wire-rimmed glasses. Mr. Ross raised his voice over Wilcox's and demanded that he leave. Wilcox receded from the room amid muttered threats, which lingered like bloodstains on the light-blue carpet.

Colberg called Eric into his office. "I need to give you a heads-up on something."

"Yeah?"

"I'm sure you are aware that Professor Wilcox was dismissed from the faculty yesterday."

"Yes," Eric said. "I'm very well aware of that."

Colberg cleared his throat. "What you may not be aware of is that Coach Hill and Professor Wilcox are friends—very good friends," Colberg said. "And every now and then one of our players needs a little push in passing a class."

"Yeah," Eric said, sensing where Colberg was going.

"Hill knew that Ed Martin failed chemistry last year and is barely passing now. If his GPA drops any lower, we'll have to suspend him from the team next season."

Eric mulled the implications of Colberg's statement. "What exactly did Hill arrange with Wilcox?"

"As I understand it, if Martin showed up for every class Wilcox was going to pass him with a C-minus."

"All he has to do is show up?" Eric asked, tension creping into his voice.

Colberg gave Eric a moment to comprehend the situation. "Hill is aware that Kate was the principal person behind getting Wilcox dismissed."

Eric recalled the rage Coach Hill had exhibited time and again. He didn't want that fury on him. "Can we get Ed a chemistry tutor?"

"Martin hardly has time to sleep, as it is," said Colberg. "Hill knows his players. He knows his staff. He is going to say some things that aren't very nice to you."

Bewildered, Eric gazed at Colberg. For a second, he considered quitting his job.

"Just don't let Hill get the best of you—because if he does, you're time here will get exhausting," Colberg said. "Support

your wife. We both know she did the right thing."
Eric could feel the stress in his chest. He hated the position he was in—hated it with all his might. If Martin was suspended from the team, Hill would blame Eric. "Thanks, Ray," Eric said and stood.
"This thing will pass," said Colberg, trying to encourage Eric.
Eric walked back to his office in a daze.
"What happened?" Dianne asked. There was no concealing his dismay.
"If Martin doesn't pass chemistry this semester, Hill is going to put a noose around my neck."
"What?" she asked.
"Hill and that bum Wilcox had this little deal going to get Martin through chemistry. If he attended every class, Wilcox was going to pass him no matter how poorly he did."
"Yeah, so?"
Eric's jaw tensed up. "Hill is pissed off that Wilcox was fired and he knows that Kate had a lot to do with it."
"Wilcox was fired?"
Eric threw his hands up in frustration. "The guy is a jackass, anyway," he blurted. "I mean, come on, the guy fixed a test on this poor kid who's in a wheelchair, just because he didn't want him in his class."
"Maybe there was some reason to kick the kid out of his class?" Dianne speculated.
"There was no good reason, Dianne," he said. "Trust me, Wilcox just didn't have the patience to deal with Carl."
"Can they somehow delay Wilcox's dismissal until the end of the semester?" she asked.
For a brief moment, Eric considered the idea, but it was too late. He shook his head.
Dianne didn't say anything more. After six months of working with Eric, she felt that she knew him as well as anyone.

It was 8:30 on a Thursday night. Kate wasn't expecting Eric for another two hours. She lay on the futon and watched television when she heard the door. She called out and Eric answered in an edgy tone, throwing his keys down on the counter. She crawled into the hallway.
"How was your day?" she asked, sensing his dark mood.

"Great," he said sarcastically into the refrigerator.

"What's the matter?"

"Nothing."

She crawled into the kitchen and leaned against the wall. "Eric, what's the matter?"

"Nothing, alright," he said and closed the refrigerator door hard enough to rattle the contents.

She wasn't satisfied with his answer. "Something is obviously bothering you."

He sucked on his bottom lip. "Ed Martin is failing chemistry."

"Yeah?"

"Ed failed last year and if he doesn't get at least a C this time, he'll be suspended from the team."

Kate looked at him with an inquiring gaze. "And?"

"Coach Hill had some stupid arrangement with Wilcox that if Martin showed up to every class, Wilcox would give Ed a C no matter how badly he did."

"No matter what?"

"Yes, no matter what." He nodded. "Everybody knows that you were behind Wilcox getting dismissed and it's already coming around to me."

She didn't know whether to feel sorry for her husband, or be angry at him. "So, what are you saying to these people, Eric?"

"I don't know, I'm in a difficult position," he said. "I need to watch out for the players."

"You're a trainer, Eric," he said. "You have nothing to do with their education."

"I try to help when I can."

"Is that why you're never home—because you're out saving the world?" She snapped.

"Oh, here we go again," he said. "This isn't about you!"

"I think it is about me," she said. "You come home all pissed off and I don't know why. I think you're doing too much, hon."

"I know you worked hard on the Wilcox thing. And it was the right thing to do. I'm not questioning that. I'm just in a tough spot, is all."

"You know all the crap I went through with that jerk," she said.

"I'm not asking you to do anything!" Eric shouted, his voice rising with his temper. The exhausting day had taken toll on his nerves.

"It sounds like you are," she said, trying to remain composed. "Why can't Ed get a tutor for chemistry?"

"I thought of that. He doesn't have time."

She needed to refocus her thoughts. She looked at her tormented husband and her frustration turned into concern. "I don't know what to say to make you feel better," she said, calmly. "This is not your problem. It's really not. If people are expecting more of you, then you may just need to say no a little more often. Do what you think is right."

"You're not hearing what I'm saying, Kate," he said.

"So, what are you saying, Eric?" she asked, sternly. Down deep, she knew what he was really saying to her and she understood his frustration, but he needed to get it out for himself.

He stared at the floor, unable to say he was angry at her for getting Wilcox dismissed. He knew that his anger was unwarranted and that his frustration was toward his job, but he couldn't let go. "I don't have any more to say."

"Fine," she said, feeling more defeated than she imagined. "I'm tired. By the way, I called Dr. Wells today. She says everything's fine."

"Good," he said, dismissively.

They retired for the night—in silence.

Chapter 11

Winter wore on. The snow fell and the howling wind blew. Kate immersed herself in work. Day and night, she sat in front of the computer until she was too tired to continue. Then, she would fall asleep on the futon. The sound of the front door would awaken her, but she would remain silent unless she needed Eric to take her to the bathroom. She listened, as he moved through the apartment. She would hear the refrigerator door opening and closing. She would hear the water running in the kitchen and then the bathroom. She would hear the toilet flushing. On the nights when she didn't call out to him, she desperately hoped he would lie down beside her like he used to. Hearing him climb into their bed without her was agony.

Tears rolled down her nose and fell onto the flannel sheet. It became a nightly ritual. The quietness of the apartment was deafening and sleep did not come easily to Kate. It was also deserting Eric a room away.

Kate questioned if there would come a day when they would speak more than a few words to each other, discuss more than just what items they needed at the grocery store, give more than a quick glance at each other. She wondered when they would discuss starting a family. Time was running short. *Time will hold all the answers,* she thought.

Eric was at an away game, so she spent the day with Roberta. They had grown close over the months and she felt at ease around Roberta, who by now was almost as adept as Eric at understanding her speech. Despite feeling so somber, Kate tried to display a happy attitude. They sat around and watched movies. Occasionally, Kate looked at the falling snow outside.

"You think it's ever going to stop?" asked Roberta.

Kate startled.

"Oh, I'm sorry," Roberta said.

"Maybe it'll stop by June."

"Is everything all right, Kate?" Roberta ventured.

The question took her by surprise. She looked at Roberta and then at the television.

"I apologize. It's none of my business," said Roberta.

"Oh, no, it's okay," she said. "I'm just not sure myself."

"John told me about the situation with Ed Martin."

"Did he?" Kate murmured. "Eric seems to think it's my fault."

"Wilcox brought it on himself. You didn't get him dismissed for some minor violation. This was a big deal, Kate!"

"I know it was a big deal," she said, "but Eric wants to help the world and the team is his world right now."

Roberta touched her shoulders. "What can I do, Kate?"

"Oh, we'll be okay," she said. "He just has to come to his senses." She laughed, demonstrating she was not worried about the situation. Roberta laughed, also.

Before they knew, the credits were rolling at the end of the movie.

It freed Kate acknowledging the feud with her husband. She prayed the rest of the heaviness would lift soon.

Cold air followed Eric and John into the apartment. Eric glanced briefly at Kate and ventured a hi before carrying his duffel bags into the bedroom. Roberta hurried to her feet before John had a chance to unzip his jacket. Eric offered the Griffys some food and drink, but Roberta declined his offer. Four turned into two.

Kate broke the silence. "How was the trip?"

"Okay," Eric said. His body language suggested that he would rather be watching television than talking to her.

"Are things okay?" she asked.

"Super, Kate," he said, mordantly.

"I just want to talk to you," she said.

"What would you like to talk about?" he asked with an edge.

Sadness overtook her. "I don't deserve this," she said.

"It's been so hard, Kate."

"What?"

"Having to deal with Hill and all his obnoxious comments," he said angrily. "He just keeps going."

She'd never seen her husband so defeated. "Don't let him get the best of you," she said.

"Oh, do you think that is so easy, Kate?" he asked, explosively. "I spend at least two hours with this monster in his office and when we're out on the road I see his pudgy face every time I turn around. There he is, just staring at me with those eyes of his, knowing he can make my life a living hell if Martin fails!"

"This is not your fault, Eric."

"It will be if Martin doesn't play next year."

She looked at him, concerned. "It won't be your fault," she repeated. "Eric, I know you're taking the blame for this and I'm the one who did it. I'm the one who got rid of Wilcox and that pisses you off!" Before continuing, she had to gather herself. "I can't handle you taking it out on me anymore."

"I'm not taking it out on you!" he exclaimed.

"Then why are you yelling at me?"

"Jesus Christ, Kate, I'm just trying to hold this team together until the season's over!"

"What about *our* team, Eric?" she asked. "Who's gonna hold us together?" The lump in her throat grew to the size of a hailstone. "I thought..." she began, but got overwhelmed by what she was about to say. Tears rolled down her face. "I thought one of these days we were going to talk about having kids."

"I don't need this, Kate—I really don't," he said and walked into the bedroom. He came out moments later wearing his jacket. "I'm going out for a while. Do you need anything before I go?" he asked with muted feeling.

"No," she answered, even though her bladder was near capacity.

She fought back the tears, but the weight upon her soul was too much for her. Finally, she succumbed to her sorrow. The telephone rang and startled her. It was Meg on the answering machine. Hearing her best friend's caused Kate to crumble. Hiding was all she could think to do to avoid the barrage of questions that would arise.

The tears slowed and she crawled toward the bathroom in search for a towel to dry her face. She remembered her bladder, but the urge was no greater than before. The towel rack was just inside the door, so Kate didn't have to kneel on the hard tile. She reached for the towel, but her first attempt to pull it down failed. She tried again and succeeded. Exhausted, she crawled into the den and lay down on the futon.

The next day, Eric went off to tend to a player who had come down with a fever. Kate resolved to call Meg, while he was out. As she dialed the phone, a nervous twinge emerged. It was like a contest, a marathon, to hide her emotions as best she could. The conversation proceeded like any other conversation they had had in the past. When Eric became the topic, her voice lost strength, her chest became tight, and her throat constricted. Meg had to ask her to repeat several things, and Kate forced the words out again. She clearly heard the sadness. She was familiar with Kate's attempts to cover up things she didn't want anyone else, not even Meg, to know. Meg sensed Kate was fragile. She refrained from pushing Kate to talk. Meg reminded Kate that her line was open anytime. Kate noticed the lump in her throat again, as she thanked her friend. They rang off. For Kate, the curtain fell and the act was over.

Super Bowl Sunday: every boy's dream to play in or at least to sit in the stadium. The living room filled up with guests, some of whom Kate had never met. She felt out of place in her own home. Her only comfort was that Roberta and John were there. The familiar faces eased her. Eric sat on the other end of the couch, putting on a far better act than she.

Dianne showed up just before kickoff. Kate hated surprises and particularly hated this surprise. Dianne sat on the floor, two feet in front of Kate, but never acknowledged her. Kate raged inwardly, as Eric went to the kitchen and grabbed Dianne a beer.

The outcome was decided halfway into the fourth quarter. San Francisco had a sizable lead over San Diego. Kate was silently begging everyone to leave. Eight minutes remained on the game clock. In real time, it was at least half an hour more. She tried to conceal her irritation. The last two minutes seemed like an eternity.

Guests began to depart. Dianne waited for the last seconds to tick away before she was ready to leave. John and Roberta lingered to help Eric clean up. He insisted that they go home. Husband and wife were alone at last.

"Where the hell do you get off inviting her here?!" she asked, angrily.

Eric returned to the living room. "What was I gonna do, Kate, invite everyone except Dianne?!" he asked. "I thought she wasn't coming."

"She didn't even look at me, Eric!"

"Dianne doesn't know what to say to you," he said and retreated into the kitchen. "Did you ever think of that?!" Eric asked, raising his voice.

She crawled into the kitchen. "Five months and she still can't say 'Hi'? What the hell is her problem?"

"What would you like me to do, Kate? Force Dianne to like you? Force her to say 'Hi' to you?"

"This is my home, too," she argued. "If someone can't look at me, she shouldn't come in!" Her anger showed in her jerky movements. "All I want is a little respect, Eric!"

He turned back to the dishes.

"You don't have anything more to say?" she asked to his back.

"What do you want me to say?" he returned, without turning around.

"I just want you to take my side," she answered. "I guess that's too much to ask for these days."

She withdrew to the den. He was too exhausted to respond.

She turned on the television and lay down on the familiar futon that was now her primary bed. She waited for Eric to finish up in the kitchen. Her attention was always on him. Without a word, he put her on the toilet and dressed her for bed. They had become intimate strangers. Although he had the ability to conceal his, she could not conceal her nakedness from him. Like a leaf recoiling from a killing frost, Kate curled herself up to hide her body. His ire scared her. *Will he be attracted to me again after this madness is over?* The gentleness of his hands made it hard for her to ignore his presence, aware of the love they had the ability to share.

He went into the bedroom and closed the door behind him. This was something new. She was crushed.

"I see you read my note," Mr. Leonard said, as he entered Kate's office.

"Yes," she typed. "I'll ask Sue to call Emily Harrod and invite her to the meeting."

"This Pamela Dixon didn't sound too happy on the phone," he said.

"How so?" she asked in her natural voice.

"Well," Mr. Leonard said, "she seems to think she's the only counselor in the State of New York. She says she can only spend about ten minutes with us."

Kate felt defeated already, telling Mr. Leonard she'd written out what she wanted to say to Ms. Dixon.

"Do the best you can," Mr. Leonard said.

Kate typed: "Thank you."

"You're welcome, Kate," he said. "Good luck."

As she immersed herself in work, Kate's constant, aching thoughts about Eric receded. *Perhaps Ms. Dixon will turn out to be very nice in person,* Kate mused; but deep down she knew this wouldn't be the case. She was getting keyed up for an unpleasant encounter with this Dixon woman.

It was almost five and Ms. Dixon still hadn't arrived. She was due at 4:30. Kate and Emily waited patiently, along with her friend Carla. Fifteen more minutes and Kate would miss her van ride home. She apologized to Emily and Carla for the delay.

Ten minutes later, Pamela Dixon blew in the door, dressed smartly in a black dress under a tan overcoat.

"I'm looking for Kate Hollis," she said. She was in a hurry.

Kate typed on her laptop: "I'm Kate. You must be Pam Dixon."

"It's Pamela," Ms. Dixon said. "You're not the person I talked to on the phone."

"No, you spoke with Mr. Leonard this morning," said the computer.

"And where is he?" she asked.

As Kate typed, she sensed Ms. Dixon's growing impatience. "He left for the night," she explained. "I'm the one who wanted to speak to you. This is Emily Harrod and her friend, Carla. Please make yourself comfortable next to Emily."

Kate was angry by Ms. Dixon's failure to say hello to Emily. "Can I assume you have met Emily before?"

"Yes, I have," Ms. Dixon said.

Kate pressed on: "I believe that Emily would benefit from having her own computer."

"What makes you think Emily needs her own computer?" Ms. Dixon asked.

"With the correct software, it would enable her to read

independently. She would be able to take notes and then the computer could read them back to her," Kate replied.

"How will we know she won't use it for something else?" asked Ms. Dixon.

"What the hell do you think I'm going to use it for—International drug smuggling?" Emily quipped.

The remark surprised Ms. Dixon. All fell silent, as Kate scrolled down to a sentence she had typed earlier: "Emily has worked through all the frustrations of depending on other people to read for her, take class notes for her, and type for her. Emily could do all those things for herself with a simple laptop."

"Computers cost money," said Ms. Dixon. "All these things cost money."

Kate typed: "Isn't your job as vocational counselor to help people like Emily reach their goals for the future?"

"We feel that Emily is doing fine. We see no need for her to have a computer," Ms. Dixon said.

"Who's 'we'?" asked Emily.

"John Coneroy, my supervisor."

"I have never met John Coneroy in my entire life," said Emily in exasperation. "Who is he to judge what I need for college?"

As the conversation veered toward impasse, Kate tried to stay positive. "Emily has a 3.7 grade point average," she typed.

"That's my point," Ms. Dixon said. "If she's doing so well, I can't see why a computer would be a benefit."

Kate's nerves began to fray. No doubt the van had come and gone by now. "The computer will give her independence," Kate typed—she wanted to scream at her.

"We don't buy independence for our clients, Ms. Hollis."

"What exactly do you do for your clients, Ms. Dixon?" Kate typed. She wished her synthesizer had the ability to speak in italics.

"We guide our clients into the workforce and into the community," Ms. Dixon said, as if she read a cue card.

"Don't bother, Kate," Emily said. "We can argue until we're blue in the face, but this loon isn't going to bat for me."

"Hey," Ms. Dixon snapped back, "be my guest and do my job for just one day, with 75 clients on my docket, and then tell me how easy it is to give everyone what they want."

"Gladly," Emily said. "I'm sure I'd be able to do *something*."
Without another word, Ms. Dixon picked up and left the office.
"Did she just leave?" Emily asked.
"Yeah," Kate said in her natural voice.
"Think I said too much?" Emily asked.
Kate typed: "No, I just think Ms. Dixon met her match today. You did just fine. Why don't you two go home. We'll deal with this some other day."
"Alright, Kate," Emily said and rose. "Have a great night." Carla waved goodbye and led Emily outside.
"You too, Emily," Kate said, closed her laptop and took off her headstick. She looked out the window and saw darkness. She pumped herself up for the 20-minute walk home, knowing she'd catch hell from Liz for wheeling home in freezing weather. Sue dressed Kate warmly and called Liz to warn her that Kate was on her way.
The cold air scattered all the frustrations of the day. Kate realized she hadn't focused on Eric. Super Bowl Sunday seemed like ages ago, barely remembering what they fought about. Kate refused to live in a dark, cold existence. She loved Eric more than he would ever know. Optimism propelled her forward, into the night. Carefully, she made her way home over the ruts and bumps on every sidewalk. She got home in 15 minutes—record time.
Liz had cleaned the dinner dishes and gone home for the night. Kate lingered by the window and looked out across the street. Her body shifted erratically from knee to knee in a nervous motion. The neighborhood was coated in snow. She strained to see something, signs of life, anything across the street. Her thoughts turned to Eric and soon her mind was consumed with him. She exhausted herself, trying to figure out how to make things right again. What frightened her was how fighting had become so easy.
To comfort herself, she thought back to when they lived in Boston. What she would give to turn back the hands of time! The etching on the wall carried her back to Meg's barn—to a distant place. It seemed like a fairytale. Her lovely beginning with Eric was now as remote. Where had those two people disappeared to? She prayed for their safe return.

Eric was an hour late getting home. He looked bedraggled, carrying his orange-and-blue duffel bag over his shoulder. He apologized to Liz and began to explain his tale. Kate allowed brief eye contact, despite being tremendously relieved at the splendid sight of him. His plane sat on the runway for two hours. A plate of chicken, potatoes and string beans waited in the oven. Eric sent Liz home. Kate's plate sat half empty. She was still hungry, but debated whether to finish. Without a word, Eric fed her. The television occupied their attention. Lacking a proper subject to begin a conversation, she stayed silent for the rest of the night.

Utterly engaged in his work, Eric didn't hear Stuart's quiet knock on the door. The visitor knocked again, a bit louder.

Eric looked up. "Hey Stu, how are you doing?"

"I'm fine," he said.

Eric rose to stretch out his back. "What's up?"

Stuart plopped down in the chair. "Oh, nothing," he said. "One of my classes was cancelled, so I thought I'd come bother you."

"I feel so honored, Stu," Eric said. "What class got cancelled?"

"Intro to Economics."

"Is it boring?" Eric asked.

"I hope the professor picks up the pace a little bit."

"I think I took that class when I was in college. I forget how I did," Eric said.

"If I know you, you probably got an A in every single class," said Stuart.

Eric laughed and shook his head. "Not even close, Stu. I had my moments, but I wasn't a nerd."

"You're just being modest."

"No, it's true," said Eric, twirling a pen between his fingers. "I had to be the good son because my brother definitely wasn't."

"Yeah, I have one of those brothers, too," Stuart said. "He lives on the edge. We're all just waiting for him to take that one wrong step."

Eric glanced at Stuart. He realized he was not alone. "Is he older?"

"No, he's four years younger than I am," said Stuart. "He's a smart kid, but he just doesn't see things the way they are. He has his own rules."

Something in the way Stuart spoke about his brother struck a familiar chord with Eric. He saw himself in Stuart.

"Oh crap! What day is it?" Stuart asked.

"It's the seventh," Eric answered. "Why?"

"I'm supposed to get my bike at four. I need a ride downtown. I can't believe I forgot."

"I can take you down," Eric said. "It'll only probably take an hour, right?"

"Yeah," he said. "I just gotta pick it up."

Eric nodded at Stuart. "I'll take you right now, if you want."

"Really?"

"Yeah, really."

"Thanks a lot," said Stuart. "You're not like the other white boys."

Eric laughed. "Does that mean I'm a *good* white boy?"

"Yes," Stuart answered, chuckling. "You're the best white boy that ever looked out for me."

"Well I'm glad, Stu. I'll carry that badge of honor for a long time to come. Let's go."

The fans at Seton Hall were wildly enthusiastic about the game against Syracuse. It was five minutes to tip-off and Coach Hill was giving precise instructions to each member of the team. He had to scream to be heard. Eric and Dianne sat a row behind the players.

Eric kept looking at the clock. Time was moving slowly. He wanted the game to be over. He wanted to be anywhere but where he was, but he didn't know why.

The second half began with Syracuse down by seven points. Coach Hill badgered the players to pick up the game. Time seemed to be moving even slower than before. Eric chose to focus on Stuart on the court. With seven minutes left, the team was playing hard, especially Stuart. Eric's attention was drawn away from Stuart for only a second when he heard the referee blow his whistle. The clock stopped. The crowd fell silent. Eric saw Derrick Johns waving frantically at him. Eric dashed down to the floor. The players gathered around Stuart's motionless body. Eric stared in horror.

"He just collapsed," yelled Derrick.

Eric kneeled over Stuart and determined that he wasn't breathing. "Get Colberg!" he exclaimed. "Dianne, bring everything!" He made the crucial decision to turn Stuart onto his back. "Stu! Stu!"

"I'm here," Dianne reassured Eric, as she brought down the medical kit.

"He's not breathing, Dianne!" Eric shouted, nervously. "Where is Colberg?!"

She saw the terror in Eric's eyes, as he feverishly compressed Stuart's chest.

Dianne found the breathing bag and placed it over Stuart's mouth. "I see him," she said. "He's coming."

"What the hell happened?" Colberg asked.

"He collapsed!" Eric said in distress. "I need to shock him, Ray!"

"The paramedics will be here in a minute."

"We don't have a minute, Ray!" Eric shouted angrily.

"Okay," Colberg said. He knelt down and prepared Stuart for defibrillations. "Ready."

As Eric picked up the paddles, he realized that he had only done this once—in school on a dummy. "Charge to 120," he said. He put the paddles on Stuart's chest and side, and triggered the electricity through his heart. Stuart's body thrashed. Eric watched the ECG intently.

"Nothing," he said, looking up at Colberg.

"I'll put it on 200," said Colberg.

"Clear!" Eric yelled and sent more voltage through Stuart's struggling heart. The second shock was unsuccessful. "Put it up to 300!" Eric was about to shock Stuart again when the paramedics arrived.

"Sir, let me evaluate him before you shock him," the paramedic said to Eric.

"He's in full cardiac arrest!" Eric screamed. "Clear!" Eric sent a bigger pulse of electricity through Stuart's heart.

"Sir," the paramedic called out, "we need to get him to the hospital now."

Stuart was close to death. Eric deferred to the paramedics

and helped lift Stuart onto the stretcher, accompanying Stuart through the corridors and out to the ambulance, giving him chest compressions along the way. Eric was numb to everything else. He didn't notice the 20-degree temperatures outside. He didn't hear the chaos around him. When they reached the ambulance, he sat on the bench while the paramedics tried to save Stuart. Stuart was rushed to the emergency room. Eric followed, accepting that the situation was out of his hands. He watched hopelessly, as the doctors and nurses tried to save Stuart. He began to cry. Dianne found him and tried to comfort him, but he was inconsolable.

Kate heard the news about Stuart and her heart dropped. Roberta came over and stayed with her until Liz arrived later that evening. John called before six to confirm Stuart's death. He spoke very little about Eric's state of mind. Kate wanted more information, but she didn't press John. They expected to return to Syracuse by ten, leaving Kate with four agonizing hours to worry about her husband. She recognized the possibility he might shut her out of his sadness, but hoped he would allow her to share in his grief.

At about half past ten, Kate heard the door on the truck close and his footsteps coming up the front steps. Eric's gait was slow and heavy. Kate conjectured his mood would be the same. She held her breath until she saw him.

"Please, Kate," he said mournfully, "don't start crying."

"Are you okay?" she asked.

He stared vacantly in her direction. "I guess." He dropped his bags on the floor. "Where's Liz?" One of the bags had belonged to Stuart.

"She's in the bathroom," she answered.

Liz emerged and gave him a hug. "I'm sorry," she said.

"Thanks, Liz," he said. "Thanks for staying with Kate."

"Yeah, anytime." She put her jacket on. "Night guys."

"Night," Kate said, as Liz left for the night.

Kate waited for Eric to say something. She sat by the bedroom door and watched him unpack his duffel bag. "Do you want to talk?" she ventured.

"No, I don't want to talk," he said in frustration. "The last thing I wanna do is to relive this day."

She didn't have the strength to look at him. "Okay," she said. She crawled into the den and closed the door behind her.

As the days passed, Eric's anger over Stuart's death increased. He kept thinking about Stuart's ECG months earlier. He tortured himself with thoughts of failure—failure to confront Dr. Freham. He spotted Freham's car approaching the parking lot outside the athletics building. He needed to confront him. Freham parked about 20 yards away and got out of his car. Eric approached him.

"You knew all along that he had a heart defect, didn't you?" Eric asked.

Freham whistled coolly, as he headed toward the athletics building.

Eric followed him inside. "You knew," Eric said, heatedly.

Freham continued to whistle, as he entered the elevator.

Eric followed. "Say something!" he said.

Freham remained silent. The elevator opened and Freham calmly made his way to his office. He took off his camel overcoat and hung it on the rack.

"Will you stop whistling, damn you!" Eric screamed.

Freham turned to Eric. "Did you say something to me, Mr. Hollis?"

"Stuart King is dead and it's your fault!" Eric screamed.

"Is that so, Mr. Hollis?" His gaze was sharp. "Got any proof?"

"I got his ECG from September's stress test. They are doing the autopsy this morning."

Freham sat in his leather chair and scratched his chin. "Are you finished, Mr. Hollis?"

"What the hell is wrong with you, anyway?" he asked. "Do you get paid for the number of baskets each kid sinks, or what?"

"You're treading on dangerous ground, Mr. Hollis!"

The comment did not faze Eric. "I have never met a more incompetent doctor than you, Freham."

Freham pointed to the gold-framed college diplomas that hung on the wall. "Do you know what those are, Mr. Hollis?"

"They are not going to save your ass from a big lawsuit," Eric said, leaning over Freham's grand cherry desk. "I'm going to make sure they screw your ass to the wall over this, you heartless jerk!" Eric left Freham's office, without waiting for a reply. Stuart's death would haunt him forever and he continued to torture himself with blame and regret. As he returned to his office, he met Colberg in the hallway.

"Can I see you in my office, please?" Colberg asked.

"Sure," Eric said.

Colberg closed the door behind him. "Freham wants me to fire you, but I'm not going to do that," Colberg said bluntly. "There will be a lawsuit in the months to come and the truth is going to come out. Whatever happened—whether there was an oversight by Freham, or if it was just a freak thing that happened to Stuart—we'll find the truth."

Eric sat and rubbed his exhausted eyes.

"Have you gotten any sleep the past few nights?" Colberg asked.

"Nope," Eric answered, quietly. "All I do is toss and turn all night long, just thinking what I could have done to have prevented this."

"Eric," Colberg said, "this wasn't your fault. You did all you could do. Don't beat yourself up."

"No, I didn't do enough, Ray. I should have made a bigger issue of the abnormality I saw on Stuart's ECG."

"Why don't you go home; take the day off tomorrow," Colberg said, sensing Eric's fragile mood. "Stuart's wake is set for Wednesday and the funeral is Thursday morning. We're going to charter a few buses to Cleveland."

Eric slowly stood. "Alright, see you Wednesday."

Stuart's duffel bag was still lying in the corner of the bedroom. Eric trembled slightly, as he unzipped the bag and sorted through Stuart's belongings. He found a uniform and held the orange tank top up against the morning light. He laid the garment gently on the floor. He found the Walkman that Stuart always carried. Inside was a Cooke tape. He also found a Valentine's Day card, not yet inscribed. Chills ran up and down his spine, as he thought Stuart's girlfriend would hold it as a keepsake. He returned the contents to the bag and closed it. He would give the bag to Stuart's family.

Eric stopped off at Kate's office to say goodbye. She was typing at her computer.

"We are leaving for Cleveland soon," he said.

"Okay," she said, seeing his face pale and drawn. She ached to wrap her arms around him and tell him everything was going to be all right. "Call me tonight, if you get a moment."

He nodded. "Roberta is going to stay over tonight?"

"Yeah," she answered. "I'll be okay." She was trying to stay positive for him.

He wanted to say more, but it didn't feel like the right time. "I'll call you later." He went down to his truck. Catching a glimpse of his pale reflection in the rearview mirror, he barely recognized himself. He looked and felt like he had aged 20 years.

Two charter buses were idling by the athletics building. He loaded his duffel bag and then Stuart's. The buses steadily filled up with a young group of mourners. When he saw Dianne coming onto his bus, he knew which seat she was going to choose. As predicted, she took the seat next to him. He acknowledged her with a nod. Silence prevailed in the bus. The team's normally boisterous atmosphere was temporarily muted. No one knew when it would return.

He recalled taking Stuart downtown to pick up his bike and felt a tremendous wave of sorrow for Stuart's parents, who hadn't expected their eldest son to drop dead at 20 while playing the game he loved. *Damn Freham!* Eric thought and began to berate himself. He played that "if only I had" game over and over again in his mind. Somehow, he couldn't accept the situation that had unfolded before him.

The team members walked together for the three blocks from their hotel to the funeral home. The winter wind blew hard, adding to the tears. They walked in silence. For some, it was their first wake.

Eric's stomach cramped seeing Stuart's grieving parents and siblings across the room. He studied the face of Stuart's younger brother. He knew something about the boy.

As he glanced down at Stuart's body, Eric fumbled in prayer. Stuart looked peaceful. The awful scene in the emergency room flashed back—Stuart's heart in a surgeon's hand. Eric felt lightheaded. He grabbed the brass railing, knelt down, said a quick prayer and got back up on his feet. He collected himself and approached Mr. and Mrs. King. "Sorry for your loss," he said, automatically. "My name is Eric Hollis. I was Stuart's sports trainer."

"Oh, Eric, yes, yes—Stuart told us all about you," Mrs. King replied.

Mr. King extended his hand. "It's good to meet you, Eric."

"It's good to meet you both," Eric said, struck by their strength under the circumstances. Once again, he was consumed with self-loathing.

"If you have time to meet with us after the wake, we would like to speak with you," Mrs. King said, as she grasped Eric's hand.

"Certainly," Eric said. She introduced Stuart's sister, Rebecca, and his brother, Chad. As he returned into the crowd, Eric was overwhelmed by the strength the family. They were rising to the task at hand and forged on the best that they knew how. He admired their poise and dignity.

"Are you doing all right?" Dianne asked, as she sat beside him.

"I'm okay, I guess," Eric answered.

"Stuart knew a lot of people, didn't he?" she said, trying to get a conversation going.

"He sure did."

"If we get back to the hotel early enough, do you want to grab a drink with me?" she asked, fighting hard to get his attention.

"I won't be back for a while. I'm going to join the Kings after the wake."

"Oh, okay," she said. "Shall I come along?"

"Maybe it would be better if I talked to them one on one," he said.

"Sure, sure," she said quickly. She expected him to need her like he needed her that afternoon in the emergency room. Reliving that moment in her mind, she could almost feel his head on her shoulder. He was so devastated by Stuart's death. She loved comforting him. His hair felt like silk. She hoped she would have the chance to comfort him again.

As the crowd slowly cleared, Eric and Colberg remained. Rebecca and Chad went home with their aunt. As the Kings approached, Eric quickly stood. Colberg followed his lead. It felt strange to be discussing Stuart's death, with him lying in his coffin ten feet away. Eric kept reminding himself that Stuart was dead. As Colberg described what happened on the basketball court, he looked at the body often. He recalled his little anxiety attack in the game's first half—*was it a sign telling me that something was about to go tragically wrong?* Stuart's parents held each other's hands tightly. Tears ran down their sorrowful faces. Eric fought back his own tears.

Eric talked about driving Stuart downtown to pick up the bike. He became distraught and his voice quivered, as he began to recount his efforts to save Stuart. The Kings cried along. Eric hid his face in his hands, overwhelmed by a grief that cut down all the way to his soul. Mrs. King put her hand on his back. Feeling her consoling him, Eric cried openly. He hadn't expected to fall apart so utterly. Mrs. King reassured him that Stuart's death wasn't his fault. Her voice was as sweet as a song bird's. Even so, her gentle words made him cry harder. He still blamed himself for not standing up to Freham.

He realized he needed to pull himself together for Stuart's parents. He needed to be strong for them. Eric gave Stuart's duffel bag to his parents. The Kings thanked him profusely.

He gathered himself in the winter night, brutally aware that a certain soul was missing from the land he stood upon. He looked up at the thousands of glimmering stars, renewing his strength.

As he approached his hotel room, Eric was surprised by a tap on his shoulder. He turned and saw Dianne. She was in a white bathrobe and her long curly hair was wet.

"How did things go with the Kings?" she asked. She seemed to have the energy of a person who'd a full night's sleep. Eric was struggling to keep his eyes open.

"Okay, I guess."

"Did you talk about Freham?" she asked, hoping to spark some passion in him.

"Yeah," he said, looking down and fiddling with his room key.

"I've got some beer in my room," she said. "Do you want one?"

"No, no, Dianne. I'm sorry, but I need to get to bed."

"C'mon, you can stay awake for one beer," she said, turning on the charm. It was as if she had forgotten that they were at a funeral.

He breathed a surrendering sigh. "Okay, but just one," he said and followed her to her room.

She opened a bottle of beer for him. "Do you think the Kings are going to sue Syracuse?" she asked.

"Most likely," he answered, staring at the television and sipping his beer.

"Did they find out anything in the autopsy?"

He was in no mood to rehash the details of Stuart's death and struggled to answer. "They believe he had Long QT syndrome that was undiagnosed. He may have been borderline. It's very difficult to prove Long QT after death because it usually shows up in the ECG." He swallowed a gulp of beer. It went down easy. Before he knew it, the bottle was empty.

"Want another beer?"

He thought about it. If he had a second beer, there was a chance he would want a third, fourth, a fifth. "Yeah, I'll have one more."

"You were right all along about Stuart."

"And now he's dead and I can't do too much about that." The beer numbed his pain. He hadn't felt so relaxed in days. His mind was empty. The stress he had been putting on himself slowly dissipated.

"It wasn't your fault, Eric," she said, hoping to comfort him again. "You did all you could."

"If everyone keeps on saying that, I might start believing it," he said, and drained half of his beer.

"You *can* believe it, Eric," she said. She slid off the bed and knelt before him. "You did nothing wrong, Eric." She put her hand on his knee.

He looked down and saw her bare leg. He stood. "I think I've had enough beer. Thanks, Dianne."

Before she had a chance to follow him, he disappeared.

Rows of gravestones went on as far as the eye could see. The funeral procession arrived at its final stop. It was a very lonely place: Stuart's final resting place. Eric was thankful it was nearly over. They watched in silence, as the pallbearers set the coffin by the grave. Stuart's girlfriend lay a red rose on the coffin. The winter wind blew the rose off onto the frozen ground. Eric cursed the wind. The minister said his final words giving Stuart to the Earth and to Heaven. A tear rolled down Eric's cold face. He had failed Stuart.

Kate heard the truck pull in to the driveway, desperately wanting to see him. The front door opened and Eric stood before her.

"Hi," he said calmly. He looked worn out.

"Hi," she said. "Did everything go all right?"

"As well as a funeral can go, I guess." He put his arms around her. She'd almost forgot what his embrace felt like and savored the moment.

"How come you didn't call last night?" she asked.

"We got back late from the funeral home. Ray and I stayed and talked with Stuart's parents." The previous night came rushing back to him. He refrained from telling Kate how he had lost his composure in front of them.

"Are you going to work tomorrow?"

"Yeah. We have practice," he answered. "Why?"

"Oh, I was just wondering," she said, trying to stay positive. "I thought if you had the day off, I might take the day off, too."

"Sorry," he said. He went into the bedroom to drop his duffel bag. Soon, he returned and sat on the couch.

"Okay, okay," she said. "Maybe some other day?"

He nodded and stared at the television.

She surrendered in silence. He needed time to heal. She felt relieved to be in his company. She settled by his side and they watched TV without exchanging a word. After dinner, he dressed her for bed and then retreated into the bedroom, leaving her to sleep alone on the futon once again.

Chapter 12

Syracuse played their last games of the regular season in the closing weeks before the NCAA tournament got underway. Kate rarely saw Eric. At times, she barely remembered what he looked like, smelled like, felt like—it had been so long since she had felt the caress of his strong, gentle hands. Sometimes, she played back old messages on the answering machine just to hear his voice, so strong and cheerful.

Nights: she would spend endless hours at the computer. This gave her more time for her students during the day. Work kept her mind off her frustrations at home. She was usually asleep in the den when he arrived home in the late hours of the night. Painfully aware of the harm she was causing herself by working too many hours, she continued her tiring schedule—drowning herself in something other than Eric. Some mornings, she awoke around four o'clock, sometimes needing to go to the bathroom. She would wait until Liz arrived rather than bother Eric, even when he was getting ready for work. It was a great effort for her to eat. Liz worried, but she continued to smile to disguise her deep sorrow.

Dark circles appeared under her eyes, but she reassured Liz she was fine. Weight started to drop off her like leaves from an autumn tree. She made every effort to appear content. Liz had no recourse. She sensed Kate's sadness but didn't want to upset her further. In her irresolute plight, Kate's spirit grew weaker. She questioned Eric's love for her. She questioned their marriage. She questioned everything around her.

The clock read 11:45 and Eric hadn't arrived home. Usually around eleven, she awoke to the sound of his keys jingling in the door. On this night, she was awake and needed to use the bathroom. Frustrated with his lateness, she watched the late show, as she waited to relieve her bladder. Another 17 minutes went by before Eric came home. She kicked off the covers and crawled into the hallway. He was in the kitchen. It was the first time she had seen him in five days. "You're home kinda late," she said.

"How come you're not asleep?" he asked.

"I have to pee," she said and began to crawl toward the

bathroom. He helped her onto the toilet. She smelled a combination of smoke and alcohol reeking from him. "Where were you?" she asked.

He looked at her strangely and rolled his eyes. "Kate."

"What? Where did you go?" she asked.

"You got to be kidding?" He put Kate back on the floor.

Her eyes didn't waver from his glare. "I'm just asking you a question, Eric."

"I went for a drink, alright?" he said sharply.

"Who were you with?"

"What the hell is this—the third degree?"

Anger spread through her chest. "You know, I haven't seen or talked to you in five days," she said boldly. "I would just like to know where you were!"

"Jesus Christ, Kate. I had a drink with Dianne and Ray." He looked down at her with animosity.

"Why are you drinking?" she asked in a hushed tone. "You know you shouldn't."

"I just had a couple drinks," he said, wanting her to believe him and stop pestering.

"You had more than two, Eric. I know you." Tears filled her eyes, as she stared at her pitiful husband. "Please don't drink. We've been through this."

"I'm not drunk!" he exclaimed and retreated into the dark bedroom, leaving her in the hallway. He started to undress.

She tried to hold it together. "You are still upset about Stuart and I understand that," she said into the darkness.

"You don't understand anything, Kate," he shot back. "Please don't analyze me. It's late and I want to go to sleep."

"How could I understand? You never talk to me anymore." Anger crept into her tone.

"I'm tired of this conversation. I'm going to bed."

"Conversation?" she yelled. "We haven't had a conversation in two months!" She paused to breathe. "We are falling apart and you don't seem to care!"

There was no response. He sat on the bed and stared into the blackness.

There was another question she wanted to ask, but she was deathly afraid of his answer. She peered into the darkness, barely seeing the outline of her husband. The question in her mind lingered, while she rallied her courage. "Do you care about us anymore, Eric?"

He raised his head and looked at her. "I don't know."

After those wounding words, she forgot how to breathe. Everything was shrouded in black. Automatically, she returned to the den, numb, almost in a stupor. She closed the door behind her. She was alone. Her entire body quivered like a lost bird in a fierce rainstorm. She began to sob. Disappointment shook her to the core. She buried her face in the futon, so as to not disturb Eric. She unleashed the emotions within her.

The next morning, the team left for the Big East Tournament in New York City. Another snowstorm disrupted flights and unsettled the players. Eric was tense. He thought little about the previous night. On the flight, he and Dianne talked constantly, always about work.

That evening, the team went to Madison Square Garden for a two-hour practice. The arena was grander than he ever imagined. He always wanted to play basketball in a place like this. This was the closest he would ever get to playing pro ball. It was all he could do to keep his attention on the team.

Back at the hotel, he looked out the window of his room on the 34th floor. He could see the gargoyles lunging out from the Chrysler Building. Light snowfall lulled him into a daydream. He wanted to sleep, but there was a staff meeting set for after dinner. He tried to keep his mind off the reason he had gotten so little sleep the night before.

She awoke in an unfamiliar room: her own, in their bed. The bed was uncomfortable. She reacquainted herself with the things in the room: the trinkets on the bureaus, their wedding picture. The photograph became the object of her rapt attention. Nothing else existed but this photograph. She was haunted by Eric's words. As she fixated on the picture, sadness flooded her. Their vows echoed in her mind. She fought to keep the tears from falling, as she thought about that beautiful day. She didn't want that day to be all for nothing. Life without Eric—she didn't want to consider it even for a second. There was tightness to her chest that she never felt before. It was stress, she knew, and it would not leave her until everything was

settled.
Liz arrived and Kate put on her best disguise. It was a struggle for her to smile. It was a struggle for her to exist. Her eyes were heavy, demanding more sleep, but she didn't falter in keeping them open and alert. It took tremendous energy to maintain her false tranquility.
Liz looked at her warily. "Is everything alright, Kate?"
The question startled her and her left hand struck the underside of the counter in front of her. Pain shot through her knuckles. Kate nodded to answer Liz.
Liz looked at her with trepidation. "Are you sure?" she asked, "because you haven't been quite yourself for the last couple weeks."
"Yeah, I'm fine," she feigned.
Liz removed a bagel from the toaster. "How come I don't believe you?"
"I'm just a little tired, that's all."
Liz spread some cream cheese on the bagel and put it on the plate for her.
"Okay," she said.
The ringing of the telephone interrupted their flagging communication. Liz answered and put the call on speakerphone. It was Meg.
Kate reached deep to find the strength to deal with her curiosity about life. For the first minute or two, she mostly talked and Kate listened. She soon sensed something amiss in Kate's voice. She tried to get to the issue, but Kate concealed her torment, insisting everything was fine. Kate realized Meg knew she was lying and apologized. Liz went out to run an errand. Kate still could not bring herself to talk about Eric, fearing she would never stop crying if she did. She asked Meg if she could call her back in a few days. Meg said she would, then said goodbye. The apartment fell silent. Kate was all alone.
Syracuse lost to Providence College by two points in overtime. The game ended after midnight. Eric lingered in the Garden until all the people had left their seats. Soaring above him were the rays of steel that formed the grand dome.
"Are you ready to get on the bus?" asked Dianne.
"Yeah, I guess."

"Are you up for a drink when we get back to the hotel?"

"Nah, I'm ready to crash," he said. Dark circles under his eyes supported his claim.

"Just one beer?" she pursued.

"I'm pretty beat."

She smiled at him. "Okay."

They walked though the locker rooms out to the bus. The bright lights of Midtown Manhattan on a Friday night failed to hold Eric's interest. All he wanted to do was sleep. At the door of his hotel room, he struggled to get the card in the slot.

"Let me help you with that," she offered.

"You must think I'm a complete idiot not being able to unlock my own door."

"No, no," she said. "Sometimes these cards get bent or screwed up." It took her only a few seconds to thread the card into the slot. She turned the knob and the door opened. "There you go."

"I have clumsy hands," he explained. "Thank you and have a good night."

"Good night, Eric,"

The door shut behind him. He slid into his bed and fell asleep.

The players gathered at Coach Hill's house to watch the announcement of the 64 teams for the NCAA tournament. The living room erupted when they announced Syracuse was headed to Austin, Texas for their shot at the Final Four. Eric and Dianne clanked their beer bottles together.

The jubilation continued for several minutes. Then the room fell quiet, as the players remembered their fallen teammate. They held hands and prayed for Stuart King. Dianne kept holding Eric's hand well after the prayer ended. Eric either didn't notice or didn't care. For a moment, he neglected to pull it away. She loved the way her hand sat in his. It felt so strong and so soft.

By nine o'clock, he was ready to leave. He said goodbye to all and headed out to his truck. He put the key in the ignition and turned it. The engine wouldn't start. He pumped furiously on the gas pedal and turned the key once again, but his efforts were in vain. He got out and ran across the street to catch

Dianne to get a ride home.

He and Dianne conversed easily. They had worked side by side for the past eight months. She frequently glanced over at him and debated whether to move her hand from the stick shift to his hand. She resisted. When she pulled up to his apartment, she looked up at the bay window and saw no lights on inside. He opened the car door. She touched his jacket and took hold of his hand. Thanking her for the ride home, he asked if she could pick him up in the morning. She happily agreed. She sat there for several minutes and watched the lights in the apartment went on, and then off. She drove off, in her own darkness.

Kate awoke when Liz closed the living room door, sleeping for only four hours. A warm shower roused her somewhat, as she geared up for another Monday.

The phone rang and Liz answered. It was for Eric. Joe was in trouble again. The van picked up Kate. She thought about how to tell him the news. She was tense, as she got off the van. She said hello to Sue and then headed to the athletics building. Mrs. Colenza motioned her to go in.

Kate drove to his office door.

Eric greeted her with a lift of his brow. "What's going on?"

"Somebody called from the Boston police," she said. "Joe was arrested last night."

"For what?" he asked harshly, looking away.

His reaction unsettled her. She struggled to answer him. "He hit a car full of kids. He was drunk."

"He was driving?" he asked.

She nodded.

This news brought him to his knees. He held his head in his hands. "Oh God," he said. "Was anyone killed?"

"The guy said a 16-year-old girl is pretty bad."

He trembled.

She resisted her strong urge to touch him. He walked out of the office. She waited for him to return.

Just then, Dianne walked in. She noticed Kate and quickly retreated into the hallway.

There was nothing Kate could feel: no anger, no hurt. She continued to wait.

Eric returned. "I'm gonna catch a flight to Boston this afternoon," he said. "I'll stay the night and fly to Texas tomorrow."

"Okay," she said. "I guess I won't see you until next week."

He looked confused. "Yeah, I guess, if everything goes well," he said.

They searched for words to say to each other.

"Umm," he began, "the truck is at Mike's Garage. It'll be ready probably on Wednesday."

"What's wrong with it now?" she asked, irritated over the truck's chronic problems.

"It died on me last night at Hill's."

"How did you get home?"

He became annoyed. "Dianne brought me home and drove me to work this morning," he said angrily.

She was unwilling to make a scene in his office, so she let his spiteful tone pass. "How much is it gonna be?" she asked.

"About $450," he said.

"Oh, come on," she said, surrendering to her frustration. "We can't afford to put $450 into that truck." She raised her voice. "We could be making a down payment on something else, Eric."

"Just get someone to pick it up," he said and hung the keys on her control stick.

She reminded herself why she was in his office. "Good luck with Joe," she said.

"I'll call," he said.

She nodded and headed back to her office, recovering from yet another unfriendly encounter with her husband.

Chapter 13

The plane was jammed with graying men in business suits. Eric fought a strong temptation to have a drink. The past few weeks had taken a toll that he had not realized. He blamed his exhausting travel schedule. *Soon, it would be over,* he told himself over and over again.

He hurried through the Logan Airport terminal and hailed a cab. On the ride in, he took in the familiar sights of his hometown. For a moment he forgot all about Syracuse, imagining he was going to see his parents in the house he grew up in. The cold reality set in: he wasn't going to see his childhood home; he wasn't going to see his parents. Never would he do these things again.

The cab pulled up to the police station. He paid his fare and went inside. The woman at the front desk explained all the circumstances surrounding Joe's case. The more Eric listened, the more he crumbled inside. She asked Eric for his bag and directed him down the hall to another officer. The clanking of steel bars terrified him. Beads of sweat ran down his temples. His heart raced. An officer directed him into a small room and closed the door. The gray walls seemed to be closing in around him. The only window was a Plexiglas barrier. He felt trapped.

The door opened in the adjacent room and Joe appeared, escorted by a policeman. Joe's face was skeleton-like and unshaven, very different from Christmas Day. *He fit the profile of a criminal,* Eric thought.

"I don't want to hear any excuses coming out of your mouth," he shouted through the holes in the Plexiglas. "Do you hear me?!"

"I didn't do anything!" Joe exclaimed.

Enraged by Joe's denial, Eric put his face closer to the glass and pointed at him. "Own it up, Joe! You're screwed now!" He took a breath and sat down. "You know, if that girl dies you're looking at many years in prison. And I don't give a damn if you spend the rest of your life in prison, Joe."

Joe looked at his brother in disgust. "You can go to hell," he muttered.

"You know what?" Eric said, wearing a slight smirk. "Maybe I will. I'll just leave you to rot here, 'cause that's what you were put on this earth to do."

"I was always the bad seed, wasn't I, Eric?" Joe said, raising his voice. "You were always the apple of Mom's eye. And Dad didn't give a damn about any of us. He would just get drunk off his ass every time he came home."

"Are you blaming him for your crappy life now?" Eric asked.

"Yes, I am," Joe cried out.

"What about Mom, Joe?" asked Eric. "She took care of both of us."

"She didn't love me as much as her beloved little Eric," Joe said, with contempt. "I was a pain in the ass, but my little brother was her star."

"Do you hate me, Joe?" Eric asked. "Is that why you keep getting in trouble all the time, because you want go get back at me?"

"Maybe there's no reason why I am such a screw up," Joe said, calmly. "But if I had to blame someone, I'd stick it on Dad."

Eric glared at his brother. "You never appreciated one thing I did for you!" he snapped.

"I don't need you," Joe said. "I never needed you."

"You know what?" Eric said. "You can bail out your own sorry ass!" Eric left the room and didn't stop walking until he reached the front desk. Outside, the brisk air filled his lungs.

It would take days, maybe weeks for him to recover from the last 40 minutes. It would take longer to get Joe's gaunt appearance out of his head. As he walked, h e examined the streets and buildings. The city was busy. Cars and people moved about, briskly and purposefully, as darkness fell on the day.

Eric got a room at the Holiday Inn. He took a shower to get all the remnants of his horrendous day off of him. Every crevasse of his body was exhausted. The television kept him company, as he succumbed to sleep.

Eric was feeling sluggish and irritable, as he lugged his duffel bag through the labyrinth of the Dallas/Fort Worth airport. He sat in a bar near where he was to meet the team.

A voice on one of the television sets overhead speculated on Syracuse's chances of getting past the round of 64. The commentator picked through every Syracuse weakness, including the tragic loss of Stuart King. The grim day came surging back and Eric's breathing became irregular. His chest tightened. He closed his eyes and wished he was somewhere else, preferably somewhere far away. Opening his eyes, he found himself sitting in the same chair, at the same bar, staring at the same television.

In Austin, he lived within his own tortured world, anguished by his thoughts. Wednesday was another merciless day. John Griffy's father passed away suddenly.

Thursday morning brought a ray of sunlight through his hotel window. He cursed it. The automated wake-up call came at seven o'clock. He cursed the telephone. Time went by slowly. He looked at his watch a thousand times that morning, as if he expected something to happen.

After practice, the team returned to the hotel and got ready for dinner. Eric's beeper went off. It was Kate. A pain impaled his stomach. It seemed to take days for the elevator to get him up to the fourth floor. His legs felt disconnected from his brain.

Liz answered the phone and put Kate on. He listened hard to Kate's clumsy speech. He slid down to the floor and was in a fetal position, as he continued to listen to his wife. The teenage girl had died from her injuries. Kate repeatedly offered support and comfort. Eric felt nothing. He said goodbye and sat motionless at the foot of the bed.

Eric was living in slow motion. He could not distract himself from the empty feeling that seized him. It was almost nine o'clock at night and he hadn't moved from where he had called Kate. He was still as destroyed and ashamed as when he had first heard the cataclysmic news. He was the brother of a murderer, and the son of a lying, drunken, adulterous father. He thought about his mother, whom he loved so much and whom he'd cared for in her last days. He looked vacantly out his hotel window into the night. There was a knock on his door. He sluggishly rose to his feet and opened the door to find Dianne.

"Oh, did I wake you?" she asked, seeing his dark room.

"No, no, I was just watching television," he improvised.

"Why don't you come down and have a drink with us in the

bar?"

He recoiled from the prospect of making cheerful small talk, but figured a drink or two might soothe his mind. "Okay," he mumbled.

They went down to the bar and he wasted no time ordering some beers. A stream of Heinekens soon stripped his anxieties. He drained bottle after bottle. The bar thinned out, as the other staff members retired for the night. Soon, he and Dianne were the only ones left from Syracuse crew.

"My own brother is a murderer," he said without emotion.

"What?" she asked, shocked.

He took a gulp of beer. "He was driving drunk the other night and plowed into a car full of kids," he said. "A 16-year-old girl died this morning."

"Oh, Eric," she said. "I'm so sorry. Is that why you went to Boston?"

"You bet."

She put her arm around him.

"I tried to do everything for the guy. I tried everything!" he said.

"Will he go to jail?" she asked.

"He's already in jail. I hope he stays there for a long time," he said and ordered his seventh beer. "I have to piss again—excuse me."

A few minutes later, he stumbled back to his seat. She grabbed his arm to prevent him from falling.

"Why don't we go upstairs now," she said.

He leaned on her shoulder, as they walked to the elevator.

The door closed, but the elevator remained motionless. She propped him in the corner.

"Can I help you feel better?" she whispered into his ear.

He was oblivious to everything and didn't respond. His eyes were closed.

Dianne boldly made up his mind for him and gently pressed her lips to his, waiting for a reaction. His eyes opened slightly.

He continued to let her kiss him.

"You just need someone to take care of you," she whispered excitedly, kissing him again. She pressed the button and the elevator started its upward motion. She led him quietly to her room and quickly unlocked the door.

At around three in the morning, the bile and beer in Eric's stomach started revolting against him. He awoke in darkness. Dianne was asleep beside him. He rolled and fell hard onto the floor, and crawled into the bathroom to empty out the contents of his stomach.

The floor's cold tiles made him aware of his nakedness. A light went on in the bedroom and he hastily shut the bathroom door. He heard her voice, suddenly realizing his dreadful mistake. He huddled over the toilet again, took a deep breath and asked Dianne to retrieve his clothes.

He crawled behind the bathroom door. She opened it slightly and passed his clothes to him. The door closed and he switched on the bathroom light. As he struggled to dress himself, the pain inside his skull multiplied tenfold.

When he came out of the bathroom, she was waiting for him, wearing nothing. The pain in worsened. He opened the door to the hallway, not uttering a word. A moment later, he was in his own bathroom, huddling over the toilet.

There were many salutes to Saint Patrick on this Friday, but Kate wasn't feeling all that lucky. Eric's devastated voice from the day before echoed in her mind. She asked Carl over to watch the NCAA tournament. Entertaining Carl kept her mind off her husband. It was the first time in a long while that Liz saw a smile on Kate's gaunt face.

The Orangemen were up against Razorbacks of Arkansas. During the game, Carl made it his goal to scout out Eric on the television. "There he is!" Carl exclaimed, pointing to the top-right corner of the screen. By the time Kate fixed her eyes upon the television, Eric was gone.

"Sorry, Kate," said Carl. "Hey, are you coming down with something?"

"No, no—I'm fine," she said.

"Are you sure? Because I've seen you look a hell of a lot better."

She laughed. "Thank you very much."

"You know what I mean," he said.

"Yeah, I do," she said. "I guess I'm just sick of all the snow."

"I second that," he said. "Hey, there's Eric again! He's' coming out onto the court. See him?"

This time, Kate saw him, surrounded by his teammates. He kept his head down, as he walked. Dianne walked behind him, wearing a grin that disturbed Kate.

"He doesn't look happy," Carl said.

"I'm sure he would appreciate that."

"I'm only kidding," he said.

"I know you are," she said, and yet she agreed with Carl's perceptions. She desperately wanted Syracuse to get the win, so Eric would feel something positive in his life. It wasn't to be. The Razorbacks advanced to the round of 32. The season was over for Syracuse.

She wondered about the future and grew anxious. She didn't know what to expect from Eric after his terrible week. She didn't know how they would communicate after two months of arguing. It would be half of a day before she knew.

On the trip back to Syracuse, disappointment weighed heavily on the faces of the team. Eric could not face Dianne, who sat next to him on the plane. Thursday night haunted him, feeling overwhelming guilt. It consumed him. His chest felt like a ton of steel sat upon it. Breathing was difficult. Swallowing was difficult. He felt her hand on his. Instantly, he pulled his hand away.

Dianne pressed for a conversation with him, but he stayed quiet and stared out the window at the clouds. The plane neared Syracuse. He would soon see Kate. It would be hard to look at her. His mouth was dry and his stomach began to cramp.

It was 2:30 in the afternoon when Eric returned home. Kate was working at the computer. He put his bag on the bed.

"Hi," she said softly.

"Hi," he said. "How are things?"

"Things are fine," she said. "Are you alright?"

He didn't know how to answer. "I guess so," he said, unconvincingly. "It's been a tough week."

"Yeah, I know," she said. "Did it go okay with Joe?"

He shook his head. "You know Joe. He denies everything and blames everyone else for his rotten life."

She saw his tremendous distress and knew not to push him

about Joe. "The boys did a good job last night," she said.

"Yeah, they did, they did," he said. He struggled to keep the doomed conversation going, but a long and awkward silence punctuated his words. The longer he failed to speak, the more agitated he became. "I might lie on the couch for a while. I'm beat," he said.

"Okay," she said and tried in vain to look into his eyes before he retreated to the couch. She grew apprehensive about what he was keeping from her, but continued to work.

He turned on the television, breaking the silence in the apartment. She debated whether to join him in the living room and decided not to. It had been months since they had a civil conversation, and she wasn't up to starting one at the moment.

The phone rang. He picked it up. The television muffled his voice, as he spoke to Dianne. She had found his watch in her suitcase and wanted him to come get it. He ruefully agreed to meet her. He got up and went into the den. "That was John," he said. Mindful of his lie, he searched for his next words. "I'm going to go over there for a little while. You need anything before I go?"

"No, I'm fine," she said. "Please tell him how sorry I am about his father."

"I will," he said. "I'll be back soon."

"Okay," she said. "The keys are on the counter."

"Thanks," he said and disappeared.

When he pulled into Dianne's driveway, she was waiting on the front steps. He hurriedly asked for his watch and repeatedly declined her invitations to come inside for a beer. The sun was sinking behind the horizon. He just wanted his watch. She went inside to get it. He wanted to get as far away from Dianne as possible, as soon as possible. She returned with the watch and he grabbed it from her hands. She talked but he wasn't listening. He got into his truck and drove away.

He drove up and down the streets of Syracuse and tried to get his mind off of the tremendous burden he carried. He found a bar and went in. The bar was empty and dark. The television kept his attention, as he sipped a Coke for the better part of an hour.

There was a knock on the door. Kate was startled. She crawled out to the living room and pressed the button that unlocked the door. It was Roberta and John.

"Hi," said Roberta.

"Please, come in," Kate said.

Roberta knelt down and hugged Kate. John did the same.

Kate expressed her sorrow for the loss of his father.

"Thanks, Kate," he said.

"Where's the big guy?" John asked, as he removed his jacket.

"I thought he was with you," she said.

Roberta repeated Kate's words for John.

"No, no, Kate. I haven't seen him since Wednesday morning," he said.

Nervousness overtook her like a strong gust of wind. "He said he was going to see you about an hour ago. Right after you called," she said.

John had trouble comprehending, so Roberta repeated what Kate said.

"Today?" John asked. "I haven't talked to him today, Kate. He said I called?"

"Yeah," she whispered.

"I'm sure he's fine," Roberta said.

Kate felt worthless—worthless as a wife and worthless as a friend in her own home.

Roberta gestured toward John and he withdrew to the bathroom. "What can I do?" she asked, seeing the pain in Kate's eyes.

"I don't know," Kate answered flatly. "He said he'd be back soon."

"Okay," Roberta said. "Would it be better if we left?"

"Yeah, probably," Kate said, confounded.

"Okay, but if he's not back by six, please call me, all right?"

Kate nodded.

Roberta put on her coat. John emerged. "Are we leaving?"

"Yes," answered Roberta.

"Thank you," Kate said and in a moment, she was alone again. Each agonizing minute she waited for him felt like it took a day away from her life. Her mind raced. She thought of every conceivable explanation he might offer for his behavior. Whatever he was hiding, she knew it had to be hurtful. She startled when she heard the truck's door.

She breathed, as he entered the room. "I was waiting for you," she said, amazed how clearly she spoke. "How's John?"

"He's okay," he answered, looking away.

His response tore into her like a knife to her chest. She swallowed hard. "Was Roberta home?" Her voice started to fail.

He hesitated. Her questions made him uneasy. "I think she was at her sister's."

"That's kinda funny," she said, changing to a sharp tone, "because John and Roberta were both here a little while ago. John said he hadn't talked to you today."

Eric struggled to remain standing. He leaned on a chair and slowly sat down in it. He brought his cold hands to his face and stared at the blackness of the night.

"Did you go out to get a drink?"

He looked at the floor. "No, I haven't had a drink today," he murmured.

"Ever since you got home, you haven't looked me in the eye," e said. "Just tell me why?" She was holding herself together by a thread.

Tears welled in his eyes, as he witnessed his wife's longing for the truth.

"Please tell me, Eric," she pleaded.

Thursday night came back like a nightmare. His trembling hands were locked together against his chin. He couldn't tell her. Seconds crept by. As he attempted to speak, his voice shook. "I, ah." He paused to gather himself. "I drank Thursday night. I drank a lot."

She listened and waited. Tears fell from her eyes.

Emotions engulfed Eric and he began to sob. "I didn't mean to—I never meant to hurt you."

She sat like a stone, waiting for him to plow her over. "What happened Thursday night?"

"I didn't make it back to my room, Kate," he said through tears. "I had to get my watch back from Dianne this afternoon."

"Dianne?" she said. He nodded in despair. Unable to look at him, her eyes found the same dark sky. The weight of this crushing news hit her and she began to shake.

He extended his hand and touched her shoulder. "I'm so sorry," he dared.

She turned away and irately pushed his hand away from her. He got up and disappeared into the bedroom. Moments later, he reappeared with his duffel bag and left. She sat alone in the failing light. She heard the whine of the truck, as Eric drove away. She could do nothing but cry.

Eric drove aimlessly and wound up at the Griffys'. While Kate was home crying, he lingered by their door without knocking. After a long moment of miserable indecision, he knocked. It was barely heard. John opened the door.

Roberta asked Eric if he was all right. He did his best to explain and apologized for putting them in an awkward situation. His hands trembled, as he moved his house key from his keychain. John and Roberta looked at each other nervously. Eric gave the key to Roberta and urged her to go to Kate. Roberta's expression turned to extreme concern. John handed her the car keys. Roberta squeezed her husband's forearm and left, all the while avoiding eye contact with Eric.

Kate was still sobbing in front of the couch when Roberta rushed inside. She knelt down and gently stroked Kate's hair. After a few minutes, she was able to get Kate to sit back against the couch; Kate still sobbed uncontrollably. Roberta was still oblivious to what had happened. She held Kate close in her arms for a long time.

The phone rang, surprising them both. They let the answering machine pick up the call. It was John. Kate urged Roberta to take the call. The conversation was brief, but when Roberta hung up tears were running down her face. She turned away from Kate.

The phone rang again. This time it was Brian. Roberta took the cordless receiver into the den and proceeded to tell Brian what had happened. He said he would fly to Syracuse that night. Roberta told him to call from the airport and John would pick him up. Roberta called Liz and asked her to come over.

An hour passed and Kate grew tired of crying. She hated being seen in such a state. She tried to occupy her thoughts, but her mind was in a daze. Roberta returned from the den and offered to get Kate a drink, but she declined. Roberta searched for words that might soothe Kate's pain, but she found none. She offered Kate her shoulder.

Kate startled upon seeing Liz. She began to cry again. Even

though she wanted to be strong, it was all too much to handle. Fifteen minutes went by without a word being spoken. Liz broke the silence. She offered to give Kate a shower. It was only then that Kate realized she hadn't been to the bathroom in five hours.

As she slowly crawled toward the bathroom, Liz conferred with Roberta in the kitchen.

"So, where's the little two-timing bastard now?" Liz asked Roberta in a hushed voice.

"My house," Roberta answered. "He gave me the key to the apartment and said I better come to see Kate. She's been sitting there crying all afternoon."

"She's pretty destroyed," Liz said.

"Yep, she sure is."

"It'll be good to have Brian here," Liz said.

Roberta nodded and an awkward silence enveloped the entire apartment.

"How could he do this to Kate?" Liz whispered.

"I have no idea," Roberta answered. "I can't imagine what she's going through, my God."

"Neither can I," Liz said and headed for the bathroom.

That night, Kate was haunted by the silence that shrouded the apartment. She lied on the futon in the den—her refuge from the rest of the world—and watched TV. Her body fought to get warm under two heavy comforters. Chills traveled up and down her spine like drops from melting icicles. She imagined the long nights ahead. Sleep would evade her. Reliving the previous hours in her mind, she felt like something less than a woman, less than a human being. She convinced herself that she had driven Eric away—her body, so awkward and plastic, nauseated him. Her inadequacies had pushed him to Dianne. The image of Eric in the act of intimacy with Dianne drove all other thoughts out of Kate's head. She thought that Dianne was the better woman. Dianne was able to give him more than Kate ever could. *No longer will he need to worry about coming home to take me to the bathroom,* Kate thought. *No more will he have to feed me every time he ate at home. No more will he have to love me.* She rationalized every negative thing about her marriage as being her fault. Nothing was his responsibility in her manic judgment.

This senseless way of responding to the devastating news was almost a source of relief for Kate. She would never be a soulmate to anyone. No one could ever stay married to this thing—to her. *Maybe my mind is human,* Kate concluded. *But my body isn't.* Now, Eric was free from it.

Hushed voices from the living room awakened Kate. It was eleven o'clock. When she saw Brian in the doorway, tears overcame her again. Brian kneeled on the futon and held her. He stayed by her side until the darkness was wiped away.

Brian awoke and got up without disturbing his sister. As though she didn't have a single worry, Kate was so calm and so peaceful in sleep.

Brian roamed the apartment. The pictures of family gatherings made him smile at first, but then he became angry at Eric. The refrigerator only had a quart of milk and some leftovers. He searched the cabinets and closets for some breakfast, but all he could find was a half-empty box of Special K. He finished it.

As he ate, he looked out the window. The houses across the street were bathed in morning sunlight.

Kate emerged from the den and he greeted her with a smile. He went over and wrapped his arms around her.

She felt embarrassed about her night of crying.

"I thought you would have slept a little longer," he said.

Something about his tone brought out a grin. "It will probably be the last time I ever sleep," she said.

"Oh, Katie," he said and they held each other tighter.

"I don't want to cry anymore," she said, as she fought back tears.

"Okay, okay, we won't cry anymore," he said. "Do you know you hardly have any food?"

"No, really?"

"Yep, no food," he said. "I had to eat some old Special K crap." Hearing Kate laugh was heaven for him. "Can I go out and get you something to eat, Kate?"

"Oh God, no—I couldn't eat anything."

"You need to eat something," he said, gently. "At least have some tea and try eating some toast for me, please."

"Okay, I'll try," she said. "There's some bread on top of the fridge." She watched him. "Does Mom know you're here?"

"No," he said. "I told her I was going on a business trip."

A tiny giggle came from Kate. "You never go on business trips. You sell sports apparel."

"Hell, maybe we had a problem with one of our distributors or something. How would she know?"

"Well, it *is* a little fishy, going on a business trip on a Saturday night."

"Hey, don't worry about what Mom is going to think," Brian said. He turned and looked her straight in the eye. "This wasn't your fault. He's the one who screwed up here."

Humiliated, she looked at the floor. "I didn't help."

"What the hell does that mean?" he asked. "You are not to blame for this, and if you think differently you're very much mistaken." He put his hand on her shoulder. "What did you do?"

"I made him love me," she said and started to cry.

"Oh, Katie," he said. He was consumed with her grief. Anger started to rage inside of him. He wanted to see Eric, but worried what he might do once he saw him. He turned his attention back to relieving Kate's pain. The teakettle whistled.

Sleep evaded Kate again. She felt she was teetering on the edge of a cliff. She stayed in the den, refusing to sleep in their bed. She found no comfort anywhere. Eric was everywhere, like a ghost, and she could not escape his presence. It was only when she was in Brian's comforting arms that she felt safe and could drift into a deep sleep.

Brian dared not move from the couch, fearing he might wake her. He worried about what was going to happen. He did not want her to grow old alone. He ran his fingers through her hair, careful not to disturb her as she slept.

Meg called and mistook Brian's voice for Eric's. Brian was glad to hear Meg's voice and quickly explained Kate's plight. The news confounded Meg and she fought to control her anger and sadness. She grew worried about how little Kate was eating. Meg urged Brian to get Kate to eat and drink.

Eric's name barely came up, as the two grappled with the cruelty of his conduct toward Kate. They reflected on all their years of happiness. No one knew what the future held, especially for Kate. Brian promised Meg he would keep in touch. Meg wanted Kate to call her whenever she was ready.

On Monday morning, Kate persuaded Brian to let her go to work. Spring was approaching and sunlight splashed on the kitchen floor, as he prepared breakfast. He told Kate tasteless and dirty jokes. Her laughter masked her tremendous sadness in her heart. She wondered how she was going to get through the day. She would to stay in her office to avoid running into Eric on campus.

Soon, Liz came and introduced herself to Brian. Liz urged Kate to stay home but she refused.

Liz showered Kate and noticed her ribs were now visible. Concerned, Liz, pressed Kate to eat a full breakfast. She reluctantly agreed. Liz applied some makeup to hide Kate's ghostly pallor.

Kate felt like a circus act, waiting to be gawked at by thousands of spectators. She managed to eat a decent breakfast, her first major achievement this day, and it wouldn't be her last. Energy slowly returned to her weak body.

The sun filled the morning sky, as she made her way to campus, with Brian walking alongside. Few words were exchanged. He feared saying the wrong thing and upsetting her. They enjoyed the warm sunshine beating down. Winter would soon be gone.

Nearing the campus, Kate looked at every passing car on the off chance of spotting Eric.

"Are you sure you're going to be okay?" Brian asked outside of her office.

"Yeah, yeah, I'll be fine," she said, flatly. "What are you going to do today?"

He squatted down beside her. "I thought I'd do some grocery shopping and then stop by your office for lunch. John said I could borrow his car."

"Please don't go see Eric," she begged.

He looked away, but failed to hide his intentions.

"Brian, please, please stay away from Eric," she said, searching for his reassurance. "This is our problem. As much as you want to kick the hell out of him, we need to work this out ourselves."

"Okay," Brian mumbled and kissed her cheek. "I'll see you soon." He was uneasy about leaving her, knowing she would have a difficult time getting through the morning.

Sue greeted Kate with the usual kind words and helped set up her computer and headstick. Kate said she had an okay weekend and left it at that. She managed to disguise her overwhelming grief. As more people walked by and said hello, she started to feel herself imploding like a condemned building. She hated the attention and felt absurdly self-conscious. She swore that the words "used, damaged, foolish" were emblazoned across her chest. People stopped and chatted, but she had trouble paying attention and devoted all her effort to keeping a smile on her face. It was physically draining to keep up this manufactured facade.

A few buildings over, Eric sat with his head in his hands at his desk. The office was quiet. Colberg was busy wrapping up the last details of the basketball season. Dianne was in Albany, attending a two-day nursing conference. Eric worked because he knew she was out of town.

His images of Kate devastated haunted him. He despised himself and everything he was. He cursed himself. He cursed his dead father. Memories of his mother came flooding back. Kate's defeated expression was the same one he had seen on his mother's face, as she lay dying. He was destroying Kate, just as his father had destroyed his mother. He recalled his mother's last words: "Take care of Kate," who was at his side. Kate's presence had given him strength to get through his mother's illness. She loved Kate as much as he did and didn't want Eric to repeat the sins of his father. She wanted Eric to love Kate and knew that he would.

Sadness filled every niche of his body. Tears rolled down his face, as he recognized his failure to honor his mother's dying wish.

Kate was relieved that half the day was over. Mr. Leonard was in her office, chatting idly about various work-related issues. To Kate's relief, Brian arrived before the conversation turned personal. A big smile appeared on her worn face. He smiled back and introduced himself to Mr. Leonard.

"So, how long are you in Syracuse?" Mr. Leonard asked.

"A few days," Brian answered, concealing his uncertainty.

"Oh, good," Mr. Leonard said. "What are you two doing for lunch?

Kate looked up at Brian.

"I thought we might head down to that little falafel place near campus," said Brian. "We have some catching up to do. So much has happened since Kate and Eric moved to Syracuse."

"That's a plan," Leonard said. "Why don't you take the afternoon off. Nothing is going on later that is overly pressing."

Kate considered the offer and concluded that either she looked like a wreck, or there was indeed nothing pressing happening this afternoon. "Are you sure?" she typed.

"Yeah, I'm sure," said Leonard, cheerfully. "You haven't heard from Ms. Dixon, have you?"

"She probably won't call back before the next ice age," the computer said.

"I know, I know," said Mr. Leonard. "Go on, enjoy the afternoon."

"Thank you," she said.

"Thank you, Mr. Leonard," Brian repeated. He turned off her computer and removed her headstick.

In the sunlight, Brian detected a rosy glow to Kate's skin and was pleased to see the improvement. "You amaze me with your strength," he commented, as they walked to John's car.

"I'm not strong, Brian," she said.

They didn't speak again until they reached the restaurant. It was the kind of silence that grows from mutual respect. Speaking would have degraded the moment. As the gentle breeze stirred the trees, they delighted in the spring air.

Kate arrived home with the notion that Eric wouldn't be walking through the same door later. The mailbox held letters with his name, but he wasn't there to open them. Brian helped her into sweats and started dinner. The bedroom was eerily dark. Something inside the bedroom beckoned her to enter. She resisted as long as she could, but soon her will was broken. She crawled in. The closet door begged to be opened. As the door swung open, the light clicked on. The sight of Eric's suits arrayed on their hangers lured her within.

Her arm bounced around, as she reached up to touch the soft

fabric. She loved the feel of his clothes. She loved their smell, the smell of him. Lost in reverie and desire, she briefly forgot her pain.

She looked at Brian, as he discovered her. All her sorrow came rushing back and she crumbled into his arms.

Chapter 14

Eric awoke on his office couch, still exhausted. The office was empty and he struggled to keep busy and focus on his work. He wanted to go see Kate, but could offer no defense for his actions—and probably never would, he presumed. Every so often he picked up the phone, but he had nobody to call.

He heard the elevator doors open and peered into the hallway. A neatly attired man was holding a small boy.

Eric walked behind the reception desk. "May I help you?" he said.

"I'm looking for Dianne Jensen," said the gentleman.

Eric recoiled. "Um, Dianne isn't in right now. May I have her get in touch with you?"

"I was really hoping to catch her tonight," the man said. He reached into his back pocket and pulled out some folded papers. "I really need Dianne to sign these as soon as possible."

"Oh, okay," Eric said. "I can put them in her box if you'd like."

"I'm sorry, I'm Mark Jensen," he said and reached to shake Eric's hand.

"Yes, I'm Eric Hollis," he said. "Nice to meet you, Mark."

As the men talked, the child babbled.

"And this is our son, Jake," Mark said.

Eric looked at the young boy and smiled weakly, trying to hide his disbelief.

"He has cerebral palsy."

Eric crumbled. "I didn't know Dianne had a son." He reached out and touched Jake's dark hair.

Mark sighed and kissed his precious child. "Yeah, well, Dianne hasn't dealt with it too well. He's a good boy."

"Can I hold him?" Eric asked.

"Sure you can," Mark said. "It'll give me a chance to write Dianne a note."

Eric came around the desk and lifted up Jake's little body.

"You know," Mark said, "nobody has ever asked to hold Jake, outside of the family."

Eric imagined it was Kate he was holding in his arms. Memories from the past seven years came flooding back, as if a tidal wave swept him over, washing away everything in his path. If he ever had any doubts about how much he loved his wife, they were all washed away as he clutched little Jake.

"You have kids?" asked Mark.

"No," he said in a fragile voice. "Not yet, anyway."

"You are good with him," Mark said.

Eric was truly enthralled with this little person.

"My wife has cerebral palsy," Eric said. The full force of the mistakes he made over the past few months came crashing down on him. He whole-heartedly hated himself.

"Really?" Mark said. "How long have you been married?"

"Two years this past October. But we've been together for seven." Eric's emotions were overtaking him. He struggled to not to drown.

Mark smiled and nodded. "That's great!" Mark finished his note to Dianne and handed it to Eric. "We've been divorced for nearly two years. Jake was just one when our divorce became final," explained Mark. "It's tough to hold things together these days."

Hit by another ugly untruth from Dianne, Eric sank inside. The joy of holding Jake kept Eric afloat.

"Thanks for your help," Mark said, as he took Jake back into his arms. Mark shook Eric's hand again.

"Oh, no problem, Mark," he said. "Dianne should be home this evening. She went to an overnight conference in Albany."

"It'll be fine if she signs those papers in the morning," Mark said. "Thanks again."

"Not a problem," Eric said. He waved goodbye to Jake, as they disappeared into the elevator.

Eric slumped against his desk and slid down onto the carpet. He couldn't think. In his confusion, all he could see was Kate. He wanted to touch her and to hold her. He created this mad eruption in their lives and now it was up to him to rectify it. Angry, he knew he needed to confront Dianne. She had used him, lied to him, and seduced him.

His gold wedding band caught his eye. It had been a long time since he had touched the ring against Kate's. As he considered his next step, he rotated the ring around his finger. His mind became clearer once he realized what was ahead of him.

Dianne arrived home a little before six. The night was clear and cold, but calm. The moon shone bright overhead. She saw Eric standing on the sidewalk and dashed over to him.

"What a pleasant surprise. Are you waiting for me?" she exclaimed. She attempted to kiss him. He took a quick step backwards.

"I held your son today," he said.

The words left her dumbfounded. "My son—I don't have any kids, I told you."

The denial outraged him. "Oh God," he said, as he looked to the star-filled sky. "You are truly unbelievable." He couldn't bring himself to look at Dianne, for if he did, she would reflect all the mistakes he had made in the past months. "I came to drop off papers that Mark needs you to sign," he said, enraged.

She took the papers and shoved them in her jacket pocket. "Come inside, I'll explain everything," she said.

"I'm not coming inside!" he shouted. "I don't care if I ever see you again!" He looked straight into her ebony eyes. He turned around and headed for his truck. She pulled violently on his jacket.

"What are you doing?!" he said.

"We love each other!" she shouted.

He was startled by her sudden loss of composure. He realized he might be in danger. He grabbed her wrists and exclaimed, "Dianne, don't do this!"

"Let me go!" she squealed and pulled him toward the ground. Eric fell onto her.

"I don't love you, Dianne!" he said, emphatically.

"You do love me!" she protested. He tried to scramble away, but she prevented him from standing. "Remember Thursday night?" He slipped and fell hard onto the pavement. "I love you!"

He panicked, as he struggled to get away. "I don't love you," he yelled, squeezing and twisting her wrists. "Thursday night was a mistake, alright?" he said. The strong grip she had on his jacket withstood all of his efforts to break free. "I love my wife!" he said.

"How can you love something like that?" she said, insanely.

A rush of adrenaline propelled him free and he left her on the ground. In his rush to get away, he tripped and grabbed onto the hood of his truck. She caught him by the ankle.

"Let go of me, Dianne!" he said. His heart was pounding harder and harder, as he clambered into his truck and locked the doors. He turned the key, but the truck didn't start. Ruthlessly, he pumped the gas pedal before the engine started.

She stood in front of his truck. Her expression was both beseeching and menacing. Without a second thought, he threw the truck into reverse and punched the accelerator. The tires spun wildly and the truck lurched away from her. He sped off.

Eric found himself parked in an empty lot at Syracuse University. He was still breathing heavy, but his adrenaline was slowly subsiding. The darkness that surrounded him put fear into his soul. He looked into the rearview mirror to be sure she hadn't followed him.

His body shook and tears streamed down his face. His chest swelled with every cruel breath he gasped. Shrouded in darkness, he wept endlessly as he reflected on the past year. The anger, the frustration, the sadness poured out of him like a burst dam. On the passenger's seat, something glimmered in the darkness. It was his gold watch, which he placed there three days ago. He picked it up and ran his fingers gently over the engraved letters on the reverse side. He didn't need to read the inscription. He knew the words by heart. It was too much for him to bear. He hated himself for breaking her dreams. He hated himself for breaking her. He wept hard.

Kate said on the floor in the kitchen, as Brian prepared dinner. She had successfully made it through another day. In recent days, her goals consisted of holding herself together. "How long are you going to stay?" she asked him.

He stopped peeling the potato and looked down at her. "As long as you need me here."

"Don't you miss Allison?" she asked.

"Of course I do, but I'm here for you," he said in a caring voice. "Don't worry about me right now."

She sighed and smiled up at him. "Thank you for being here."

He kneeled in front of her. "Hey, I'm your brother and you needed me." He kissed her forehead.

The phone rang and he went into the living room to answer

it. "This woman wants to talk to you," he called out to her.

"Who is it?"

"I don't know—she won't say," he answered, perplexed.

"Put her on speakerphone," she said, crawling toward the phone.

He nodded. "Hold on, I'm going to put you on the speakerphone." He carried the phone close to her and pressed the button.

"Hello," she tried to say clearly.

"Is this Kate Hollis?" the caller asked.

"Yes," she answered, not recognizing the voice.

"This is Dianne Jensen."

Immediately, she grew anxious. "Dianne?"

"Well, I just wanted to tell you that I plan to get Eric back," Dianne said.

Brian stared at the phone and Kate looked hopelessly at him.

"So I advise you to watch your back." *Click.*

Kate and Brian gazed at each other in disbelief. Then reality set in and she began to quiver with fright.

"I'm calling Roberta," he said, decisively. He pressed the speed-dial button marked with her name and waited anxiously until she picked up. "Hi Roberta, this is Brian."

Fear started playing havoc with Kate's vital organs: her heart pumped faster, her lungs breathed irregularly, her intestines started to cramp. All her energy drained from her body. Her face turned porcelain white.

"We got a strange phone call from Dianne," Brian said to Roberta. "She threatened Kate."

Roberta responded with outrage. Brian never took his eyes off of Kate.

"He's there?" he said, and Kate knew who Brian was referring to. "Okay."

"What?"

"Eric's on his way over," he said.

Kate closed her eyes for several seconds. "I have to go sit in the bathroom for a while."

"Okay, Katie, let's go," Brian said. Even though his sister's fragile state frightened him, He tried to remain calm. She had lost a noticeable amount of weight over the past couple of days and Brian wasn't sure how much more of this she could take.

He started wondering how much more he could endure.

In a few minutes, he would face Eric. Anger built up inside of him, donning an invisible coat of armor. Brian was preparing for war—a war he wanted to fight on behalf of his sister. He desperately wanted to give her strength, but all he could give was hope.

Eric knocked on his own door. Brian appeared and stared harshly at him. Several seconds passed without a word exchanged between them. Brian's intense glare consumed every good intention Eric possessed.

"May I come in?" Eric asked with a wavering voice.

"It's your apartment," said Brian. His first instinct was to punch Eric in the stomach, but his conscience restrained him.

As he cautiously walked into the living room, Eric's cold hands were in his pockets.

"Remember that promise you made me last year?" Brian heatedly asked. "Congratulations for blowing it all to hell."

Shame overtook Eric hard. No response could redeem him. He looked away in disgrace. "Where's Kate?" he asked. The words dropped uninflected from his lips.

"Right now she's in the bathroom, shitting out the last of her nerves from her skinny little body," Brian said in frustration.

Eric's hands trembled. "Oh, God," he said, bracing his head in his hands.

Brian directed his loathing gaze at Eric's flushed face.

"If she's up to it, I'd like to see my wife, please," Eric said, bravely.

Brian stepped forward. "I'm gonna tell you now, if you dare upset Kate again, I'm going to tear your spine out. Understand?!"

Eric nodded, convincingly. Brian's gaze impaled him with daggers. Brian went to check on Kate. Eric paced, searching for some object to distract him. He found nothing. He felt like something in the room was out of place. He realized it was he that was out of place—in his own home.

Brian gently sat her down in front of the couch. "Be strong," he whispered into her ear and left.

Eric was struck by Kate's withered form. Her face was turned away from him. He slid out of his chair and kneeled in front of her. "I'm so sorry, Kate," he said in a low, agonized voice.

She startled upon hearing his voice. It was a voice she had loved for many years, and now it equated betrayal. She could not look him in the eye. If she did, she would lose her strength altogether. She peered glumly into the darkness beyond the window.

He moved closer. "Please look at me, Kate," he said, almost begging.

Tears filled her eyes. She swallowed again and again, but couldn't bring herself to look at him.

"Please, Kate," Eric pleaded, sorrowfully.

It was inevitable that she had to look at him. It was time to do so now. She bowed her head to the floor and then slowly lifted her drawn face for his inspection.

Upon seeing the brutal consequences of his actions upon her expression, he spoke through tears. "I never meant for any of this to happen."

Consumed by her emotions, she was unable to respond the way she wanted. Words gathered in her throat like a blockade. "But..." she managed to say. She swallowed hard and tried again. "But it did."

Through his stream of tears, he could not disagree.

She used all her energy to push the next words from her heavy chest. "Why did she..."

"Why did she call?" he guessed, trying to finish the sentence. She nodded. "Mark dropped by the office today, looking for Dianne," he said. "She was in Albany for a conference. I had never met Mark before today. He came in with their son, Jake." He took a deep breath. "Jake has CP."

"She has a kid?"

He nodded. "I held him," he said. A gentle smile momentarily diverted his tears. "I remembered how good it was to hold you."

She abruptly looked away from him, trying to hold together.

"And so I went and confronted Dianne," he said. "She denied even having a son!" He heard Kate's sobs. He debated whether she could handle hearing the rest of the story. He pressed on. It had to be told. "She just snapped. First, she begs me to stay; then she tells me that I love her, so I said no I don't—I told her I love you."

The lump in Kate's throat doubled in size. "Did you ever..." she said before pausing to take a breath, fighting back her sadness. Words wouldn't come freely. She resolved to head-spell the rest.

He focused intently on her eyes. "L?" he guessed.

She nodded and drew the second letter.

"O?"

She drew the third letter, a V.

"Do I love—did I ever love Dianne?" he asked. His tone already answered his wife's question.

"Yeah," she said, eager to hear his answer.

"No. God no," he said, without hesitation. "I love you. I always have and I always will. I was so upset that night in Austin, about everything, about Joe, about Stuart, and I just wanted the pain to go away. I didn't know how to deal with it. I knew that drinking myself into oblivious would take it all away for a while."

"I wanted to talk to you," she said, strongly. "I've wanted to talk to you for months, but you've been shutting me out!" Tears streamed down her face. She looked him in the eye.

"I know I have, Kate," he said, "and I'm sorry. I know I've hurt you deeply." He resisted the urge to touch her. "It's been a tough year."

She nodded in agreement.

He gazed around the dimly lit room. He wanted so badly to tell her how he had rebuffed Dianne time and again, how she had preyed on him that night in Austin—that he had no idea what, if anything, happened on her bed in that hotel room—and how disgusted he had been with himself. Kate had been through enough. "You know you're the only one I have, Kate. I don't want to lose you."

She wanted more than anything to accept him back, but she didn't know how. "What now?" she asked.

Before he tried to answer, the phone rang. He picked up the receiver. "Hello?" As he listened, he grew enraged. "If you dare call here again and threaten my wife, I'll have you arrested!" he shouted and slammed the phone down.

"Oh, God," she said.

Brian emerged from the den. "Was that her again?" he asked,

comforting Kate.

"Yeah," Eric answered. *What crazy stunt will Dianne try next?* "I would like to stay the night, just in case she tries something else," Eric said. He knelt down in front of Kate. "Can I stay?"

Kate naively looked to Brian for an answer.

"It's up to you," he said.

The decision was about more than just letting Eric stay overnight. For Kate, it was about forgiving him. She tried to imagine the future. It was hard to imagine her life without him. She loved him so much. "You can stay," she answered, meeting his tired gaze.

"Thanks," Eric said, with a slight smile.

"You need to drink something, Katie," Brian demanded.

"Okay," she said.

"I'll get it," Eric said, willing.

Eric woke up when Liz arrived. She did not speak to him, but only gave a blazing glare when she walked by. Brian informed Liz about the events of the previous night. She grew anxious and went to check on Kate in the den. She was fast asleep. She looked so peaceful. Liz reluctantly awakened her.

Kate smiled when she saw the numbers on the clock: it was by far the longest rest she'd had in months. Now, there was another day to conquer in this painful week, but today she felt more prepared. After her shower, she spoke to Eric. With a sincere voice, he told Kate his plans for the day. Out the living room window, Kate watched him drive off.

It was a beautiful morning in late March. Wispy clouds floated overhead. As Kate rolled down the driveway, she recalled her fascination with the couple across the street. The young woman appeared and walked toward her car, cradling a newborn child. The man emerged and opened the car door for her. The smile on her face told of the sweetness of the new life that reposed in her embrace.

Brian sensed the process of healing had begun. Kate watched the familiar car, as it disappeared around the corner. She resolved not to worry about the mysterious couple from this moment forward. She knew their precious child would hold them together. She looked up at Brian and smiled. They set out on their long walk to campus.

She looked forward to her meeting with Carl, but feared he would notice her frail appearance. The spring air helped her feel closer to her old self, even though her body was slower to recover. The main campus library was her destination. She knew all the short cuts and was familiar with all the sidewalks. Kate looked up. *Leaves will soon appear,* Kate imagined.

She heard someone call out her name. She turned around and was terrified to see Dianne walking toward her.

"You ruined him," Dianne said. "How can he love you?"

Fear overtook her entire body. Her heart was beating faster and faster. She struggled to control her muscles, trying desperately to keep her hand on the wheelchair's joystick. Dianne was ten feet away, looking crazed.

"Do you love him?" Dianne asked and stepped closer.

Kate didn't know what to do. She looked around for help, but saw nobody. Dianne was fidgeting with something in her pocket of her denim jacket.

"Do you love him?!" Dianne repeated, only louder, startling Kate.

"Yes!" Kate exclaimed.

"What did you say?" Dianne asked. "You're just like my son, who can't walk or talk! He's retarded!" She was growing more agitated. "How can Eric love you? I can love him so much better than you can. You've ruined him."

Frustrated and fearful, Kate had to get away from Dianne. She succeeded in getting her hand on the joystick and took off at full speed. She put all her effort into keeping her hand on the joystick and didn't look back. She sped toward the athletics building.

Kate was fighting her own adrenaline. She kept the joystick pressed forward until she reached the building. A passing student held the door open for her, and she passed quickly into the lobby and headed for the elevator.

She labored to reach out to press the call button. Her clenched knuckles skimmed past the target button on several attempts. Every muscle in her body was rigid. She rested her arm and tried again, this time holding her breath in the hope of steadying her hand. Finally, she hit the button. Inside, the elevator started traveling upward.

Getting her hand back on the joystick took a strenuous effort. The elevator doors opened onto Eric's floor. She slammed her hand down violently on the joystick. The wheelchair jerked forward and nearly hit the reception desk.

Mrs. Colenza alerted Eric to Kate's arrival, giving a friendly nod to Kate to head down to his office.

Eric stepped out of his office and saw Kate battling to control her wheelchair. "Oh God," he murmured. "You saw her, didn't you?" Out of breath, Kate vigorously nodded her head. He took hold of the joystick and steered she into his office. "Where?" he asked.

She breathed deeply several times, trying to calm down. He put his hand on her shoulder, as she started to head-spell. He looked on intently.

B...E...H...

"Behind?" he conjectured.

She nodded. L...I...B...R—

"Behind the library?!" He became tense, as the realization set in that something dreadful could have happened to Kate. "Are you okay?" With a tender hand, he touched her face. "I'll call security."

He stood and dialed the phone. "I'm so sorry, Sweetie," he whispered, as he waited on the line for an answer.

"She's really sick, Eric," Kate managed to say.

"I'm discovering how sick she really is," he said.

Kate remained in his office for the entire afternoon. He called Meg and arranged for Kate to stay with her in New Hampshire through college break. Eric stumbled over his words in obvious embarrassment, explaining the recent events to Meg. It was gut-wrenching for him. Anguished, he admitted everything to one of his dearest friends.

He called Mr. Leonard and explained that Kate needed to leave for break a few days early due to a family emergency. He relayed her disappointment about missing her meeting with Carl. Mr. Leonard would take care of Carl and apologize for her absence.

The afternoon went by slowly. Kate sat next to the window, as he worked at his desk. There was so much to look out upon: students walking to and from class, the trees waving in the chilly, early spring air. Memories of her days at college came back. She wanted to return to those days when life was so ordinary. They loved each other so much. She smiled freely at the memories.

Exhaustion was written all over his body. He was in a boxing match and his opponent was himself, visibly losing in the eleventh round.

"Have I ruined you, Eric?" she asked, breaking a long silence.

"Honey, where would you get an idea like that?" he asked.

"Dianne," she answered. "She said I ruined you."

"Oh Katie, she doesn't know what she's talking about," he said.

Kate sighed deeply. "Even if she hadn't said it, have I ruined you?" she pursued, pressing him for an answer.

He stood and approached her. "How would you ruin me?"

"I don't know, I don't know," she said and became emotional. "Maybe she's right?"

"She's not right, babe," he said. "Come here." He closed the office door and brought her over to the couch. "You haven't ruined me, babe," he said, as he sat down in front of her and held her knee.

Kate saw tears welling up in his eyes. "Do I give you everything you need?"

"Katie, you do, you do," he answered without hesitation. He caressed her cheek. "I swear to God you do."

His affirmation brought tears to her eyes. "You could've had anyone in the world. You picked me," she said. "Why?"

"Do you think I spent the last seven years with you because I felt sorry for you?" he demanded.

"No," she said, "but look at me, Eric. What do you see in me?"

"Do you know why I married you—I married you because you were so strong, babe, and I needed someone who was strong. You were there, living life like anyone else. I thought you were amazing the first time I saw you."

"I'm not strong, Eric," she struggled to confess.

"Yes you are, Sweetie," he said. "If I could take back the past year and do it all over again, I would—much better this time. I've made some horrible mistakes with us, Katie, I know. I've been selfish with us."

"If I was so strong," she said, fighting tears—she had to look away in order to get the words out—"I would have made you talk to me, but I didn't have the courage."

"I was a jerk, Kate," he said. "I thought I could handle everything myself, without bothering you. I should have bothered you before things got out of hand."

She nodded and cried.

"Please stay with me, Katie," he begged.

She looked away in embarrassment. She had always imagined that it would be she who said these words, if it ever got to this moment. She still didn't believe she was worthy of his love. She had contrived Eric would be happy without her. And if he was happy without her, then she would be happy. She tried to imagine life without him.

"What are you thinking about?" he asked. She couldn't summon an answer. "I made a vow to you—I intend to keep it."

The more praise she heard from her husband, the more she cried. His tears matched hers in quantity.

"I'll tell you what," he said. "You go to Meg's, relax, eat some food, and think about us." His gaze was pure devotion. "Whatever you decide, we'll do."

She mulled his words for several seconds and nodded in affirmation.

With a gentle stroke of his thumb, he caught a tear as it slid down her flushed face. "I love you," he said.

Chapter 15

The plane landed in Manchester and Kate awakened to the captain's voice over the intercom. Brian was sitting beside her, ready to help her sit up. She looked out the window at the rush of blue and red lights. At the terminal, she and Brian waited for her wheelchair to be brought up from cargo. shee engaged in creative imagination, as she watched the line of people walking toward the exit. She speculated in their reasons for coming to Manchester, New Hampshire. *The young ones may be on break from college,* Kate thought. A middle-aged, well-dressed man was probably here on business. He looked back at Kate. *Is he guessing why I've flown to Manchester? Can he tell that my husband has behaved cruelly toward me?* She grew weary of this little game and closed her eyes. She sensed Brian's eyes upon her. When she opened her eyes, he looked away. She reassured him that she would survive this blow and thanked him for being there for her.

She and Brian sat in silence. She grew apprehensive about the upcoming weeks and feared being apart from him. He had been her fortification for the past four days and now it was time for her to begin rebuilding her life on her own.

The wheelchair came and Brian wheeled Kate out to the arrivals lounge. A slight spasm in her stomach reminded her that she was not prepared for what her reaction might be on seeing Meg. *Maybe it will be embarrassment?* she thought, taking one last deep breath before she began the next step of her reclamation.

Meg was easy to spot in the sparse crowd. Kate battled to avoid crying. She looked away, as she sought to regain her composure. Meg squatted and hugged her. They headed for baggage claim, where Allison was waiting to throw her arms around Brian. He was caught off balance by Allison's enthusiasm to see him. It pleased Kate to see them so happy and a smile broke through.

They got their luggage and made their way to the garage. Brian helped Kate into Meg's car, giving his sister a bear hug, and making her promise that she would call him if ever she needed him. They said their goodbyes. Meg started the car. As Kate waved goodbye, she already missed Brian.

The ride to Jaffrey began awkwardly, as she initially recoiled at the prospect of rehashing her story for her best friend. In the failing light, she caught her reflection in the side window and studied her image. She scrutinized her eyes for something that would make Eric desire her. This shell that was her body—she believed it was a hindrance to everyone around her. She deeply felt Eric's love for her, but still could not accept it.

Meg drove down her dirt road and pulled into the driveway. Kate wasn't ready for the overwhelming sadness she felt in being there without Eric. She could not repress the surge of memories that came along with being at Meg's house and barn.

The main house was still cherry-red. The smell of wood burning smoke from the chimney was heavenly to her. She knew she was in Jaffrey.

Meg jockeyed her wheelchair inside. Meg went out to get her luggage, while Kate looked around the familiar old farmhouse kitchen. Everything was exactly the same from her last visit. She couldn't face going inside the barn and all the memories that would come flooding back.

Meg returned with her luggage. "Want a beer? I'm gonna have one."

"No, thanks," Kate said.

"Oh, come on, have a beer with me," Meg said. She reached into the refrigerator and grabbed two beers. She put a straw in Kate's and put it in front of her. "Hungry?"

"Oh God, no."

"You look like you could use a good meal," Meg said. "You're skin and bones. How about a big breakfast tomorrow?"

Kate postured a slight grin. "Okay," she said.

Meg lit up a cigarette.

"When did you start smoking again?" Kate asked.

"Sunday night," Meg said and blew a column of smoke at the ceiling.

"Oh, lovely."

"It wasn't your fault," said Meg, reassuring her friend with a smile. "I was planning to start again anyway. Drink your beer."

Kate worried that her stomach might reject it. She did drink it, sleep would come easily. She took a sip and it settled in her empty stomach. She took a second and third sip.

"It's been a tough few days, hasn't it?" Meg asked.

Kate looked away and nodded, feeling her throat tighten.

"Want to go to bed?" Meg asked.

Kate nodded.

"Okay, let's go," Meg said. Kate collapsed in a ball of tears. "Oh, Kate," she said. Meg hugged her and was struck by how much weight Kate had lost. "Kate, you know Eric loves you. You know that," Meg said sternly. "Things are going to work out."

Meg wheeled Kate into the guest bedroom. The tears rolled down Kate's cheeks. Sleep brought a welcome close to this harrowing day.

Spending several days with Meg restored Kate's body and soul. She had always thought of this house and barn as her and Eric's place of beginning. She contemplated everything that surrounded her, and thought about her life. On weekdays, she went to work with Meg, back to the Miller School, where she and Kate first met. Old acquaintances at the school greeted her warmly. It meant a lot that she remained important to these people. Some asked about Eric. Meg deflected the bullets by explaining that he had to remain in Syracuse for spring break. Whenever his name came up, Kate would bow her head, shielding her translucent eyes. Some knew the reason why she had come to visit Meg, but none pressed the subject. In the evenings, friends gathered at Meg's. Some stayed past midnight. They saw to it that Kate ate some food and drank a beer to put some weight back on that skinny body, occasionally coaxing Kate into paying a visit to the barn. She wasn't ready to take that step. As much as she enjoyed their company, she wasn't ready to discuss her life in front of them. She wasn't in the mood to break down in front of everybody.

Mornings were difficult. It was hard waking up apart from him. Every morning, she asked herself why she wasn't in her own bed. She imagined what Eric was doing that exact moment, often wondering if he was thinking of her.

The kids at the Miller School all had serious physical and emotional problems, and Kate was moved by the tremendous love Meg and the other counselors had for the students. She remembered how Eric related to her at the start of their relationship. He would look her in the eye when she talked, determined to understand her every word. She recalled the joyful expression on his face when he understood what she was saying—he was so strong, so willing. Was she as strong as Eric said she was?

One of the younger students was struggling to communicate with a counselor by using a word board. He indicated the numbers 1, 3, and 4 on the boards; word No. 134 corresponded with the word "music." The counselor asked the student if he wanted to listen to music. The student answered with a smile. Kate admired the young man, who, despite very limited functions, had ten times the strength that she possessed. Her thoughts returned to Eric, ashamed he was carrying the burden of both of them. He had the strength of a thousand men.

She felt Meg's hand on her shoulder. It was time to go.

As Meg stirred a pot of noodles, Kate sat in the dimly lit kitchen.

"Talk to me," Meg demanded.

Deep in thought, Kate failed to register all of her friend's words. "Uh?" she said and looked up at Meg.

"Talk to me," Meg repeated, sitting down next to Kate. "You haven't really said anything significant since you got here. Five days is enough time. Tell me what's in that head of yours."

"I don't know," she said, stalling, brutally aware Meg wasn't going to let her leave the kitchen until she opened up.

"What the hell kind of answer is that, 'I don't know'?" Meg said and took a drag from her cigarette. "You've got to come up with something better than that."

"He said I was strong," Kate said.

"Who? Eric?"

She nodded.

"Are you?"

"I don't know."

"Dammit, Kate," Meg said, "you know what your problem is? You're so goddman insecure about everything in your life, namely yourself, that you drive everybody crazy. You gotta stop being so insecure, babe."

Kate knew Meg was right. "He wanted me to make him talk when things got bad, but I didn't do that," she said. She wanted to admit everything. "I didn't want to put more pressure on him."

"And you consider yourself weak because of that?" Meg asked.

"Yeah," she answered, frankly, "I guess I do." She felt relieved. "I should have known he wasn't handling things very well. I should have seen it in his eyes."

"Do you think you could have known things were tough for him?" Meg asked calmly.

"I would hope so, but apparently I didn't," she said with anguish. "I feel like I failed him."

"You didn't fail him, Kate," Meg said. "I think you both decided to take on life separately." She stamped out her cigarette.

"I knew that if he started to drink, things wouldn't be good," Kate explained. "We were always fighting and we didn't know why."

"It sounds like things all kind of piled up at once," Meg said.

Kate gave Meg an inquisitive gaze. "Have you been talking to him?"

Meg bowed her head, as if trying to hide her guilt. "Yeah," she admitted. "Eric's been calling every night since you got here."

Kate didn't know whether to feel betrayed or excited. "How is he?" she asked eagerly.

"He's doing all right," Meg said.

"Can I ask what you two talk about?" Kate was more interested than hurt.

"Mostly you," Meg said. "How you're doing—he's very concerned about you."

"What else did he say?" Kate asked, on the verge of crying again—but this time it felt like the good kind of cry.

Meg lit another cigarette. Her movements were slow and deliberate. It seemed to take forever. "He really wants you to know that he doesn't remember being with Dianne," Meg said. "All he remembers is waking up beside her."

Kate thought this over.

"Do you believe him?" Meg prompted.

"I have no reason not to," Kate said easily. "Eric never lies."

"I don't think he would lie either," she said. Meg got up and gave the noodles a stir.

Kate gazed upward. "You think he's tired of taking care of me?"

Meg laughed in irritation. "What? Did he think you would be running the marathon by now? Come on, Eric knew this was a lifetime commitment going in. All of us should be so lucky. How many women do you know who get showered by their husbands all the time, uh? I can't even get my own boyfriend to take a shower with me."

Kate cracked a smile.

"He just made a mistake," said Meg. "And how good could the sex have been? He doesn't even remember; he was so drunk."

Kate chuckled through the last of her tears.

"Am I right?" Meg playfully demanded, sensing a break in the tension.

Kate nodded.

"Has he ever been drunk with you?"

Kate thought for a moment. "I don't think so," she said. "He felt strongly about not drinking because of his Dad and Joe."

"I'm telling you, he really loves you," said Meg. "I think you guys should have a kid."

Kate looked strangely at Meg.

"What the hell was that look for?" she said. "I really think it's time you guys had a baby."

Kate arched her back and closed her eyes. "Maybe we should start out with a dog and see if we can handle that first."

Meg laughed in relief that Kate was getting her sense of humor back. "You always said you wanted kids."

"Yeah, well, I don't really know how he feels about it."

"I thought you two were going to talk about it?"

"We didn't get around to it," Kate said. "If I had a kid, I worried that it would hate me."

"What makes you say that?"

"The whole bonding thing. I'm not sure how that would work. The poor kid will probably need therapy all his life."

Meg shook her head. "Come on, babies are very resilient. You two are going to be great parents."

"Do you think Eric is going to do this again?" Kate asked.

"No, Kate," said Meg. "Would you stop being so insecure?

You're the only one he has in his life that he really loves. He can count on you. He just found that out the hard way."

"Brian hates him," Kate said.

"Yeah, well, Brian's going to hate him for a while, until he can trust him again." Meg drained the pasta and served dinner. Kate recognized that this was the best she had felt in several weeks. She wanted it to continue. She wanted Eric back by her side.

"Let's say we eat in the barn tonight?" Meg suggested keenly, intuiting Kate's rising spirits. "Let's get out of this boring kitchen."

Overcoming a lot in the past few days, Kate was ready to conquer this. "Okay," she said.

Meg opened the heavy wooden doors to the barn. Cold air poured into the kitchen. Meg disappeared into the darkness to turn the lights on. The barn was exactly as Kate remembered it.

At first, going into the barn seemed haunting, as if she was violating some place, violating history, violating the privacy of the ghosts that dwelled there. Kate, too, had a place in its archives.

The same old oars, nets, and lanterns still hung from the purling above. The loft was still overcrowded with old furniture covered with worn blankets. At the far end was the brick fireplace. A great peace came over Kate. Being there felt so right. It brought back powerful memories, powerful feelings of love she shared with Eric. She loved this great, old structure. She loved Eric.

Meg studied her reaction. "You're okay?" Meg asked.

"Yeah," she said.

Eric used the apartment only to sleep. The walls spoke to him with wrath. They longed for Kate's return. It was too much for him to bear. Only his own shadows kept him company. Every room felt lonely. He slept in the den. He spent most evenings with John and Roberta. Gradually, Roberta trusted him again. Eric thanked them both profusely for their caring and hospitality. He wished Dianne would disappear. There was nothing anyone could do unless she attempted to follow through on her threats. His chest constricted with anger. He desperately needed to solve this crisis.

Kate was on his mind continually. Talking to Meg had eased his worry. They talked about what Kate did during the day, what she ate and how she slept. He didn't want to disrupt her recovery by talking directly to her, out of fear he might worry her needlessly. It pleased him to know she had gone into the barn. He ached to go to her.

Kate was accustomed to spending time in the barn. She was increasingly hopeful about her future. Looking back wasn't going to mend the broken pieces.

Meg appeared from the front hallway.

"Your Mom is here," she said.

Kate's stomach tensed up, as her mother came into view.

"I'll be in the laundry room," Meg said. Mother and daughter were alone.

"Surprised to see me?" Mrs. Reed asked.

"Yeah," Kate answered, thinking of a way to survive this encounter. "How did you know I was here?"

"I overheard Brian talking to you last night, and after an hour trying to pry it out of him, he finally told me," Mrs. Reed said and sat down next to Kate.

Kate looked away. "What did he tell you?"

"Enough," said Mrs. Reed. "I want you to move back home."

Kate chuckled derisively. "Is that why you're here—to bring me home?"

"Yes," said Mrs. Reed, as if the decision was already made. "Syracuse is too far away for you to be alone."

"Who says I'm going to be alone?" Kate demanded.

"How can you possibly stay with him, Kate?" asked Mrs. Reed. "He's just like his father!"

Kate overcame the impulse to second-guess herself. "Eric is nothing like his father," she said flatly.

"He's just like his father," said Mrs. Reed, vehemently.

"How can you say that?!" Kate exclaimed. She was determined to stay focused, in control. "You've never even met Mr. Hollis. And you hardly even know Eric!"

"I know Eric enough to know he isn't for you," she said.

"Okay, Ma, then who is?" Kate said. Her voice started to break.

"All I know is Eric's not the one."

"Why?" Kate asked. Mrs. Reed seemed to think she knew Kate's life inside and out.

"Stop kidding yourself, Kate," Mrs. Reed said, bluntly. "Eric is not going to want to stay with someone who can't give him children."

Kate neared defeat. All of her muscles became rigid. She knew what she wanted to say, but she was unable to get the words out. This was her chance to show her mother who she was, how strong she was. She fought off tears and stood her ground. "I'm gonna stay with Eric." The words came out loud and clear. "We're going to try to have kids."

"How the hell are you going to do that?" Mrs. Reed asked, abhorred by the notion.

"Like everybody else, Ma," Kate answered.

"You're crazy—you know that?!"

Looking into her mother's stony eyes, she found her true courage. "Maybe I am," she said, "but I don't want to go through life alone." She looked over at the fireplace. "I matter to him, Ma," she said. "That's all I want from life. All I want is to matter to someone."

"You matter to the family," Mrs. Reed said.

"No, I don't, Ma," she said. "I come home and everyone seems happy to see me, but nobody really talks to me, only Brian."

"How can Eric know you better than your own family?" asked Mrs. Reed, impervious to the substance of her daughter's words.

"He does, Ma," she said. "This guy fell in love with me; me who can't walk, who can't talk right, who can't do a lot without help. I don't think I would find anyone like him again. He loves me and I love him very much."

Mrs. Reed gazed down at the floor. "You do what you want," she said, cuttingly.

Stung by her mother's coarse demeanor, she remained strong. "Why can't you ever be happy for me?" she asked.

"Because I think you are making a big mistake, Kate!"

Rendered speechless by this last hurtful conjecture, she looked into her mother's eyes and recognized what her mother was lacking in her own life.

Mrs. Reed stood. "I have to leave," she said and withdrew from the barn without looking back.

At first, emptiness filled Kate's heart, but the feeling soon dissipated, like air seeping out of a tiny hole in a child's balloon. She felt strangely invigorated, as if she had just won a bullfight. Meg returned and found her in surprisingly good spirits. Kate welcomed a warm embrace from her best friend.

The last Wednesday of March was cloudy and cool in Syracuse. It was spring break, and the streets around campus were quiet. Eric pulled into his driveway a little after seven. He went in and dropped his bag of Chinese take-out on the kitchen counter. He was leafing through the mail when the doorbell rang. It was Dianne.

"What the hell are you doing here?" he asked with contempt.

"I just, I just want to explain some things to you," she expressed in a wavering voice.

"I don't think I want to listen to anymore of your lies, Dianne." He started to close the door.

"Please, please Eric," she said desperately, "just give me a few minutes."

He stared at her apprehensively. "What?"

She was lost in her words, trying to find a place to begin. "After I had Jake, I became extremely depressed. I had to be hospitalized because I got so bad." He watched her trembling hands. "I was in the hospital for two months."

"Was it post-partum depression?"

"They thought it was post-partum at first, but I didn't get any better with time. Soon, I was diagnosed with bi-polar."

He felt sympathy for her. What she was telling him, in her unusual calmness made sense. He invited her inside. She sat defenseless on the couch. He sat on the arm of the chair.

"Once I got the job at Syracuse, I was certain that I didn't need to take my medication anymore, and I stopped." She told him how she internalized everything that he was to her into much more than it was. She took every kind thing that he did for her and believed he loved her. "You wouldn't touch me," she said.

"I have no intentions of hurting you, Dianne," he said. "You need to get some help."

"No," she said, "that's not what I meant. That night in Texas, I tried to interest you in me, but you seemed totally immune. It wasn't like you were resisting, you just weren't interested." Her tone was strangely neutral, like they were back in the office discussing an athlete's twisted ankle.

He felt euphoric, as her words sunk in. He wanted to call Kate—and then shout the news from the rooftops. He reined in his emotions and focused on Dianne, who was, after all, confiding in him. "I have always loved my wife and I'll always love my wife," he said. "You shouldn't take my rejection in you for any other reason than I'm happily married." He spoke from the heart. He could tell by her demeanor that something had changed inside her, no longer sensing she was a threat to him or Kate.

"I always knew that you loved your wife dearly," She returned, fighting back tears. "I think I was jealous of you that you loved your wife so much, and I couldn't love my son in the same way." She took a deep breath between her tears. "Sometimes, it's just easier to tell people that I don't have a little boy than to explain to people why he doesn't live with his Mom."

He moved to the couch and put his hand on her shoulder. She sobbed easily in his presence. He went to the kitchen and got her a glass of ginger ale.

"I'm sorry for all the trouble I caused you," she said. "I should have known that stopping my drugs was a big mistake."

"Are you taking them again?"

"Yeah," she answered, apprehensively. "It's awfully difficult to accept that you might be on these drugs for the rest of your life." She took another sip of ginger ale. "Would you mind if I stay a bit longer?" she asked.

"No, not at all," he said. They talked for about an hour, first about her family, her childhood in Nebraska, how she and Mark were high school sweethearts. The conversation turned to the team and they went over the various injuries the players had sustained during the season. She seemed more like the person he remembered from when they first met.

"Mark says that if I go home to Omaha, he'll bring Jake back every now and then, and he might even be willing to move back there if I do. I've been thinking about it. At least until my Mom is done with her cancer treatments."

Eric told her how smitten he had been with Jake that day when Mark brought him to the office, and how lucky she was to have him.

"Would you mind taking me home now?" she asked. "I'm exhausted after all this talking."

"Sure," he said. "I'd be glad to."

Eric made his nightly call to Meg after midnight. This time, he also talked to his wife. He told her about the arduous events of his night. Both he and Kate became emotional on the telephone. He loved hearing her voice. He promised he would come get her; he would drive to New Hampshire the next day to surprise her.

Chapter 16

Evening fell on another New Hampshire day. It was clear and cool, and the wind blew gently. Inside, the two friends sat at the long table. In the fireplace, the last embers scented the barn with the most pleasant of smells.

The two women chortled jubilantly, talking about anything and everything. Kate wanted more than anything to see Eric. There was no need to dwell on the past anymore. The future was straight in front of her, within her grasp.

There was a knock on the front door. The two friends looked at each other in wonder. They weren't expecting any visitors.

Meg got up and went to the door. When she returned, she announced that they had a surprise guest for dinner. Raising her head, Kate recognized her husband's silhouette standing in the entrance to the barn. As she trembled, Kate forgot how to breathe.

Eric hurried into the barn and kneeled down in front of her. "I'm okay, Sweetie," he said and lifted her downward into his lap. "I'm okay, I'm okay," he repeated and cried along with his wife.

She quivered with happiness, as he held her close.

"It's so good to hold you again," he whispered, as he rocked her back and forth. "I love you," he proclaimed and pressed his lips to her forehead.

Emotion overcame her, as she reached her unruly arm around his neck.

"I'm so sorry all this happened, Sweetie," he said. "I've missed you."

She looked into his beautiful eyes and knew his words were true. "Me, too."

She let her lips caress his for several sweet seconds. She did not want to stop kissing him. She looked up into his loving gaze. "We haven't done that in a while."

"Yes, I know," he said tenderly and kissed her again. "Come home with me?"

"Yes, I will." Feeling his strong arms holding her tightly was all she needed. "I'm sorry," she said.

"For what?" he asked. "What do you have to apologize to me for?"

"I wasn't there," she said.

"You weren't where, Sweetie?"

"I didn't push you," she said with emotion. "I didn't push you to talk to me after Stuart died. I knew how much he meant to you."

"Oh, Katie," he said. "Please don't worry about that."

"And Joe," she added.

"Don't worry about that," he said. "I was the jerk and messed everything up. It was never you."

"Are you sure?"

"Look at me," he demanded. "You did nothing wrong. It was me who didn't talk to you when I really needed to. It was me who decided to drink that night and almost threw my life away, the life I have with you."

"I love you so much," she said with all of her emotion, kissing him passionately. He smiled and gently clutched her to his chest. Running his hands up and down her back, he looked upward around the barn. "This place hasn't changed, has it?"

She raised her head up off his chest to look for herself. "Not really."

"You think we could buy this place someday?"

This question surprised her. "You want to buy this house?" The idea pleased her.

"Not right now, obviously, but some day," he said, "maybe fill it with kids." He gauged her reaction.

She grinned. "Have you been talking to Meg?"

"Is that so wrong?" he asked. The funny expression on his face brought a giggle.

"No," she said, "but I didn't know how you felt. After I saw the doctor, you didn't seem to want to talk about it."

"I didn't seem to want to talk about anything, did I?" he conjectured and kissed her forehead. "You know, my father wasn't so good at being a father, or a husband, for that matter. I just didn't know how I would do at being a father."

She gazed at him with compassion. "I know how you are with me," she said, "and if you are half that with our kids, you'll be a wonderful dad." She put her arms around him.

He put his arms around her.

"How many kids were you thinking about?" she asked.

"Five, six—maybe seven or eight," he answered, playfully.

The sound of her laugh was the best gift he could receive. "I know that the children we have together will be beautiful."

She loved these words. He embraced her with all of his love. "Hold me," she said.

His love met her wishes.

The barn found them once again.

Made in the USA
Charleston, SC
15 September 2011